TASTE OF VICTORY

Taste of Victory

SANDY DENGLER

BETHANY HOUSE PUBLISHERS
MINNEAPOLIS, MINNESOTA 55438
A Division of Bethany Fellowship, Inc.

Manuscript edited by Penelope J. Stokes.

Cover illustration by Dan Thornberg,
Bethany House Publishers staff artist.

Copyright © 1989
Sandy Dengler
All Rights Reserved

Published by Bethany House Publishers
A Division of Bethany Fellowship, Inc.
6820 Auto Club Road, Minneapolis, Minnesota 55438

Printed in the United States of America

Library of Congress Cataloging-in-Publication Data
Dengler, Sandy.
    Taste of victory / Sandy Dengler.
        p. cm. — (Australian destiny ; book 3)
    I. Title. II. Series. III. Series: Dengler, Sandy.
    Australian destiny ; 3.
    PS3554.E524T3   1989
813'.54—dc20   89–18075
ISBN 1-55661-085-8   CIP

SANDY DENGLER is a freelance writer whose wide range of books has a strong record in the Christian bookselling market. Twenty-six published books over the last nine years include juvenile historical novels, biographies, and adult historical romances. She has a master's degree in natural sciences and her husband is a national park ranger. They make their home in Ashford, Washington, and their family includes two grown daughters.

AUSTRALIAN DESTINY SERIES

Code of Honor
Power of Pinjarra
Taste of Victory

Contents

1. Angel Reginald 9
2. Sydney Silvertail 19
3. Linnet's Song 31
4. Trouble 43
5. Echuca Charlene 59
6. Barmah....................................... 73
7. A Paid Engagement 89
8. The Wharfmaster's Lackey 101
9. Fantasia on a Pair of Songbirds 115
10. Variation on a Christmas Present 127
11. Intermezzo With Old Friends 139
12. Recitative on Love and Handel 151
13. Cutting Deals 165
14. Air on a Shoestring 179
15. Counterpoint on a Heart's Theme 191
16. Betrayal 203
17. In Pursuit of Fame and Fortune 217
18. Hymn for Him 227
19. Tangled Threads 243
20. Flood and Crescendo 259
21. Coda 271

Chapter One

Angel Reginald
1906

Nothing. Nothing but nothing. She stood in the very center of nothing and turned slowly in a complete circle. Everywhere she looked—absolutely everywhere—she saw nothing.

Samantha Connolly, now nearly twenty-nine years old, had been many places, but never before had she been nowhere. She had done many things, but never had she stood like this in a totally flat, totally lifeless plain. *How far can the human eye see?* she wondered. *Miles, no doubt. Miles and miles.* And in all directions, for hundreds of square miles, stretched pink dirt and blue sky; and that was all.

Once she had rather liked certain shades of pink and old rose, because they complemented her reddish-brown hair and pale Irish complexion. Now she was beginning to detest the color.

According to the locals here in New South Wales, this thoroughfare was a "track." Apparently the country had no roads, for everything Samantha would have called a road was a "track." It was not just an exercise in semantics. No road, or track, tracing its long straight lines across this land, was paved or cobbled. All were made of the same dirt as the land itself. In short, she was traversing a pink road the same color as the world stretching featureless to the horizon.

She glanced down at her black skirt flapping around her ankles. Pink dust had muted her meticulous laundering. Her white blouse, once crisp, was smudged dark and pinkish at the cuffs—no doubt at the collar, too. What was in her carpetbag that she could not live without? The all-important papers describing her status as a legal immigrant from Ireland with the full right to work here in Australia. She dug them out. What else? Nothing worth lugging the carpetbag through this, certainly. Already a barely noticeable film of pink dust tinged her papers. With a sigh she jammed them into her beaded reticule and stood erect.

Samantha walked for perhaps ten minutes, she estimated—it was difficult to tell. She glanced back. She could still see her abandoned carpetbag, a tiny dark blip on the smooth pink track. She turned her back on her worldly possessions and continued on.

And on.

And on.

The horizon began undulating in gentle, nauseating waves. The inside of her head buzzed. Despite so many miles of nothing stretching round about, she could see only the brilliance immediately in front of her.

Samantha sat down in the middle of the track. There was no danger of her being run over; no vehicles were in sight for miles. The heat penetrated her skirt instantly and made her hot legs much hotter. Her ravenous hunger had subsided, but now she was outrageously thirsty. She ran her tongue across her lips and felt how dry and cracked they were, like a fever line. They probably matched her nose, which had begun to peel on the voyage from the old country almost two years ago and was still peeling today. Her nose had never forgiven her for leaving the Auld Sod. Perhaps her nose was right.

Her mind hovered near total panic, but her body was

too weak, too tired to pay any attention to her mind. She would sit like this, her head bowed beneath her broad-brimmed hat, until later in the day when the sun did not burn quite so fiercely. Then she would rise and continue her odyssey.

Intense warmth bathed her right side, her right arm, her right cheek. She seemed to float. Somewhere on high sang a solitary angel—a tenor angel, specifically.

Did God care so little for Samantha Connolly that He sent only one angel? Humph. On the other hand, why should He bother to serenade her with a full chorus? What, specifically, had she ever done for Him? Novenas, on occasion; the usual motions of worship. Well, perhaps not lately. Not since she arrived in Australia. After all, there was no appropriate church up by Mossman where she worked. Besides, she'd been busy. God knew that.

Ocean waves crashed upon her face. She licked the water off her parched lips and wished for more. It was pouring in her mouth, running out again. Pity. She would so enjoy a drink. Here came more, cool and wet. She swallowed some and inhaled some. The puddles in her lungs set her to coughing. Lovely cool trees blocked out the sun, swathing her in darkness.

Ocean? Trees? Despite the tenor angel's warning, Samantha started to sit erect. Her head clunked against the tree overhead. She coughed the last of the water from her tortured lungs and lay still to assess the situation more rationally.

But there was nothing rational about this situation. The angel had made himself visible. He smiled cheerfully. He was dressed not in gleaming white but utilitarian brown. His thinning plain brown hair, combed straight back, could hardly be mistaken for a halo. And he wore glasses, squarish little half glasses that perched midway down his nose so that his gentle brown eyes could peer out over them. One rather assumes prophets are all bearded, but angels? This one sported a short, very neatly trimmed beard that nicely complemented his roundish face.

"Good afternoon, miss. My name is Reginald Otis."

An angel named Reginald? Why not? Samantha tried to force a smile, but her poor dry lips would not stretch. "Sthamant-tha Connolly, sthir. How tdo ye tdo?" Whatever was wrong with her tongue? It kept sticking to the roof of her mouth.

"I am delighted to make your acquaintance, Miss Connolly." Either God's angels are by nature extremely polite or he was enjoying some droll bit of irony at her expense, for there was nothing delightful about this situation in the least. Not only was she embarrassed nearly to tears, but her temples were beginning to throb with a most violent, massive headache.

Angel Reginald sat cross-legged in the sun before her, and Samantha lay in the shade, but it was not the dancing, leafy shade of trees. Lacking great silver wings with which to fly, the angel transported himself about in a wagon of some sort. He had parked it directly over her, a roof against the fiery sun. There stood his patient horses dozing perhaps a rod distant, a bay gelding and a coarse, oddly colored purple roan with a white face. What an ugly horse it was, with its huge, clumsy head and ragged color, to be serving as a substitute for wings! Although the angel had unhitched his horses, their harness still hung from them in drooping lines.

Careful this time to avoid bumping her head, she pulled herself to a sitting position. Without comment he offered her a tin cup of water. She gulped it down.

He refilled the cup, still smiling. Angels do smile a lot. "Now sip this one, lest your poor tummy rebel and you lose it all."

What should she say? The shame still burned hot. "I feel rather like a person who has picked up a book and begun reading on page forty-four. Might ye please apprise me of what happened in the first forty-three?"

His laugh was the warm, heavy chuckle of an earthbound mortal. "I am traveling south to Deniliquin, and perhaps thence to Echuca. I encountered a carpetbag in the track. It's in my wagon now, incidentally. I've brought it along. And then I encountered you. You seemed a bit discomfited by lack of shelter in this inferno, so I made myself helpful."

"Meself be both indebted and very grateful."

"Irish. I've not heard that lovely lilt since I left Sydney. Forgive my boldness; you've a charming voice, Miss Connolly. Now *you* must apprise *me*: why are you out here alone in the uttermost?"

"Uttermost. Me sentiments precisely." She drank again. "Meself be southbound as well. I traveled from Mossman on the coast to Torrens Creek, an area where me sister now lives. After a brief visit with her and her bridegroom, I continued this way with Cobb and Company. But the stagecoach—argh! Meself became deathly ill from the lurching. At length, I asked to be let off."

"In the middle of nowhere?"

"The driver's very words. 'In the middle of nowhere, mum?' he asked. ''Tis that or suffer most unpleasant consequences of me illness inside y'r coach,' meself replied. He let me out. I spent the better part of two days simply lying beneath a gum tree. What misery. Then a kindly squatter brought me another seventy miles before turning off toward his station to the east. He promised another Cobb coach coming through, but as yet it has not materialized."

"Nor shall it. They went to a new schedule. It's one of the reasons I purchased this rig instead of traveling by coach, as I usually do. After four days' driving in the sun, I was beginning to doubt the wisdom of my purchase. I see now it was God's plan. Glorious, is it not, the way He handles details so cleverly?"

"Me brother-in-law would be the first to agree with ye. A preacher he is, and a fine one. Luke Vinson, married to me sister Margaret."

"A preacher!" The angel brightened. In the brilliance of this penetrating sun, he shone with delight. "As am I, after a fashion. That and many other things, Miss Connolly. My rig, as you see, is covered, and is rather breezy when in motion. You will be comfortable there, and out of the sun. If you feel up to it, let us continue on. I'm sure you're just fine, but I'd like to be a bit nearer civilization, just in case . . ." He shrugged. "Your color seems better; I hardly think you'd perish now; but—well, you know."

No, she did not know, but she wasn't sure she wanted to. He bolted to his feet, very nimble for a man with thinning hair, and offered his hand. Firmly, steadily, he lifted her to her feet. His hands fascinated her. A preacher would most likely have delicate hands, soft and expressive, protected by long hours of study and meditation. This was a working man, with gnarled, tough, stubby paws.

She climbed up the wheel and settled in the seat. The horizon still undulated a little, and she felt a wee bit nauseous. She did not in the least doubt, though, that this square-built non-ethereal gentleman had just brought her back from the brink of death. A friend from north of Longreach, Marty Frobel, told lurid tales of travelers lost in the burning wastes, of tracks completely obliterated by dust storms, of men (and by inference, women) going mad just prior to a ghastly death from thirst.

This was no country to take lightly, and Samantha had made just that error. She should have stayed with the coach. She should never have . . . But it was too late now; water under the bridge, as they say. Water. She wished the angel would offer her another drink.

Mr. Otis hitched up his bay and his roan and handed her the lines. He jumped up over the wheel and settled in beside her, more a sprightly oversized elf than an angel.

He gathered the lines from her hands and clucked to the horses. They were on their way.

"Do you sing, Miss Connolly?"

"Nae, but I suspect y'rself does. Tenor."

"True. My greatest love, except for the risen Christ, of course. Do you know any of the popular hymns?"

"Popular hymns be nae a strong tradition in me own church—save, of course, those rendered by the choir."

"A man named Ira Sankey. Toured both England and America with an evangelist. Ah, Miss Connolly, now there was a voice! They would draw twenty thousand souls to a meeting hall. Then he would stand forth in song and fill that place with splendid melody. I enjoyed the privilege of hearing him several times. He wrote some lovely hymns, as well. And Florence Haverhill, and Fanny Crosby. Phillip Bliss. We have entered a Renaissance of music in the faith, and it's glorious."

"By y'r leave, Mr. Otis, perhaps ye'd provide an example."

He twisted in the wagon box to study her. His warm eyes sparkled. "I would love to. I mentioned Ira Sankey. This one is by him, keyed to tenor, of course; he was such a superb tenor." And he opened his mouth in song.

Samantha had not been mistaken in her original impression; his was the voice of an angel. But even more telling was the expression on his face. This man was alive to a reality beyond mortal ken. His whole personality reverberated to the music of the spheres. She watched and listened, rapt, and forgot how powerfully thirsty she was.

Samantha dozed despite the beauty of the concert. When she finally managed to arouse herself, the music had ceased. Mr. Otis's wagon was winding through open scrub—tiny trees, squat and scattered, that masqueraded as woodland. The pink had dulled to a pallid ocher.

Her headache had abated somewhat. She chatted with Mr. Otis, tried to sit up straight, drank quite a bit more water and began to suspect that perhaps she would survive this hideous country, after all.

They paused for an evening meal right beside the track. Mr. Otis prepared eggs, rashers of bacon and a rather heavy, dry, biscuit-like breadstuff he called damper. Samantha would have been more enthusiastic about damper if it wasn't baked right down in the ashes. She drank five cups of weak tea. Her headache gradually faded to a dull heaviness. Not until they were on the road again did it occur to her that she had not felt nature's call all day, despite so much tea and water.

How close had she come to death by dehydration? She would never know. She did know this: she owed Mr. Otis an enormous debt of gratitude, perhaps for life itself.

Very late that night they rolled into a small town called Bourke. One inn on the corner of the only major cross street provided her with her first real bed in many days. She slept through breakfast and very nearly missed luncheon. She learned from the desk clerk that Mr. Otis had continued south at daybreak.

She lingered in the village several days, regaining her strength, shedding the last vestiges of that headache, and drinking huge amounts of liquids. In long, quiet morning walks she explored the banks of the Darling, a bare trickle that these folks called a river. And what an odd and exotic lot were the birds of this area—amazing cockatoos, herons and hawks, and a startling variety of small birds in bright colors.

With considerable trepidation Samantha boarded the southbound coach. A week later she arrived in the dusty little town of Hay on the Murrumbidgee. Neither the village nor the stream called her to tarry. Desperate by now for both employment and some vestige of civilization, she continued south into Deniliquin. No positions to be had. She braved the rigors of stagecoach travel once again, and with the last of her meager funds, she arrived in Echuca.

She took a room in a little corner hotel and proceeded to the office of the *Riverine Herald*. The best place in town to ask about employment opportunities is the newspaper office. The office was closed. She stepped into the cloistered gloom of a small butcher shop.

She smiled at a chubby little man in a white smock. "G'day, sir. I be seeking employment. Might ye know of any?"

The butcher draped himself across his sausage stuffing machine and scratched his mustache. "Jobs. Jobs. Mmm. Bad time of year to be looking. Slow. Jobs. Mmm."

"Office work, domestic, child care—anything of that sort."

"Eh, now, there's one place you might try, depending how desperate you are. Some missionary bloke's putting together a sort of mission thing for the abos. Main work'll be out beyond the black stump, but there's some bookkeeping and other office work to do at his place here in town. Might talk to him."

"I'd love to. Where shall I find him?"

"He's got a little office set up behind the post office. Just ask for a Mr. Reginald Otis."

Chapter Two

Sydney Silvertail

At the base of an ancient, sprawling gum tree, a cricket tuned up. All around, in the grass and under the shrubbery, a hundred other crickets were already casting their strident songs into the warm and muggy night air. A block away, the bells of St. Mary's sang out their announcement of another wedding, very nearly drowning the Hyde Park crickets' song. And the song of the bells was muffled by the clamor of the street—horses clopping, fine carriages rattling as discordantly across the bricks and cobbles as battered hacks, and the occasional sputtering chug of one of those curious motor automobiles.

Cole Sloan stood beside his open brougham and eyed one such horseless doover clattering by. If the cockeyed idea persisted a few years, if these horseless carriages were not just a passing fancy, he ought to consider buying one. They might, before long, carry quite a bit of prestige.

"Watch your step, luv." He offered Hilary a hand down. The coachman and footman stretched out their hands as well. She laid dainty gloved fingers upon the hand closest and descended from coach to brass footstep to solid ground.

Hilary. Gorgeous, alluring Hilary. When a man put her on his arm, everyone took note. Should anyone engage Hilary in five minutes of conversation, though, or even two minutes, the world would instantly realize that her mind came nowhere near matching her face and figure. Too bad a bobby-dazzler like this possessed the depth of spilled coffee. *Ah, well. No woman reaches perfection.* Sloan's thoughts reined up suddenly. *But there is one woman who comes very, very close.*

Samantha. Where was Sam now?

He forced his thoughts back to the moment as Hilary arranged her hand on his arm. He had to shorten his stride considerably to fit it to her mincing walk.

"All this traffic!" she cooed. "Who would think it at eight at night?"

This much traffic at eight was normal for the height of the social season, particularly with the weather this warm. Sloan held his peace. Letting her babble on was a lot less taxing than trying to educate her constantly. She had grown up here in Sydney, as had Sloan himself, but she somehow seemed a stranger wandering absently through the fields of life.

Bright light poured out the great opened doors of Exeter Hall and evaporated into the damp darkness. Sloan escorted her into the hall, from subtropic Sydney, Australia, into merrie olde England. Servants, attendants, the doormen were standing about with nothing to do—all decked out in court livery. A couple of the major domos even sported powdered wigs. Here it was 1906, with 1907 looming perilously close, and these people were still clinging to the eighteenth century. No wonder Australia sloshed in the backwaters of progress.

The unnatural brilliance from electric chandeliers altered colors and gave the vast open room a garish intensity. Several hundred people milled about here, fashionable high-society ladies escorted by prominent men, every one. Sloan grew up in this sort of pretentious atmosphere, for his mother was as pretentious a person as you'd ever find. It bored him.

He guided Hilary over to the punch table, greeting acquaintances along the way, smiling affably on the outside and grinning smugly on the inside. He was comfortable in this milieu, but you could detect in an instant who was not. This assemblage of men from all over the fledgling federation included backblockers and city people, pastoralists and bankers. The men with tanned and leathery hides shifted from foot to foot and tried to look as if they belonged. Their ladies gazed open-mouthed at the opulence and usually approached the refreshment table with their gloves on.

Carroll Swipes, fifty-ish, gray, paunchy, and worth at least two hundred thousand pounds, motioned to Sloan. Hilary was digging deep into the refreshments, so Sloan whispered in her ear and left her there. He crossed to Swipes alone.

"Glad you could make it tonight, Cole." Swipes extended a broad, tender hand for a handshake. "I want you to meet the pastoralists' conference representative from the Mitchell District up in Queensland. He's a pastoral tenant of the Crown like his father before him, and shows great promise as a leader. . . ."

Sloan listened to the extravagant introduction with only half an ear. Swipes was always promoting some jackaroo as the next prime minister. This fellow was as good a candidate as any. He was a backblocker; you could see that from his deep suntan and the looseness in his stance. But he knew how to wear a suit, and he didn't seem ill at ease in the midst of all this power and prestige. What held the bulk of Sloan's attention, though, was the beauty on this fellow's arm. She was a natural blond, tall and graceful and obviously in complete charge of herself. This lady used money and held responsibility; you could read it in the way she moved, even in the way she stood still. Her mien of confidence stopped just a shade short of haughtiness. He admired that in a woman.

His attention and his thoughts slammed to a halt.

"Martin Frobel . . ." Swipes was saying, and he had just spoken Sloan's full name.

Sloan could feel himself gaping, and this young Frobel had frozen just as solidly. Yes, you could see the family resemblance there, especially in the chocolate-colored eyes. The Martin Frobel, Jr., before him reflected the ghost of the Martin Frobel, Sr., he knew too well.

Young Frobel snapped out of it first. He extended his hand. "Pleased. Isn't too often I get to meet someone who shot it out with my father."

It was Swipes' turn to gape.

Sloan gripped Frobel's warm hand, rough and calloused. "My pleasure. Hope he's doing well."

"Very well. I'll tell him you inquired." He nodded toward the blond beauty. "My wife, Pearl."

"Delighted." And Sloan was. He scooped up the graceful hand and kissed it.

Pearl Frobel smiled, radiant as the sun. "Now I see why Margaret's sister gets stars in her eyes when she talks about you. You're a handsome and gracious man, Mr. Sloan."

"Samantha! You've seen her recently. How is she?"

"Fine. She should be in Melbourne by now. She thought she'd try there for a domestic position since jobs like that are scarce here in Sydney."

Sloan nodded. "She shouldn't have any trouble. She's the best employee I ever had." *Melbourne. Buried in a bustling city. I'll never find her again . . . not that I want to, of course.*

Not too many months ago, Sloan had defended himself against an old nemesis from his past, and in the process had ended up in a gunfight with this fellow's father. Did the young man harbor any animosity toward the person who could easily have killed dear old dad? He ought to. Yet Sloan could feel no tension, no malice. Strange. Surely

Sloan couldn't be so quickly absolved. And Luke Vinson. Had Vinson not been carrying a big thick Bible, Sloan's bullet would have nailed him for sure.

"How's Luke Vinson? Doing well with his pastorate, I trust. You do know him, I assume."

Frobel was probably Samantha's age, but he looked like a grammar school lad when he grinned like that. "He married us."

Pearl was smiling also. "The stockmen's association needed a representative for the conference down here, and we needed somewhere to honeymoon." She shrugged fetchingly. "We never imagined meeting you, though. Fascinating." Her voice dropped, sobered. "Marty's father and Samantha described that battle, and the destruction . . . You lost a great deal."

"Enough that I decided to give up sugar and tea." He nodded to young Frobel. "My warmest congratulations. I wish you a long and happy life together." Not only could Sloan detect no animosity; this young woman, a complete stranger, sounded genuinely solicitous. The sincerity of her interest made him uncomfortable. She should be distant, cool toward him. And young Frobel appeared just as concerned. Sloan would frankly have preferred some plain old hostility; it was what he deserved.

From nowhere, Hilary latched on to his arm. A few cake crumbs clung to the corner of her mouth. "They're readying the orchestra. A waltz, I heard someone say."

Sloan made introductions and Swipes, with a few words, excused himself. The usual pleasantries were exchanged; Hilary was very good at surface pleasantries; but Sloan's mind worked on other things. The string quartet Hilary had called an orchestra opened with a moderately paced waltz and Sloan knew what he wanted to do.

"Mr. Frobel, may I have a waltz with your lovely bride?"

Frobel caught his wife's eye briefly, and in that swift glance they spoke volumes to each other. These two were not just bride and groom; they were good friends. Pure, unadulterated jealousy wrenched Sloan's heart. How much would he give for a happy union like this with a smart, sensible, beautiful woman? Frobel here had everything Sloan wanted and more.

"Certainly," the young pastoralist said, and Sloan swept her away lest the lad change his mind. From the corner of his eye Sloan watched Frobel lead Hilary out toward the dance floor.

"Mrs. Frobel, your man seems at home here, as do you. Are you both originally from Sydney?"

She smiled as she laid a hand firmly on his shoulder. "I was born in Parramatta and raised here and in Brisbane. He spent his whole life in the outback. He calls all the big-city financiers silvertails, and suspects every city bloke of being a lurk merchant out to get the backblockers. Other than that, he has a fairly healthy attitude toward urban life."

Sloan chuckled. *Silvertail. Obviously that includes me. You're just polite enough not to say so.*

Pearl Frobel was not one to waltz in silence. "So you gave up growing sugar and tea in the jungle. What has replaced it?"

"Commodities trade. Broker. I'm finding I enjoy it very much. A different sort of jungle, this, but still a jungle."

She laughed, and her voice lilted. "When Mr. Swipes first spotted you here, he instantly launched into a lengthy explanation about how you can help sell Queensland beef. Export markets?"

"Who is the stockmen's representative, you or your husband?"

She smiled knowingly. "Behind the scenes, Mr. Sloan, or in front of them?" She was a wonderful dancer; for a woman so cocksure of herself, she followed well and smoothly. "Marty has an excellent business acumen. He established and kept his station through the worst drought in many years, and he's displayed a fine political sense. But I've a head for business also, and he trusts my judgment. We work well together."

"That I don't doubt." The knife of jealousy stabbed anew.

They completed the waltz with not-so-small talk about cattle and sheep and the difficulty of procuring dependable markets. Sloan reluctantly returned her to her bridegroom and made a business appointment with them both for the following morning in Crown Street.

He sought out Carroll Swipes and thanked him for the timely introduction. With some difficulty he fielded the inevitable barrage of questions about shoot-outs and hastened on to other contacts. For Hilary, this was a grand party. For most of the others there it was a means to get acquainted, both socially and for business purposes—an important place to see and be seen. But to Sloan this soiree could make or break his very living. He knew nothing of brokering. He knew precious little about the commodities he planned to handle. Here he could learn and learn quickly while he still had the capital to maintain a well-appointed office in one of Australia's two most expensive cities. He poised on the brink of either ruin or glory; how much he learned and how quickly he acted would determine his future.

On the brink. The story of his life was that simple phrase. He always and ever seemed to be leaping from crisis to crisis. Why could he not just enjoy a peaceful, stable means of living with a comfortable financial return? Even in the heat of some heady deal, he yearned for quiet stability.

Curious, the way he loathed this frantic struggle and yet played the game so eagerly. Once he established himself—if ever he did—perhaps he could relax a bit. He was not yet thirty-one, and he was beginning to feel tired. He'd watched men drop over from nothing more than keeping a constant frantic pace. If this weariness was his body telling him something, his very health might depend upon success.

"Well, Sloan! Never expected you here."

Sloan wheeled. Here it came. He adjusted his voice and his mien to communicate confidence, friendliness. "Mr. Beckerstaff, good evening. How's the sugar business?"

The balding businessman drew himself up to his full five-feet-eight. "I think you know. Either you have more courage than a bulldog to show up at this function, or you have a stupid streak."

"Probably a little of both. Sorry you're unhappy."

"You knew, didn't you? You knew what was coming with that Kanaka business. I see now why you arranged the deal you did when I bought your plantation from you. 'Sugarlea will return her price in five years,' you said. You took me for a fool, and you were almost right."

"Sorry; I don't understand."

"Yes, you do. You knew Melbourne was going to order the repatriation of all those Kanakas. You had to know; Sugarlea used more of them than any other holder in Queensland. You knew the expense that was coming, and you left it for me to pay."

"There was a rumor going around that Melbourne was going to send the Kanakas back to the islands they came from, but that's all it was—a rumor. I figured if Melbourne wanted them sent home, Melbourne would send them home."

"And tender a bill. I've been assessed more than I paid you for the holding."

Beckerstaff raised a finger. "Rest assured you'll pay, Sloan, one way or another. I didn't know where you were until this moment, but I have you now, and I'll not lose you again."

"You're overreacting to circumstantial evidence. There's nothing to suggest I misled you when we made our deal. The courts weigh evidence, not your personal bitterness."

The man's voice dropped to a hiss. "I never resort to the courts, Sloan. Takes too long, and it's expensive. No. No, I'll ruin you. Smarter men than you have tried to best me. Now they're picking rags behind the buildings by the bridge. Your ruin will bring me great personal satisfaction."

Sloan held the man's piercing little eyes firmly. "By that I take it that the gauntlet is thrown down."

"You crack hardy now. But I'll watch you come crawling to me, Sloan." Beckerstaff turned on his heel and walked away.

How much of Beckerstaff's threats were idle skitting, and how much damage could he do? Sloan was up King Street already, practically bankrupt. He smirked. Beckerstaff could have an easy go of it if he only knew.

Between dances with Hilary, Sloan made seven other contacts and arranged several more appointments. He was able to listen in on some excellent casual talk about beef raising and wine culture. When at last he called for his carriage, he could look back on the evening with a sense of satisfaction and accomplishment.

Satisfaction? Not completely. Two haunting, jarring discordances poked at the edges of his mind. On the one edge, Beckerstaff's vitriol. And on the other, Martin Frobel and Pearl. Why were they so open and friendly, so ready to discuss business? Why of all the people in this great nation were they the ones here tonight? Might they, as it appeared, give Sloan an inside track to a major source of cheap beef, or was he being set up for some elaborate plan of revenge and retribution? What if they were somehow allied with Beckerstaff—he the snarling dog out front, and they the snakes waiting in the grass? Sloan didn't dare trust the Frobels, *pere* or *fils*. Or *femme*, for that matter; Pearl was just as crafty as any man.

"Hilary, what'd you think of that Frobel bloke?"

"Did you see his boots?"

"No, I didn't notice his boots."

"They're made out of some kind of lizard skin or snake skin. Or crocodile. I forget which. He ought to wear patent leather like everyone else when he's in town, don't you think?"

"I hadn't thought about it. Does he seem trustworthy to you?"

"He didn't make any unseemly suggestions. But of course, he just got married a month ago. I suppose I could trust him."

Sloan sighed. Why had he asked?

"Cole, you made lots of money growing sugar, didn't you?"

What should he tell her? That after the fire destroyed his home he sold off everything—land, mill and all—and worked the payments in such a way as to leave his debtors weeping? That he came away from the north Queensland coast with far fewer assets than when he had started up there? Would she appreciate the intricate deals he had wrought to save from the disaster enough money to set himself up as a broker of means? Hardly. "Enough. Yes."

"Then why aren't you a planter anymore?"

"Because, luv, a planter risks his own money, same as a pastoralist does. As a broker I risk other people's money. I much prefer it that way." He frowned. "What did he tell you, anyway, about—uh, the past?"

"Nothing. Oh, wait. He mentioned his father met you once."

"That's all?"

"What else is there?"

"Nothing." He lapsed into silence. Hilary's soft warmth pressed against his side and he thought of Samantha.

What a drongo you are, Sloan, to daydream over one stubborn Irish lass while sitting in the midst of one of the world's great cosmopolitan cities full of nubile and willing young ladies.

"Cole, don't you think crocodile boots are grotesque?"

"I own a pair."

"Oh."

Silence.

"Cole, have you ever seen a real crocodile?"

"I killed the beast that is now my boots."

"Oooh." She pondered the cosmic meaning of it all for a while. "Cole? I always thought you were more sophisticated than that."

Chapter Three

Linnet's Song

It looked almost like a cathedral, a great brick box two stories high, replete with spires and flying buttresses, and in the very top of the gable, a round rose window. "Elder Hall and Conservatorium" the sign said. Here in serene majesty were perpetuated the muses of music and the arts. Linnet Connolly climbed the steps into the high foyer. The interior, a single great and echoing hall, lacked only the stations of the cross and a few statues from being truly holy ground. No pews, though. Seating consisted of chairs, hundreds of chairs. At the far end, where one would properly expect an altar, a massive pipe organ filled a story-and-a-half alcove.

Linnet walked the length of the hall, passing the rows and rows of silent chairs. She climbed the steps of the non-altar to get a better view of the organ console—banks and banks of stops, keyboard stacked upon keyboard. More foot pedals than toes on ten feet, it seemed, jutted out of the dark paneling. What great artist could claim skill divine enough to master this amazing instrument?

"Young lady!"

Linnet gasped and wheeled as the accusing voice echoed from the cantilevered rafters. She curtsied. "G'day, sir!"

"Well." His voice rang with authority, but his slight,

sauntering appearance suggested a music hall comedian or juggler—an entertainer with a strange accent Linnet had never heard before. "Perhaps you're the charwoman, hey? You here to clean the place?"

"Clean the—nae, sir. But I . . ." Linnet drew a deep breath, gathering what precious little courage she had. "Are ye saying they've need of a cleaning woman here?"

"They need everything here. What is your business, please?"

"I'm a . . . I hope to be . . ." She took one last glance at the organ console and stepped down to floor level.

He was smaller than she had guessed, hardly taller than her own five feet five inches. What a wonderful, thick, healthy looking head of hair he had, all black ringlets! His olive skin suggested that his accent was probably Italian or Greek, neither of which Linnet would recognize. He looked . . . well, he looked classic, a minor Greek god in a strange and rather threadbare velvet jacket. He couldn't be any older than her sister Meg—twenty-five perhaps. And yet he left no doubt that he could rule the world, given the opportunity. Imperious. That was the adjective. Imperious.

"Your name, miss?"

"Linnet Connolly, sir."

"Irish."

"Emigrated a year and ten months ago with me two sisters. Me papers be in order, sir."

"I'm sure. Your purpose?"

"Twofold, sir. I'm seeking employment, and I hope to enroll in the University of Adelaide here."

"Which curriculum?"

"Meself has always loved music, sir."

"Prior training?"

"Nae training, sir. Me parents could ill afford lessons beyond those I learned in school. I learned some music in school."

"With no education and no training, you purpose to enter the university. You are very bold, young lady, or very naive." He studied her a moment. "Or you are a very fine musician. Sing for me."

"Sir?"

"Sing for me!"

A small voice at the back of her mind warned her that this young man had no right or cause to make such a demand, but she stilled the voice. Flustered, she could think of no song except "Brennan on the Moor," and that was hardly appropriate to the situation. Better that than no song at all. " 'Tis of a brave young highwayman / this story I will tell . . ."

Why wasn't he stopping her? She continued with the next line. "His name was Willie Brennan / and in Ireland he did dwell." In fact, the actual Willie Brennan, dead by hanging some hundred years ago, plied his trade and forged his legend in the hills right behind her native Cork.

The dark young gentleman stood there, his head cocked slightly aside, his arms folded. He gave no direction yea or nae, so she continued.

"It was on the Kilwood mountain / he commenced his wild career, and many a wealthy nobleman / before him shook with fear." She completed the chorus and the three verses she knew. At last she ran out of song, and still he did not speak.

Suddenly he lurched into motion. "Come with me, please, Miss Connolly."

She followed him to a grand piano in the far corner. A magnificent instrument it was, gleaming black. Carelessly he shoved the lid open and propped it up, then bared the keyboard in the same manner. "Play."

This was getting to be a bit much. She took a deep breath. "Meself lately informed ye, sir, that I cannae play. Sister Bertrand taught me some etudes and such, but I cannae remember them."

Eyelashes. He had the most wonderful long black eyelashes. "I want to hear 'Brennan on the Moor' rendered on the piano." The dark, dark eyes behind those lashes softened. "As best you can. Please. Perhaps the key of one flat?"

Why was she doing this? Why was she making an utter fool of herself at his behest? Obediently she sat down on the slick, stiff stool. One flat. F. She struck the F chord, hummed the first line to herself and picked it out. She hummed the second.

"Very good. In the key of E, please."

This time she had to really think; four sharps were involved. She got as far as the wealthy nobleman when he laid his warm hand on hers. The silence rang.

He smiled, and in smiling glowed. "You have a wonderful ear! And a splendid voice. Untrained, but beautiful." He dropped the lid unceremoniously, as if this lovely piano were nothing more than a glove box.

From the doorway came a girl's voice. "Chris! Is that you?"

"At the piano," he called.

That was silly; surely she could see them here. No, she could not. As she approached, tapping with a white cane, Linnet saw the unfocused, sightless eyes, and understood. Linnet stood up as Chris introduced them.

"Elizabeth, this is Linnet Connolly, a girl of perhaps eighteen—" He turned to Linnet. "Eighteen? Yes. And seeking to enter the music program. She is perhaps five feet five, weighs I'd say ten stone, gray-green eyes and lovely auburn hair. Light auburn, on the red side. Fair complexioned. Linnet, Elizabeth Mapes here is a third-year music student majoring in violin."

"How do you do." Elizabeth smiled and extended her hand before her.

Linnet curtsied, realized in a flash of embarrassment that the gesture had gone unseen, and took the proffered hand briefly. "How do ye do."

"You two just met?" With her flat brown hair and rather coarse, plump frame, Elizabeth appeared, frankly, quite plain. But when she smiled so warmly like this, the plainness disappeared.

"Yes. She just wandered in." Chris's eyes twinkled.

Elizabeth shook her head. "Then, Miss Connolly, I'll bet he didn't introduce himself. He never does. This is Esmond Christenikos Yorke, a fourth-year piano and organ student. Did he mention that his father is a diplomat?"

"No. Uh, he didn't. That's, uh, very nice." Linnet smiled because it seemed the right thing to do. What was the relationship between these two? Cozy, it would seem. And what was their role in the University of Adelaide? She felt dreadfully confused and out of place. This notion of coming to a university, of all places, was so absurd! Whatever made her think a simple servant girl and clerk had any business at all here?

"Now, I like that!" Yorke beamed. "You don't seem the least bit impressed with my father's trade. There's hope for you, Miss Connolly. Come, we'll introduce you to the registrar and see what we can do for you. The term has started, but that shouldn't bar your entry."

Elizabeth turned and Chris Yorke took her arm, ushering her toward the door. Linnet fell in beside them, the fifth wheel on a buggy. Elizabeth tucked her cane under her arm. "So you think the girl shows promise?"

"Wait until you hear her sing!"

Linnet followed them from the dark and sonorous cave of Elder Hall into the blinding light of day. A brilliant little red and blue parrot sort of bird lifted off the green lawn before them, flew a few yards, and settled again into the grass. Poor Elizabeth! She missed so much beauty!

Yorke glanced at Linnet. "Since you're a special case, we'll take you directly to the vice chancellor, Dr. Barlow. You'll sing for him—an audition, as it were—and probably you'll sing for Guli Hack, too. Women's vocal instructor. So you might fetch up in your mind something besides 'Brennan on the Moor,' right?"

Two days later, Linnet gradually began to realize just how special a case she was. As if she were a horse tendered for sale at a great academic horse auction, professors poked and prodded at her, intellectually. They quizzed her and drilled her. Parse this sentence. Do that long division problem without use of paper and pencil. What poetry can you recite from memory? What is the story behind Handel's Water Music? Name the capital of Canada. They frowned at her a lot. They muttered and rumbled among themselves and entered her into the university music program with a big red *conditional* stamped across her papers.

But that was the least of it. This university regimen could hardly be termed "school," as Linnet knew school. She had grown up under the tutelage of nuns in a parochial girls' school in Cork. Some of the awesomeness of God sort of rubbed off on nuns and invested them with authority. Linnet would never in a million years dream of talking back to a nun. But these professors—and that included Miss Hack, the vocal instructor—basked mysteriously in the power of their own authority, answering neither to God nor man. Linnet would never in a million years dream of talking to one of these professors at all.

And the classes! Somehow it just wasn't school without a uniform. Men and women attended together. Unnatural! Students wandered from building to building as their schedule dictated, unprotected by either walls or the watchful eye of the Mother Superior.

And Papa was not paying for it. How would Linnet ever meet the tuition costs and bills? She was assessed fourteen pounds three. Chris insisted she apply for an indigent's scholarship, and the bill dropped to nine pounds twelve. She had not two pounds to her name. She wrote urgent letters to her sisters, Margaret and Samantha. Meg was probably doomed to penury as a pastor's wife, but possibly Sam had found work by now. Maybe Sam could help.

Through a counselor, who apparently did nothing all day but sort out problems such as hers, Linnet obtained a position as part-time maid in the home of an assistant professor. She performed her household duties morning and evening, and attended class between times. In a stroke of munificence, her employer, Onslow Warner, gave her half days off on Saturday afternoon and Sunday morning, without loss of pay. Yet he paid her not much more than her former employer Cole Sloan had under terms of indenture. It would take her forever to accumulate nine pounds twelve. She needed it now.

Saturday noon she cleaned up the luncheon remains and left the house. Until tomorrow noon she was free. By Monday she would owe more than she could pay. With a heavy heart she strolled through the summer heat, headed for the practice rooms. She might as well soak up just as much music as she could until they kicked her out.

"Ahoy, the fair Irish lass!" Chris Yorke's lilting voice instantly lifted away all the weight of the world that had been plaguing her. She turned and watched him come bounding across the broad, stately lawn between the conservatorium and North Terrace. He wore a startling blue silk shirt. She'd never seen anything quite like it. Come to think of it, neither had she seen anything like the flowered silk ascot he wore last week. Or any of the other details of outrageous costume he obviously loved.

With a broad, happy grin he dropped to a walk beside her. "My piano student extraordinaire! You're on your way to the practice rooms, right? Good girl! I'll come along. So, now that you've tasted academic life, what do you think?"

"It's lovely . . . different . . ."

He stopped so suddenly she ran into him. Those anthracite eyes bored into her. "What's wrong? Warner is behaving himself, isn't he?"

"Behav— You mean . . . yes! No problem."

"You are frightened of something. Fearful."

"Chris, I cannae afford this. I've nae money at all. And they want so much."

"What else?"

"What else? What more need there be?"

"Just money? Why, Linnet, there's always a quid or two lying about waiting to be found. We'll go practice, but first join me for a pause and conversation at the Goat's Beard. It's too fine an afternoon to waste with mundane scales and etudes."

She froze in place. "Oh no. Thank ye. Uh. . . .no. I, uh, thank ye, but I never frequent pubs."

"Then you'll never eat in Adelaide, for the best places are all fully licensed. You may have tea if you wish, and if you further wish, I shall have tea also."

"Well, uh—"

"There's a clever girl." He swiftly headed out across the lawn, almost dragging her along. She nearly had to trot to keep up. "For a talented young woman like you, Linnet, money will never be a problem."

"Easy enough for y'rself to say, with y'r own dear father sending ye funds. Me papa has me mum and grandmum and brother Ellis, and nae income save his own. He cannae help; I wouldnae ask him."

"Then we'll ask Brennan."

"Brennan who?"

"Why, the only Brennan you know, 'Brennan on the Moor.' "

Linnet had no idea what he might be thinking, but it didn't sound good.

She had seen the Goat's Beard in passing, but never had she gone inside this pub or any other. *Nice* girls didn't do that sort of thing. Papa would have a first-rate conniption, and rightly so, were he ever to learn what she was doing just now. And think what Meg and Sam would say!

They stepped from daybright into hot, stuffy gloom.

Chris waited in the doorway a moment; no doubt his eyes took as long to adjust as did hers. A bar, armpit high, made a varnished mahogany U in the middle of the room. Matching booths studded the walls. At the back, where the U connected to the far wall, a wonderful variety of goat figurines marched along a shelf above a huge mirror. Cabinets on both sides of the mirror held bottles of every imaginable sort, in clear, green, brown and blue. Stem glasses of all sizes hung head down from racks above the barman. Except for one woman with her hair piled high on her head, every soul here was male. And they were every one of them looking at Linnet.

Chris dragged her forward. "Anybody here Irish? Hurlihy, I know you are. Hurlihy, my brawny lad, I'm about to bring a tear to your eye. Jemmy, let me borrow your guitar."

And Linnet realized with a shocking jolt like lightning what Chris had in store. She shook her head, her mind full of protests, but no words came out of her dry mouth. He couldn't be serious about this! He had duped her. Tea? Conversation? Ha! He intended all along to put her on display like the two-headed calf at the fair. She had been betrayed by one of the few people in Australia she felt like trusting.

Chris rotated slowly, addressing the room in general. "This young woman has never been in a pub before. She's quite shy, and as you can see, that adds immensely to her stupendous charm. But her voice, gentlemen. Wait until you hear her voice!"

Chris pulled her closer to him. "I present with enthusiasm Miss Linnet Connolly, a music student of very limited means, performing one of the great ballads from the Auld Sod. Miss Connolly?" He propped his foot up on a chair rung to support the guitar and strummed several chords.

What could she do? It was no longer a matter of avoiding shame. Her goal now was to minimize it. Should she run out the door and leave Chris there strumming, as he so richly deserved? What if she met one or more of these persons in the days to come? She wouldn't know them, but they would surely know her. And they would laugh. Almost querulously, she began to sing.

The chorus came easier. Her throat loosened up enough that she could make it through the next verse without choking. Not only was Chris an excellent pianist, he was an accomplished guitarist as well. Was he one of those persons, like her sister Sam, who could do anything at all and do it well?

The song ended. Linnet glanced at the burly man identified as Hurlihy. Just as Chris had promised, his eyes were glistening! "Speak something, lass," he murmured.

She licked her lips. "Uh, sure 'n I'm glad ye liked me song, sir."

"Real!" he purred in a heavy Galway burr. "Y're realer than real!" He dug into his pocket. With one smooth stroke he transferred something from his pocket to her hand. He clasped both his huge hands over hers. "God bless ye, lass! And God bless the fine folks what raised ye free of pubs and shame!"

"Thank ye. God bless y'rself, Mr. Hurlihy."

Chris grabbed her elbow and guided her toward a booth. There was an other-worldly feel to this whole unimaginable escapade. It made her almost numb. Too many weird things were happening too quickly. And it was so hot in here. Three others on the way pressed coins into her hand. She sat down because Chris sat her down. He muttered, "Count it later," and flung himself carelessly into the seat across.

She whispered hoarsely, "Had I known y'r intent, *Mr.* Yorke, I'd not have come here. Ye know that."

"I know that. Do you want to learn music?"

"Yes, but—"

"Do you have the resources?"

"No." A thousand lessons and homilies from her past flooded in. The end does not justify the means. Walk uprightly. Avoid temptation. God judges. Sin not. And flooding in from the other side came *Where do you plan to get money, Linnet? How will you support yourself and pay tuition? Is this so terribly bad? See, the tea has arrived, and scones. You're not drinking alcohol. Yes, but . . . No buts. Yes, but . . .*

The heat, plus the clamor of conflicting thoughts, wilted her resolve to do either good or bad. She sat like a lump and sipped at her tea. "Chris, I don't know—"

"Life isn't perfect black and white, Linnet. And what you just did is a very light shade of gray, if it's gray at all. You're not accustomed to this, I understand. But you have a lovely gift—a voice like an angel's—and you might as well use it to further your education."

"But ye dinnae understand."

"And frankly, neither do you. Had I proposed this while we were walking out on the lawn, you would have refused flat out, not because it's wrong but because it's unknown. Now it's known, if only slightly. Think about it." With that irresistible grin he raised his teacup. "To the long and successful career of one of the world's great sopranos."

She giggled suddenly. "Here now, ye scoundrel. And what great soprano would fain sing 'Brennan on the Moor'?"

Chapter Four

TROUBLE

Sloan enjoyed most this aspect of Sydney's racing season: behind the scenes. With Hilary on his arm as decoration, he strolled among the long white barns behind the racetrack. Here and there horses sneezed or whinnied. Iron-shod hoofs raised a gentle haze of dust. Diminutive jockeys, burly trainers, quiet grooms all wore bright colors and laughed a lot.

Sloan loved the smells—yes, all of them. He particularly liked the clean, honest smell of horse sweat. He liked the odor of freshly saddle-soaped leather. Foremost, the sweet aroma of hay jogged memories of his boyhood, when he dallied around these very barns and stables. Long ago he dreamed of owning the world's finest racehorse, and of riding it to victory. Now he smiled to himself at the idea of a six-foot-plus jockey.

And the horses . . . Nothing—absolutely nothing—can match a fine horse well groomed. Sloan paused to admire a glistening bay stallion being led out to the track. The long neck arched gracefully as the impatient steed sidled and pranced, anxious to be moving faster than his groom was walking. His jockey, in vivid yellow and blue silks, couldn't be more than sixteen. Did the lad appreciate the glamor of his calling?

Sloan paused at the corner of Barn C, looking around

intently. Ah! There he was in the distance, outside stall 7, just like years ago. The groom was preparing a sorrel for the next race. Sloan turned Hilary aside and escorted her beneath the aging gum trees down the powdered dirt pathway along Barn C.

Most of the gum trees shading the racetrack stables had been cut down. The stalls in Barn C were the few still protected from the heartless sun, and Barn C was therefore the abode of the elite, the old-timers, the established professionals, the few favored by man and Lady Luck. Oblivious to the honor of living in Barn C, the horses hung their heads out over their stall doors surveying the scene, ever ready to accept a carrot or sugar lump from the passing parade.

The sorrel outside stall 7, its neck already lathered, danced about and shook its head. Sloan disengaged Hilary from his arm, stepped in close and gripped the horse's bridle.

The groom's head snapped around. He stared a moment. Coal-black eyes deep in the equally black face danced to life. "Mistuh Sloan! Been too long gone!"

"Too right, Chester. How're you doing?"

"Doon fine, doon fine. How yuh like this Red Pepper beauty, hey? Best gelding Boss ever had." He elevated his voice to bullhorn loudness. "Boss Clyde! Looka here!"

Sloan heard the shuffling behind him. He kept one hand on the horse and extended the other.

Clyde Armbruster must be seventy years old now; he had seemed older than Methuselah when Sloan first met him twenty years ago, and the years clearly were not treating him kindly. He used to walk with a limp. These days he needed a cane just to limp slower. He had always been a squat, tough fellow. Now his neck had disappeared completely and his back was compressed like a folded telescope; the whole body bowed and hunched.

He came lurching up. With a trembling hand on his

cane, he leaned tri-cornered as he shook. The broad grin on his pudgy, drooping face said *welcome* more clearly than the hoarse and faltering voice ever could. "Good to see you, Cole!" The hand left Sloan's and waved toward the sorrel. "Whatcha think?"

"How, Clyde, do you always manage to find horses that are a nervous wreck from the day they're born and eat all your profits? Look at the loins on this beast. Long and sunken. A poor keeper if ever I saw one. This thing must put away a fortune in corn and hay, and it's as fat as a match."

The old trainer's throaty chuckle told Sloan he had pegged this splendid gelding's few shortcomings exactly.

"And how, Cole boy, do you always manage to find the loveliest lass in New South Wales?"

Sloan introduced Hilary around. Normally, she would speak the correct opening phrases, the pleasantries and small talk. This time she seemed distracted, at a loss. Her lovely eyes never touched Clyde's face. They kept flitting to the horse. The horse. That was it. She was absolutely stone-petrified of the horse.

Clyde leaned both hands on the cane and sagged forward. "You couldn't have come by at a better time, Cole boy." The vinegar voice dropped lower. "Got my eye on the finest colt you've ever seen. Promising. Melbourne Cup sort, as I know horses. Come in on it with me."

"To the tune of—?"

"Five, six hundred pounds; I want a majority ownership in him, but you can buy up to half."

Sloan licked his lips. "I have a couple of investments in mind, Clyde, but none of them's horses."

"None of them'll bring you the return this colt will, I vow."

"I don't follow the races as closely as I once did, but I keep an eye sharp for your name. You haven't been winning enough to buy a colt that size. Or did I miss something while I was up north?"

The old man chuckled. His ancient head dipped toward the sorrel. "Red Pepper's splendid, Cole boy, but for the first time in my life, I'm looking at something better than what I have. Pep here is going to buy me that colt. This race and one or two others will do it."

Cole studied the watery eyes. "Clyde, you've never talked like this before. The horses you already own have always been the light of your life. You ought to be in love with this sorrel right now, and calling it the wonder of the century."

"Right you are. And I would have been satisfied with this little beaut had I not seen the other. Pep runs next. When he's won the purse and he's back cooling out, I'll take you to see this other." He glanced at Hilary. "That is, if you've got the time, of course." The gravel voice purred. "Eh, Cole boy, I've waited my whole life for this. The perfect horse to keep me in my dotage."

The sorrel suddenly dipped and shied, wide-eyed, at some imagined threat. Sloan latched on with both hands. Hilary shrieked. The horse reared, hauling Sloan straight up. He sensed vaguely that Chester, too, was being dragged aloft. Old Clyde lunged at its head, but the horse was already falling back, sitting down. Clyde flopped forward on his face.

Sloan hung on. If the horse bolted forward it would run right over Clyde. He managed to grab a leathery ear. Together he and Chester twisted the panicked gelding's head around and threw it on its side, its head literally in Sloan's lap. Chester clapped a broad black hand down across Pepper's nostrils. They waited while the horse struggled. The struggling eased.

By the time they had the horse back on its feet and under control, Clyde was back on his feet, too. He propped himself, wavering, against his cane. "Bit high-strung, but a winner."

A knot of excited onlookers had collected instantly;

where did they all come from? Sloan expected some larrikin to dive in and give a hand, now that the situation was well in order. None stepped up to help with the horse, but three were offering their services to Hilary. She sat in a gorgeous heap, her face pallid, taking deep breaths.

Clyde's stableboy was on the horse now, too. The horse in good hands, Sloan turned away and helped Hilary to her feet. She craned her neck to look around him briefly at the trembling animal. She shuddered.

Then Sloan happened to glance toward the far end of Barn C. Frobel! That was young Frobel standing there, watching. Sloan recognized the backblocker's hat, the easy stance. His blond beauty, that absolutely unmistakable woman, at his side. Frobel smiled and waved and turned away. They strolled off.

What is that cocky doing here?

Hilary peered over her shoulder. "What's wrong?"

"Nothing." Sloan dug into his rapidly emptying pocket and handed her two quid. "Here you go, luv. Go pick yourself a winner."

She accepted the money without hesitation and took two steps backward. "Ta. What is the name of this one?"

"Red Pepper," Sloan replied.

She wrinkled her nose. "How did you know? You never saw it before."

"Just a sanguine hunch. Get on now, luv, and enjoy the races. I'll be back in the box directly."

She nodded, walked off ten feet, and turned. She smiled brightly. "I think it's ever so exciting, you buying a racehorse. The very best people do that, you know. Then we could watch the race from the owners' box." She waved and walked off.

Clyde snorted and mumbled, "Ever so exciting, eh? So long as she needn't get too close to one. Women!"

"Not all women. Just that one. I know a woman who would have been right in there with us, sitting on Pep's head before all was done. No fear of horses. Good hand with them. And game."

Clyde's eyes narrowed. "Then don't hang about with this dotty old woman, Cole boy. Go marry her. Now."

"Wish I could." The silent voice in his mind repeated it: *Wish I could. And she wouldn't worry about what all the best people did, either. Samantha.*

Clyde instructed the stableboy to lead Red Pepper out into the green beyond the barn, to settle him lest he be too upset to run well. The lad hurried off, the horse dancing and sidling beside him.

Sloan talked a few minutes more with the ancient trainer, engaged Chester in a bit of berley for old time's sake, and excused himself. He could return to the box and listen to Hilary's inanity or he could walk out across the paddocks for a while in relative quiet. He looked briefly around at the strutting, posturing, preening racing enthusiasts. The paddocks won, hands down.

Sloan mused on all that weighed upon him. His precarious financial position had become a constant factor in his life these last few years; he was almost accustomed to it. Still, constantly worrying about the next penny grew burdensome. He always seemed to be flat broke. Stiff as a crutch.

And what should he do about Hilary? He certainly didn't love her, and he sometimes doubted that she was capable of any but the shallowest affection. What kind of fidelity problems would she cause him on down the line? He'd better marry soon, though, if he intended to sire any little Sloans for posterity. And for pure, eye-dazzling beauty, you couldn't beat her with a stick. Look at the way that Pearl enhanced young Frobel's appearance! Sloan needed a good-looker to impress the big guns he wanted to impress.

The thought of Martin Frobel struck him like a blow. Why would the Frobels be wandering behind the track here, anyway? Certainly not to buy colts or see old friends.

Sloan wished he had six hundred pounds to invest in Clyde's deal. He'd love to buy into that. Clyde Armbruster was as fine a trainer as money can buy, and Sloan wouldn't have to buy him. Clyde would do the work; Sloan could enjoy the fun without the sweat. He could cash in on the horse, share the glory. . . .

Listen to you, you idiotic galah! You're starting to sound like Hilary!

Out across the paddock in the distance stood Red Pepper beside a little grove of wattles. The stableboy was rubbing him behind the ears, no doubt cooing and talking, though Sloan could hear nothing from this distance. The horse had settled considerably. Somehow horsemen of all stripes, some of them old vets and many of them Jacky Raws, gravitated to Clyde. All possessed a special flair for the esoteric life of horse husbandry. Sloan had been the Jacky Raw at one time, shoveling stalls out, not for the money but for the pleasure of being close to Clyde and his horses. Now this lad had that idyllic job, and Sloan was a grown man with troubles you wouldn't believe. Oh, for the old days. . . .

The back of his neck prickled. He paused in mid-step and wheeled. Two young men approached him. The situation would be unremarkable—merely a couple of young fellows headed this way—except for the intensity of their interest in Sloan. Was he imagining things?

Where are all the racing enthusiasts when you need them? Except for Red Pepper over there, the green stood abandoned, vacant. Sloan headed for the horse, quickening his stride. Behind him the men kept pace. He must stay out in the open. As long as he remained in broad view he would be safe. The predicament frightened him, not so much for its danger—when it came to a fight he was as good as there is—as for its unbelievability.

They pressed him, trying to force him back toward the

rear of the stables. He resisted by walking faster, angling outward toward the wattle grove and Red Pepper. The lad was leading the sorrel this way now, inattentive to the absurd plight before him.

Too late Sloan noticed the third man. The bloke, as young as the others and sporting a pencil mustache, popped up from nowhere, riding a mild-looking bay horse. He jogged his mount out into the paddock, partially blocking Sloan's way. Three to one, and an adversary mounted. Bad odds.

Absurdity piled upon absurdity. They were zeroing in, homing down on him like a hawk on a bandicoot. What made them think they could attack a strong man in broad daylight like this? He need only shout . . . But there were no ears to hear, save the lad's and Red Pepper's. They were crowding him toward the stables, driving him as a drover herds sheep, despite his attempt to stay in the open and clear. Something metallic—a knife blade?—flashed in the mounted fellow's hand.

With a bellow to make banshees cower, Sloan bolted forward at a dead run, straight for Red Pepper. The stableboy froze, gaping wide-eyed. Red Pepper lunged and sidestepped, instantly startled by the loud-mouthed madman coming at him.

Sloan reached Pepper as hoofbeats closed behind him. He grabbed the flimsy little saddle in both hands and vaulted, keeping his head low, throwing a leg over Pepper's back. With a shrill whinny the horse leaped from standstill to full gallop. Sloan hung on, barely, during those first flying moments. Pep collided shoulder-to-shoulder with the big bay horse, staggered and slammed on past. Sloan was nearly brushed off his perch. He squirmed back on and gathered up the reins.

He had to ride through the barns, among people, into safety. Right now this brainless horse was headed straight for a windbreak of woody shrubs at the far end of the green.

As panicky and wild-eyed as this beast was, it could well blast mindlessly right into the bushes. Sloan hauled and dragged. Nothing he did with the reins changed the horse's mind. Sloan had just exchanged one peril for another.

At least he was leaving his pursuer behind. Or was he? He glanced back. The pencil-mustached pursuer was whipping his bay horse, trying to keep up. Flecks of foam from Pepper's mouth splacked Sloan in the face. He sawed on the reins, violently wrenched the frantic horse's head aside—anything to turn him! At the last possible moment Sloan fell low across the horse's neck and pressed his face into the stinging mane.

They hit the windbreak full tilt.

Branches snapped, leaves thrashed, the sorrel squealed, Sloan's very soul cried out to God. A half ton of momentum drove horse and rider through the shrubbery. Sloan could feel himself flying, with the saddle nowhere near. He *whumped* the ground pile-driver hard and skidded.

Where was his pursuer? Surely his pursuer was not so foolish as to—

Hoofbeats! The horse was nearly on him. Dazed, Sloan lurched to his knees and twisted to meet the enemy.

"Grab!" yelled a vaguely familiar voice; a broad suntanned hand reached down to him. This pursuer wasn't the bay; its belly was white. He reached up and gripped the arm, snatching at salvation.

Smoothly, mightily, the rider hauled Sloan to his feet and on upward. Sloan swung a leg up, jumping; he was again on horseback, albeit a bit skewed. The rider dragged the horse around even as he urged it to an instant canter. They were headed for the barns.

Frobel! Of all the people on God's green earth . . .

They rode in among the sheds. Sloan glanced back just as a stable blotted the green from view. The fellow on the bay had abandoned pursuit and was whipping his horse off in the other direction.

This Frobel jackaroo was one splendid horseman. Almost effortlessly he wound their mount at a canter among the barns as onlookers in summer finery paused to turn and stare. Where was he going?

He hauled their horse to a halt at the corner of Barn A. Before Sloan could move, Frobel had swung a leg over the horse's neck and was sliding to the ground. As if Sloan were some little old lady, Frobel gave him a hand to dismount.

Sloan disdained the help. He should have held on to the saddle, though, as he slipped to the ground, for he nearly fell when his feet touched dirt. Only Frobel's strong arm kept him vertical.

"In here." Frobel piloted him into the second stall from the end. They stepped from blazing sun into warm, stuffy gloom. Frobel waved toward a three-legged stool. "Sit before you flop."

Not a bad idea. Sloan's ears buzzed and he felt dizzy. More than the breathless action and the jolt of being thrown through that hedge, incredulity was knocking him down. Why? Why would those insane fellows set upon him like that? Of all the hundreds at this race course, why Cole Sloan? And in broad daylight?

The little painted pony they had ridden to safety stood outside this stall. Sloan recognized the piebald as one of the docile nags used to lead racehorses out onto the track. Down its black-splotched white flank ran a broad splash of red blood. Frobel was peeling Sloan's jacket off, and still Sloan was slow to realize: the blood was not the horse's.

The inevitable mob of onlookers clustered about outside, second-guessing what must have happened. Drongos, every one of them. In here, in what was a stall being used as a tack room, a certain peace prevailed. A curious peace it was, born of what—confidence? This Frobel seemed to exude confident contentment. Sloan did not. He envied Frobel's peace.

Sloan leaned back heavily against the wall and inhaled deep draughts of hay-and-soaped-leather aroma. He closed his eyes. They burned. His left arm burned. His whole body ached.

"You're still bleeding, but this seems to be slowing it down pretty well." Frobel knelt beside him wrapping a cloth around Sloan's left arm, up near the shoulder. "Looks like a knife slice."

"I remember brushing against the nark, but I didn't realize he stuck me. How did you just happen along?"

"Pearl and I were wandering around among the barns, looking the place over. We enjoy the horses a lot more than the races. We happened to see your sorrel do his dance there, and we saw you didn't need any help with it. We wandered out to the back green and were just returning when Pearl noticed you walking out. She saw those three closing in on you. We were too far away to do anything directly, so she went for help and I grabbed the first warm body with four feet and a saddle."

The buzzing in his head had eased. His arm felt as if a camel were standing on it.

"So tell me, Frobel; who were they?"

Pearl Frobel's voice called from the distance. "Marty?"

"Here! Second one in."

Outside the stall door, the sea of the curious parted and a racetrack constable came shoving through with Pearl at his heels. He stopped and stared at Sloan's arm.

Sloan's feeling of peace fled. "Three young men, one with a pencil mustache riding a stocky bay. May still be in the area."

"Stay here. I'll need your statement." The constable turned and pushed his way out through the mob.

Sloan watched this blond beauty, who was obviously as much a part of it as her husband. "How did you know where to come?"

She frowned and shrugged. "Marty yelled 'Barn A' as he took off, so I ran for help and brought the constable here."

Sloan was beginning to notice other parts of his body that had been treated very badly by this whole affair. And he was *really* going to feel it tomorrow. "I'll tell you one thing—I don't know what you're playing, but it's a great game."

Frobel sat down in the dirt, drew his knees up and draped his arms across them. The blood on his hands was beginning to dry. "I don't play games, Sloan. When we talked in your office there, what I said was what I meant. And I'm not playing games now."

"Something like this doesn't just happen. I was singled out. Chosen. Of all the people in this place, they picked Cole Sloan. Of all the people in this place to lend a hand, fate picks Martin Frobel. And here's lovely Pearl, fetching the gendarmes as her husband fetches the luckless victim to an assigned place."

"You're saying this was arranged?" Frobel rubbed his chin with the back of his wrist, the only clean part left. Those chocolate-brown eyes fixed upon Sloan's steadily, without wavering.

"That's what I'm saying. There's no sense to it otherwise. And no chance it would all happen by accident."

Pearl was livid; Sloan could read the tension in her face. Frobel seemed not the least put off.

"Yes, I can see you'd think we set it up." The chocolate eyes hardened. "Your horse punched a hole in the shrubbery big enough to let a lorry through. The drongo on the bay was coming at you to finish what he started, Sloan. The only thing that turned him around was a rider coming at him, and then I wasn't sure he wouldn't reconsider and try some more. You were in more trouble than you could handle."

"Manufactured trouble. Why, Frobel? Why try to make

me feel some debt to you? Get a better deal on beef transport? Is this part of some even bigger setup, to get back at me? I see all kinds of possibilities. But I don't see anything that came out of pure chance."

"We agree there. Not chance. Pearl and I belong to God, Sloan, in a way you can't understand. Whatever those three were up to, it's God's providence that we happened to see them stalking you, and it's His doing that we—both of us—could do something to help you."

"Don't give me that—"

"If you owe a debt, it's to God, not us. And for the record, no. We didn't set it up." Frobel popped to his feet smoothly, powerfully. "I doubt those three are still here, but I'll hang around outside until the constable gets back, just in case. Pearl, maybe you can go tell his lady what's happening."

She nodded, glared at Sloan a moment, and left. If she were so angry with him, why was she off doing him a favor?

Sloan ended up sending Hilary home in his carriage. The racetrack hired its own doctor and its own constable, both of whom poked and prodded and otherwise attended him. Still, until everything was done, Sloan didn't climb into the hired cab until dark. He fell into bed the moment he arrived home. Hideous dreams marred his sleep that night, and in the morning he could not remember what they were.

He ought to take the day off. He should just sit around licking his wounds. With great and admirable force of will—plus the necessity of hustling if he was going to earn a quid today—he walked over to his office early, before breakfast. The walk shook some of the pain and stiffness out of his beleaguered body, but only some of it.

As he turned into Crown Street a fire engine passed, bound for the station. The men hanging on its rails looked grimy, weary-looking. Must have been a big one. What was this? A pumper and a hook-and-ladder stood parked by his door, their horses not yet hitched back up to them. Wet, flaccid hose lay all around the two-wheeled hose cart. Clumps and crowds of onlookers stood about. Sloan was beginning to despise onlookers.

A drift of dark gray smoke still floated out from—from—from *his* first-floor window ten feet above the street!

He approached a fireman in a spiked brass helmet. "I'm Cole Sloan. That's my office!"

"Come with me, Mr. Sloan." The fellow led the way through the door. "We confined damage to the first floor up there. Watch walking on this ground floor, though. Water makes it treacherous."

The stench of burned wood hung even thicker than the smoke. Water stood on the ground floor an inch deep. It still cascaded down the stairs they climbed. Sloan's boots were soaked through instantly.

His office. Black. Charred. Reeking. Hot, dark, humid. Curls of smoke and steam filled the room in spite of the bellows device a fireman was using to blow the stuff out the window. Sloan would salvage nothing here. Not a single thing.

"Mr. Sloan, do you smoke?"

"No."

"Did a client or visitor smoke here yesterday?"

"It was locked up yesterday. No one here."

"Your electrical system?"

"A light in the ceiling. That's all."

"I am required to determine a cause. No one here, you say. Can you offer any suggestion as to what caused it?"

"I don't know *who*, but I can tell you *what*. Arson." He stared at the mess that had been his desk, his records, his life.

He turned abruptly and headed back down the sooty, dripping stairs. He shoved past two firemen with a hose, out into the clarity of day.

And he stopped cold. A familiar black face, very sad,

approached him from the street side.

Chester, aged Chester the groom, doffed his hat and stepped up to him. "Mistuh Sloan. Track constable, he told me where to find you. Mistuh Sloan, Boss's Red Pepper horse: his leg was broke. We had to put him down. Boss ain't got no horse no more."

Chapter Five

Echuca Charlene

November 3, 1906

Dearest Mum and Papa,

I am situated in the town of Echuca in the state of Victoria. I had planned to travel to Melbourne, but an interesting position came up here. I am the secretarial assistant to Reginald Otis, a missionary to area aborigines. He is building a facility somewhere to the east, as I, here in town, handle the correspondence, requisitions, and such that his project generates. The work is very challenging, as he is building in the state of New South Wales and must adhere both to their governmental rules and hoop-de-doo and to Victoria's. What an inevitable mountain of paperwork is involved in an essentially profitless enterprise! Imagine what it would be like were he determined to make money!

Linnet has enrolled part time as a music student at the University of Adelaide, South Australia. She says she is taking voice lessons from a brilliant tiger of a woman named Guli Hack, and is engaged in violin and piano lessons as well. She has also taken a position as maid to a professor. I'll enclose her address and mine. She says she likes her professor's family and enjoys her job, but she may quit as her work load is onerous. Her note to me sounded bright and happy.

Before coming south, I visited awhile with Margaret up in central Queensland. I am pleased to report Meg appears to have married wisely. Her young man is quite attentive and utterly smitten with her. You would like him very much. He has a sly sense of humor much like Papa's.

At this moment (just past dawn) I am looking out my window at a medium-sized green and yellow parrot, quite wild, nipping berries off a bush. And in the chimney of a building across the way, a pair of kookaburras (no, I'm not making the name up) is nesting. A cockerel is not so noisy as are these big blue-gray birds. They call the sun up each morning and then complain about it all day.

Much more than the north Queensland coast, this area reminds me of home. And yet there are differences, just discordant enough to make one feel "this is not quite right." It is unsettling, and yet, very beautiful. I'm sure I'll get used to it, given time.

There are many more trees here than you know in Ireland, groves of short sparse ones scattered through an otherwise featureless landscape, and thicker forests of quite tall ones along the riverbank. The River Murray is apparently one of the continent's largest, and yet I can almost peg a stone across it from shore to shore. Papa, you would love to watch the boats. Some are smaller than a dory and others respectable enough in size to haul cattle, lumber, and great bales of wool. There are side-wheelers and barges and little steam tugs. Apparently there used to be many more. Mr. Otis says the river trade is past its heyday. If so, it must have been great indeed.

Lumbering and wool trade are the chief industries here. And eating. Echuca boasts quite a number of restaurants, cafes and hotel dining rooms. There is the American, which used to cater to that particular foreign element (I hear they're as raucous as the kookaburras), and several that court the trade of riverboat officers. My favorite is a little tea garden with outdoor seating under a bower. Very pleasant.

Indeed, there is so much to this land that is pleasant. God bless you both.

> With warmest love,
> I am your dutiful daughter,
> Samantha

Samantha glanced out the window as she addressed and sealed the envelope. A great white cockatoo with yellow feathers in its crest had joined the parrot. And a honeyeater of some sort scrambled about in the bush near the window. The honeyeater clattered and chattered obnoxiously. Did none of these birds sing sweetly? She wished she knew more about these striking birds.

Samantha took up her hat and beaded reticule, locked her door behind her, and strolled out into the golden morning sun. No need for a shawl in this hot summer weather. Summer in November! Honestly! With ample time to take the long way to the office and still arrive early, she walked down Leslie Street and angled across to the river shore.

Either Echuca was built on a rise or the Murray cut its bed very deep here, for the riverbanks fell away at least thirty feet in a stark, vertical cliff to meet the water below her. Samantha stood a few moments on the grassy lip of the cutbank and watched the brown satin water glide by. A large snow-white heron—or perhaps it was an egret— came flapping across the water and lit on its stilt legs on the cabin roof of a small paddle boat. Very peaceful, this, before the cranes and the steam engines began their day's activities.

She wandered out onto the great wharf. *The Great Echuca Wharf, the Marvel of the Age*, boasted the local *Riverine Herald*. Marvel? Well, yes, perhaps it was. For three quarters of a mile this engineering masterpiece in red gumwood linked the river below with the shore above.

The upper level, along which Samantha now strolled, with its stores and sheds, stood flush with the street. Beneath the thick plank flooring, an elaborate grid work of wooden girders laced together in geometric cacophony, a tangled maze of beams and pillars filling the thirty vertical feet from esplanade to river.

Whatever the engineering involved, the myriad beams did their duty. The wharf was not only sturdy enough to receive its tons and tons of wool and lumber, it also had to support the huge iron-and-wood cranes that laded the riverboats. Samantha would like somehow to obtain a picture of the wharf to send Papa. An excellent carpenter and joiner, he would enjoy nothing better than to admire the complex joinery of all these angled supports.

"Young woman! Miss Connolly?" A rather rotund man with muttonchop whiskers draped upon a roly-poly face flagged Samantha from the doorway of the wharfmaster's office. "You work for Reginald Otis?"

"Aye. I do." She crossed to him.

"I've a message here from him, and a problem." The man bowed and extended his hand. "Forgive me! We've not met, save through correspondence. My name is Alistair Drummond. How do you do?"

Samantha accepted the hand and nodded. "How do ye do? A message from Mr. Otis?"

"A letter arriving in last night's post; I dropped by your office, but you'd left. Come in, please."

"I had a number of errands, so I closed the office early yesterday and killed all the birds with one stone. Sorry to miss ye."

"I've no idea what you're going to do with this, but I've no resources." Mr. Drummond led the way into his office.

Samantha stepped in the door, from golden light to eternal gloom. If this were her office, she would first wash the grimy windows. Then she would haul the stacked files and papers out onto the wharf and let nothing back in the door unless it had a proper place to hide. What a jumbled, disorganized mess! But this was not her office, thank goodness, and she need not consider the days of tedious work that putting it in order would require. This was someone else's woe.

"Now, where is it. . . ?" Mr. Drummond pawed and rummaged through the clutter on his desk. He had said it arrived just last night; apparently it was already lost in this mare's nest.

"Here it . . . no . . . ah!" With a little smile of triumph, all in excess of the situation, he waved it aloft. "Mr. Otis has informed me here that supplies he's sent for will arrive by rail from Melbourne. And at the same time he's bringing down a crew from his station."

"Supplies. Aye. The roofing tin, pump parts, the donkey engine, and ten iron bedsteads. Did he mention books? He's expecting several crates of schoolbooks."

Mr. Drummond looked at her oddly. "You already know about that."

"Meself processed the order, sir. I didnae know, however, that he planned to come out so soon. The last he wrote, he'd be there for the summer."

"The crew's the problem. They're blacks, I assume. And, well, ah . . . You're aware, I'm sure, that the Esplanade or the Bridge won't take them. In fact, I don't know of an accommodation in town that will. And where do you intend to put all those supplies when they arrive? Storing them on the premises here will cost a pretty penny."

"Arranging transportation out to the station should nae cause ye much of a problem. There be boats sitting about idle and to spare."

"Well, ah, Miss Connolly. You're new in town and don't understand. The river trade is seasonal. The water is down now. Most vessels, particularly the larger ones, tie up and wait for higher water, lest they run aground. There's not a boat on the river just now that's big enough to handle all this."

"Mmm." Samantha studied the grimy floor boards. (She'd have the floor scrubbed, too. And whitewash the walls.) "When may I expect the shipment and Mr. Otis?"

"I believe your freight shall arrive late this morning on the train. Your employer is coming by the river. He should be here by nightfall, if the *Kyabram* hasn't encountered problems with shallows."

"Thank ye, Mr. Drummond. I'll make arrangements today to take care of both. I was pleased to meet ye." Samantha bobbed her head. Her terse nod was not at all a curtsy, but it seemed somehow ample for the occasion.

"Miss Connolly!" he blurted. "I don't think you realize, I can't help you."

"I understand that, Mr. Drummond. Meself shall make arrangements for Mr. Otis's crew and the supply shipment. Thank ye very much for informing me." She smiled and left promptly. What a depressing place that was.

No more time for admiring the scenery. She turned her back on the wharf and on the towering gum trees along the shore. By the time she reached her little office in Hare Street, a scant hour past dawn, the sun burned hot. Another scorcher today.

She hung her hat on the clothes tree and sat down by the window at the little table she pretended was a desk. This office was half the size of Mr. Drummond's, but it presented a neat, orderly appearance—relaxing. She much preferred this little hole in the wall to the most prestigious office. She leaned back in her chair, propped her elbows on its arms, and pondered the situation.

She already knew why blacks were not welcomed in the hotels. They were black. They tore the place up. They didn't know how to behave in civilization. They got drunk. Since Americans behaved similarly, they had a hotel all for themselves; obviously the key word was "black." Where to house them?

No large boats would be on the water now, he said. If

the wharfmaster didn't know, who did? And yet, Mr. Otis needed transport for his goods now, not some bright day in the future when the water level rose. And his books had not come yet.

Somewhat ruefully, she imagined how much a devious and scheming nature would help out just now. She was far too straightforward to cajole people into serving her needs. And the thought of deviousness instantly brought Cole Sloan to mind. Where was he now? How was he doing? She found herself still daydreaming ten minutes later. Honestly! That part of her life was ended. Besides, his was a most scheming mind, albeit housed in a most attractive body. Ah, but look at what Cole's conniving had done for him! He had lost nearly everything. No, perhaps the straightforward approach was better.

She wrote a rather hasty letter to the publisher in Melbourne concerning the delinquent books. Then she adjusted her hat on her head and strode forth to right all these irksome situations— straightforwardly.

The abandoned store beside the customs house would be the most convenient place. She walked around the corner to the store and tried the doors. The front was locked but the back was open. She walked through, assaying the amount of dust and neglect, and unlatched the front door on her way out.

She stopped by the Bridge Hotel. Mr. Otis's mission, a most charitable and worthy effort, required bedding and mattresses. Might they have worn, used bedding they'd part with for a modest price? They did. She wrote a check and hired an idle lad with a fishing pole to haul her bedding down to the abandoned store.

She retraced her steps to the wharf and trotted down the east stairs almost to river level. No matter how bright and hot the day, this world beneath the wharf remained ever damp and gloomy. Although she'd been down here before, still she found herself pausing, just to look. Massive gray beams wove themselves into a colossal cantilevered lacework three stories high, practically as far as the eye could see. The *Riverine Herald* was right.

The dry pounded dirt under here was firm yet powdery. She was sorely tempted to tread this gray world barefoot someday just to feel the cool dust as it should be felt. Two small side-wheelers lay docked at this end. She made her way to the closest—a flat, squat, graying little craft named *Echuca Charlene*—and walked a rickety plank from dirt to deck.

"G'day, mum. What can I do for you?" He came popping out of the nether regions of his deck cabin, his hands all black with engine grease. Were Samantha to meet this unkempt, dumpy little man with the shaggy beard in the streets of Cork, she would have turned and hastened the other way. But this man looked no more dangerous, and smelled no worse, than any other boat captain on the river. Appearances counted for very little in this roughhewn land. He grinned with approximately half the full complement of yellowed teeth.

Samantha dipped her head. "G'day, sir. Me name is Samantha Connolly. I work for Reginald Otis's aboriginal mission near the Barmah."

"Of course. I know well whereof you speak. August Runyan. And what might this humble boat captain do for the good and esteemed reverend, guardian of men's souls? And you, bewitching beauty?"

"A large and heavy cargo is due in on the train, and it must be transported upriver. I'm given to understand not all boats can make the trip these days. I trust, perhaps, yours can."

His eyes narrowed. "Mmm hmm. I smell in this proposed enterprise the sweet aroma of charity."

"Eh, if ye wish to make it so, Captain Runyan, we accept and gladly. Every farthing saved is a coin to be used elsewhere. But we're prepared to pay, however modestly."

Somewhere deep in that whiskered face, the narrowed eyes twinkled. "Modestly. You realize, young lady, the danger in the river this time of year, the dark and lurking shadows of misfortune poised awaiting in the wings. Shoals, shallows, stumps, snags around every bend. My lowly little boat here draws shallow indeed, but that is no guarantor of safe passage."

"By which I interpret that ye would prefer being paid extra because of the hazards involved."

The brutish head wagged. "So quickly do you cut to the core of it."

"The core of it, sir, is: Are ye willing to undertake the job, and if so, what would ye expect in payment?"

The verbose riverman laughed suddenly, loud and long. "Return at noon, sweet Irish rose, and I'll see what I can have lined up. What is your cargo specifically, do you know?"

"Bedsteads, parts, roofing tin and a donkey engine."

"Mmm hmm. You'll need more tonnage than my humble scow here will afford. I'll make inquiry round about and see who, among the smaller of us, might be willing to tender an offer. I'll check the schedule for the *Etona*'s whereabouts as well. She's small—twenty-five feet—but she carries her weight and then some."

"*Etona*. The little mission boat I hear about?"

"The very same. Paid for by students at Eton, far away in merrie England, and used by the Adelaide diocese for services, baptisms, burials and marriages all up and down the noble Murray. And"—he waved a hand—"she'll take an occasional cargo for a worthy cause such as yourself."

"Y'r help is much appreciated, sir, since I know nothing at all about the trade here, and Mr. Drummond seemed at a loss."

"Drummond! The man himself is a loss! Political appointee. The bane of solid working men everywhere, political appointees. You'll return betimes, aye?"

"With pleasure, and thank ye, sir."

Samantha excused herself and walked up the steep staircase. As she topped out at street level, the train arrived. Huffing and snorting it came, radiating heat and noise. Just what this torrid summer day needed: more heat. Already the oppressive warmth sapped Samantha's energy. From the shade of a galvanized iron shed she watched unloading commence.

An hour later they carried from the third boxcar what Samantha took to be Mr. Otis's pump parts and donkey engine. Both crates stood waist high. Disassembled, the ten iron bedsteads still occupied an inordinate amount of space. Roofing tin. There ought to be roofing tin yet. From the next car back came bound pallets that shook the decking when they were set down. Samantha gasped and sighed. Here was Mr. Otis's roofing tin, and ten boats the size of *Echuca Charlene* could not hope to transport it! Perhaps Mr. Drummond's pessimism was well served. A hand touched her shoulder, and she jumped.

Captain Runyan stood beside her; Samantha had no idea why she had not smelled him coming. He patted her shoulder. "The look of distress furrowing that lovely brow tells me you doubt the wisdom of transporting heavy cargo during this season of trial and hazard."

"Meself had no idea the size of it all. The tin especially."

"Fear not, fair Celtic flower. 'Tis been arranged. Though I be no man of God, I perceive the eternal folly of failing to serve that supreme deity's appointed ministers, so I took it upon myself to line up the transport for your master's enterprise. The *Etona* is due in any moment, and I've engaged the *Cobar,* a lackluster though serviceable barge; for the *Tarella* runs too deep to be using it in this season."

"And the cost, sir?"

"Modest. Modest."

"Ye understand meself can make no deal until the price be agreed upon."

"And wise you are to proceed cautiously." He babbled on, but the verbose flowers of his speech dropped their petals far short of her ears. Should she pay to have all this carted away from the loading dock to the commandeered warehouse? Then she would have to pay to have it all brought back here for shipping. Would she save money in the long run by leaving it here until the various boats were arranged for and in place? *Pay fairly but pay minimum* were her standing orders. What in heaven's name was she going to do with all this? And how long did she have to decide before costs began to mount?

"There you are!" A cheerful voice interrupted her thoughts. The trim, slim gray-haired little man approaching seemed not the least discomfited by the heat. He wore a small, neat tie with his white shirt and trousers, and he seemed to be marching through life at a constant, rapid double-step. He paused beside them and nodded graciously to Samantha. "Gus, they said you need me."

"Ah! Captain Albert Sykes. Here is the fair lass in true and utter need. Samantha Connolly, the master of the *Etona*."

Samantha shook hands and felt decidedly odd about being considered an equal by these boat captains. Captain Runyan explained her need in his peculiarly florid way. She kept casting an eye toward the huge mound of goods that was now her responsibility. Life weighed nearly as heavy as that roofing tin just now. "That it over there?" Captain Sykes waved a finger toward the mountain.

"Aye," she nodded. "I believe so." She almost had to break into a trot to keep up with him. He led the way to the mountain of cargo and walked around it a couple times, nodding.

"Gus? You can make the run up and back for ten pounds, I'm sure. That's what you agreed, wasn't it?"

"Eh, now, Bert, you must realize I've engaged the *Cobar*, being that *Tarella* is already beached for the season, and that right there is more than—"

"Nonsense. With *Tarella* beached, the *Cobar* should be available for nothing. I'll speak to her owner. You're right that we'll need her, though. If we spread the load across three vessels we ought to make it up there. That satisfactory with you, Miss Connolly?"

"Meself trusts y'r judgment far more than me own, Captain Sykes. But I—"

Sykes bobbed his head. "Now. Crane fees are high, because they employ seven men on one crane. So you only want to transfer your goods once, if possible. I suggest storing everything aboard the *Cobar*, then transferring some to the other two vessels. Most of it to the *Echuca Charlene*. If we can keep *Etona* high, we can use her to rescue us when we get stuck."

"Concerning costs, sir, we've not yet—"

The wiry little captain beamed. "Gus cracks hardy, but he'll come through with a reasonable rate. And the *Etona* is free."

Should she trust these men, or was she—and by extension Mr. Otis—about to be taken for a ride? Her instinct said *trust Sykes; beware Runyan*. She would act upon that instinct.

She engaged a boy with a team and dray to take the disassembled bedsteads over to the warehouse. There Mr. Otis's crew could make their beds tonight in the most fundamental sense.

She invited the captains to lunch at the tea garden, and Captain Sykes, bless him, insisted upon picking up the check. She returned to the wharf to watch the roofing tin be lifted by crane onto the flatness of a low barge. Everywhere she looked, there were probably expenses involved. The boats. This barge. The crane. The stevedores. In the past, shipments had been confined to a few manageable crates. But this . . .

The *Kyabram* arrived just before dark. His head wagging, its captain mumbled and complained about the obstacles to travel in this low water and vowed to beach his boat next morning.

Mr. Otis bounced ashore as always, with a motley, fascinating bevy of black and half-caste people crowding close behind him. It occurred to Samantha that this was probably these folks' first visit to town. They would likely go away thinking every white man's town possessed a Great Echuca Wharf, the Marvel of the Age.

Mr. Otis was even bringing a horse to ride. The ugly roan with the hulking blaze face stood patiently in the stern, as if riding these noisy monstrosities were the most natural thing in the world.

Although she stood afar off to the side, Reginald Otis's darting eyes found her almost immediately. The most wondrous grin divided his round face in two. His pace quickened.

He hurried over and clasped her hands in his. "Samantha! You're looking lovely! Your letters have all sounded so very cheerful. They make me ashamed that I don't write oftener. I've no excuse."

"Delighted to see ye, sir." And indeed she was. He introduced everyone, pronouncing names Samantha would never in a million years recall. One girl, though, she would surely remember. The young woman, with skin the color of tea with cream, looked bright and sparkly, and her name was Ellen. Samantha could surely remember "Ellen."

They stood about as bags and parcels were being unloaded, and Reginald Otis spilled over with happy descriptions of his work. She listened and laughed and asked questions. But she also listened with that inner ear that hears beyond the words spoken.

Did that ear hear correctly? If so, if Samantha were reading accurately the face and the nuances, Mr. Otis was in love.

With her.

Chapter Six

Barmah

Absolute heat. Torrid brilliance bounced off the barren ground and poured from the cloudless sky. Heavy, silent air shimmered in place. Never had Samantha experienced such searing, penetrating, exquisite heat. She sat in the lacy half shade of a gangly gum tree and waved a feather fan languidly before her face. Perhaps if she could somehow move a little of this oppressive air, she would not feel so constantly suffocated.

Samantha felt miserably weak and drained simply sitting in this shade. *Just look at Reginald Otis walking around out in that hell!* she thought. He had shed his coat and tie and rolled his sleeves above the elbow. His white shirt glared bright. Beside him jogged Ellen in a loose, modest cotton dress, apparently not the least uncomfortable. They were strolling out and about through the sparse scrub.

The roan and its partner, along with a yoke of bullocks, had transported the load to the mission site here from the river wharf a quarter mile away. Now workers, both black and white, were nailing crackly sheets of tin to the roof girders of the chapel and main house. Samantha had always thought carpenters made a lot of racket, but wood carpentry is silence compared to a half dozen aboriginals with hammers, putting on tin roofs.

The new tin reflected sunlight so brilliantly that the buildings seemed roofed with a second sun. Those men up there were getting broiled like meat, yet they seemed not to mind in the least. Unacceptable, that one human being might suffer so in conditions others found not the least unpleasant!

Samantha also found it difficult to accept the extraordinary flatness of the land. Except for some slightly rolling rises near the river, the landscape stretched in all directions as level and smooth as a marble palace floor.

Reginald was standing beside a sheep brake constructed of stacked and woven brush. He waved his hand about as Ellen nodded, writing hastily upon a child's school tablet of some sort. At length they turned and started back toward where Samantha sat.

Reginald was looking at her. His broad smile reversed itself to a worried frown and he broke into a lumbering run. *He shouldn't exert himself so strenuously in this heat. It can't be good for his health.*

When he reached Samantha, he dropped to one knee beside her chair. "Samantha, you look terrible! Your face is very red. I should never have brought you out here. I'm extremely sorry."

She forced a smile she certainly did not feel. "Nonsense. By visiting the site of y'r mission here and knowing the situation, I can operate much more intelligently and responsibly at the other end. I was rather working in the dark before."

"Don't try to sugar-coat the fact that I was a fool to subject you to this. I of all people am aware you do not take heat well."

"I'm doing nothing of the sort. I mean it. Ye didnae force me, ye invited me, and I jumped at the chance to see the place. Besides, y'r crew is hard at work putting on the new tin roofs. I'll have satisfactory shade now very shortly. I look forward to sipping water on y'r brand-new verandah."

He patted her hand and hauled himself erect. "And you shall, very soon." He hastened off.

Samantha wasn't being altogether devious; she really did profit from seeing this place. On the flatness amid the sparse, ragged little trees, Reginald was planting civilization, and she had to see it to believe it. Half a dozen modest cabins, built of crooked little logs, sported roofs that looked like bark. Surely they couldn't be rainproof—but then, when did it rain? Not lately. A roofless stone chapel stood waiting for its tin lid. The simple square mud schoolhouse beside it already served seven children, Ellen said.

And Reginald's home, just now receiving its roof as well, could hardly be called sumptuous. Constructed of rough slabbed planks, it had neither paint, indoor facilities, nor any modern comfort. The kitchen, a separate building, connected to the house by a brush-roofed breezeway. The house sat squarely in the center of things, and yet no building actually stood near it. A part and yet apart. Yes, that was Reginald.

They named the mission "Barmah," apparently because of its proximity to a great and famous forest nearby. Reginald had explained the importance of the Barmah Forest, and its renown for its versatile red gum lumber. Samantha had seen the many timber barges on the wharf. Her head understood the economic significance of red gum, but in her heart, she rather felt all the many kinds of wood—gum, acacia, box—to be pretty much the same.

Ellen came by presently with a big gourd dipper of tepid water. She handed it to Samantha and sat down in the dust with her long legs stretched out straight before her. She seemed so comfortably a part of this milieu. It made Samantha feel all the more the outsider.

Ellen smiled. Her teeth were beautiful. "I grew up in Ebenezer Mission, on the Wimmera near Lake Hindmarsh. It's Moravian, and the home office would send these missionary people over from Europe. They would turn red just like you. It would take them two or three years to get used to the climate."

"Eh, lass. Y'rself is saying that in another year I'll feel much better."

Ellen laughed. "Something to look forward to!" The smile faded. "There were a few who never did get used to it. Our schoolteachers would only last a couple of years, and then they'd leave. Except Miss Tyre. She was there five years. Dear old Miss Tyre. I had no idea who Queen Victoria was, but I knew she had to be someone very important because her death was the only time Miss Tyre ever shed tears."

"Do ye ever wish to go back? To the mission, I mean."

"Can't. It's gone now. Everything's gone. Rev. Bogisch— he's the man who *was* the mission, like Mr. Otis is Barmah here—died three years ago. And the mission itself was made available for selection a year and some later."

"What does that mean?"

"Selectors are small farmers who squat on an assigned piece of government land—their selection—and develop it. They receive some government help getting started. If they're successful, the land becomes theirs. Farmers and squatters took over the mission lands. All but the cemetery. The Moravians have arranged to keep the cemetery the way it is."

"Where Rev. Bogisch is."

"Where everybody is." The sorrow in her voice made a startling contrast to her youth. She sat quietly a few moments. "My cousin Charles was buried there the beginning of winter two years ago. He was nine years old. There was such hope in him. And a year later his grandfather was dead. 'Of course he died,' everyone said. 'He was eighty-four.' I think he would have lived to be a hundred, but he died of a broken heart. Charles was everything to him."

"Why did Ebenezer Mission fail? Because Rev. Bogisch died?"

"No, not really. It was already being dismantled. The reverend may have died of a broken heart himself. He put so many years into it. You're new, so you may not know about the Act. The government decreed that adult half-castes could not receive public money anymore. They had to *make* their place in the white man's world, you might say."

"I'd hardly call Moravian church funds public money."

"Exactly. And Rev. Bogisch fought it. He tried all sorts of ways to get around it. He finally had to give in. The half-castes were the ones who really took to gardening, and they didn't mind the yard work. They had no real place in the black world, you see. They were his workers. They kept the place going. Without them . . ." She waved her hands helplessly.

Politics. Government. Samantha understood the frustration as well as anyone. The politics of the Irish unrest had killed her brother Edan in the full flower of his youth. Now here was politics extending its ugly fingers into the farthest reaches of outback Victoria. Apparently no corner of the earth was safe from politicians.

Samantha thought a moment about the rainbow of skin hues here. "Reginald seems to be untrammeled by the Act."

"Paid labor, so far. If the money gets low or support is reduced . . ." She shook her head. "At Ebenezer, the younger blacks would leave their old people at the mission to be taken care of and go off on walkabout. Rev. Bogisch was forced to reduce the mission lands several years before the end because he had no one able-bodied to keep them up. Ebenezer was grand in its day. But then it just sort of trickled to an end."

"Ebenezer ends. Barmah begins. Tear that down. Build this up. A lot of sweat for what is, ultimately, defeat. I'm sure when y'r Rev. Bogisch devoted his life to y'r Ebenezer Mission, he entertained hopes and dreams as bright as

Reginald's. I cannae help but worry that Reginald's may come to the same ignoble end."

"Defeat." Ellen studied her. She drew her knees up and folded her arms across them as a shelf to rest her chin. "Yes, I suppose. In some ways. Ebenezer served scores of blacks for a time. But for every baby born, three or four people died. The last baby born at Ebenezer was little Willie Marks. I remember because I got to help with the birthing. I was thirteen."

"What are ye now, may I ask?"

"Nineteen. Rev. Bogisch didn't fail. He wanted to bring health and prosperity and Jesus Christ to the aborigines. He did that, but only to so very few. He was defeated by the government and by the way things are. The blacks are dying out. A generation or two, and there won't be any of us left. That will be the final defeat."

What remained to be said? Samantha said nothing. In Ireland the yellow and red and black races of the world, other than being utterly alien and incomprehensible, were . . . well, they were seen as different. Freaks and curiosities. Not non-people, and yet not quite people in every sense of the word. Certainly not civilized or fully sensate.

Yet Samantha sat here listening to Ellen talk about an eighty-four-year-old man dying of a broken heart. She listened to Ellen's eloquence and thought about the deep and resourceful blacks she had known at Sugarlea when first she arrived in this upside-down land. Her racial perceptions, ingrained through a lifetime of schoolbooks in Erin, obviously needed changing. But to what? And besides, she already had a mighty headache, and it wasn't doing her attempts at thinking the least bit of good.

They dined that evening under a brand new tin verandah roof. The cooling effects of complete shade would have helped more if it were not for the heat assailing Samantha on all sides and radiating up from the very floor. The cook served mutton with onions and carrots. Samantha managed to force down a bit of the carrots. She was already slim naturally; she'd soon be too lean to cast a shadow.

Reginald—enthusiastic, cheerful, competent Reginald—kept up a constant, thoughtful attention that flattered Samantha. He was always available, but never smothered her. This was the kind of Prince Charming every woman dreamed of meeting. Much as she would have preferred wallowing in the misery of the climate, he made her smile, and he kept the conversation bright.

The sun sank low toward Echuca, but the heat did not abate. The three sat on the verandah, sipping tea and watching the changing shadows on the scraggly trees.

A black man came striding up the track from the river. Samantha recalled his name was Toby, and she had met him down at the mission's little pontoon wharf. On his shoulder he toted a canvas bag. *Rather like a lanky black Saint Nicholas.* She smiled at the thought. This would be the mail, no doubt, the last of the load in *Echuca Charlene.* He came straight to the house and plopped the bag on the verandah.

With a grin and a nod, Toby greeted Ellen and Reginald and Samantha. The grin stayed put as he studied Samantha's face. "Your nose, missy. Bad look. Too much little possum haunch, all fresh butchered."

"What a refreshingly colorful description."

"Color full. Thass it! Too much full color. Red."

Reginald was grinning, too, and his expansive smile suggested utter delight. Ellen pawed through the mailbag, handed the five or six letters to Reginald, and disappeared inside with the bag.

"River down some more." Toby sat down and leaned against a porch post. "Boat hard time, mail gunner come by skiff now and later, says Gus. Gus says he rode to Echuca on the last of the water a week ago. Don' know what he's doing here now."

"Then, Samantha," said Reginald, "we'd best cut short your stay and send you home now. I wouldn't want you stranded here."

" 'Tis quite as hot in Echuca, aye?"

"No. Nowhere in the Riverina is it cool this time of year, but Echuca has more vegetation, and it's slightly cooler along the river. Also, there is medical attention in Echuca should the heat prostrate you, and there is none out here. I'll feel much better when you're safely back in town." With his pocket knife he slit open the top letter in the stack.

"As ye wish, of course. Y're me employer. And ye understand the land. I dinnae know it yet. Still, 'tis the first time in me life I've ever been waited on hand and foot like this. Like royalty I'm being treated, and I loathe to return to being mere common folk."

"Common?" Reginald laughed. "No, Samantha, common you will never be." He paused to read his letter.

Ellen came out with the mailbag. "Here you go, Toby. Remind Mr. Runyan we need stamps, will you?"

"I do that. Tell him too much. Him say 'I got Victoria stamps. Ellen she is New South Wales.' "

"You tell him I know for a fact he can sell Victorian stamps to anyone, even if they're from the other side of the world, and he'll sell some to me."

"I tell him again." Toby lurched to his feet.

Reginald raised a hand. "Toby, will you tell Mr. Runyan I'd like to send Miss Connolly back to Echuca as soon as possible."

Toby grinned. "Letcha know." And away he went, as smoothly and swiftly as if the temperature were normal.

Ellen walked out across the commons toward a cabin that was probably her own domicile. Perhaps it was because so much land lay vacant and unused that people out here made themselves such huge yards, placing secondary structures so far out as to bring new meaning to the word *outbuilding*. You walked and walked and walked without leaving the dooryard.

Samantha pulled in a lungful of heavy air. She felt lightheaded. There was a sudden tenseness here, and she was slow to realize she was not its source. She glanced over. "Reginald?"

He was staring tight-lipped at one of his letters. Normally so cheerful and soft, his features had hardened in just plain anger. He drew a deep breath and stared at the underside of his new verandah roof awhile. His eyes returned to the letter, but his face did not soften.

"Reginald?"

He waved the letter. "Latest instructions from the home missions board. They feel I should make purchases and handle shipments directly from Barmah here. They believe the office and secretary in Echuca are an unnecessary expense."

"They're in London. How would they know what is necessary?"

"Indeed." He tossed the letter aside. "This changes everything. I must think about it. Excuse me, Samantha, please." He leaped to his feet and strode out across the yard.

Samantha was sorely tempted to scoop that letter up and read it. She must not. Although it certainly pertained to her—this was her position they were abolishing—it was not her letter. By dint of mental strength she managed to beat temptation to a nubbin, but only by practically sitting on her nervous hands.

Toby appeared from among the trees and met Reginald at the far end of the commons. They talked. Toby nodded. Reginald wagged his head. His white shirt still glowed in the sun, but it was now a yellowish glow as the sun made its final bow. Toby left. Reginald stood about awhile with his hands in his pockets, then came back toward the house. Sadness had replaced the anger in his face.

Samantha grimaced and pretended it was a smile. "Since I be nae longer in y'r employ, I shall offer unrequested advice. Get angry. Jump up and down and scream. Let it all out, as it were. Ye'll do y'rself nae bit of good stuffing it all away like this."

"I'll vent my anger tomorrow with a hammer, putting on roofing. Do you feel up to a stroll?"

"Aye. Sure 'n I ought to move about some or I'll melt into a solid mass." She stood experimentally. No weakness, no dizziness posed problems. She took his proffered hand and stepped out into the waning sun. Why did the land not cool off better when the furnace went down?

He did not release her hand. He took it in his and pinned her arm with his. It provided a welcome steadying effect. "Toby says the *Echuca Charlene* is fired up and waiting at the wharf for you. Apparently Gus loathes walking, and he's afraid he'll have to do just that if his boat strands."

"I feel like a deserter."

"By no means! I only feel terrible about giving you the sack so precipitously. I shall, of course, make your reemployment a matter of earnest prayer."

"I understand the situation, and I thank ye for y'r prayers."

He licked his lips and glanced skyward as if seeking to pluck words out of the brazen emptiness. "I believe you said you never married." They strolled out across the yard toward the track to the river.

"As me grandmum says, 'Nae even a close call.' " Grandmum. How was she tonight? She should be here instead of Samantha. Grandmum sought out heat as a moth seeks the flame. Grandmum spent most of her day curled up in the inglenook, pressed against the warm chimney.

He chuckled. "My own dear grandmama would have said the same thing about me all the way through my schooldays. Then I met Darla. When I was courting Darla Custer, my whole world turned to mush. I was just finishing seminary—tests, reports, papers. I nearly failed the next-to-final quarter, for no matter what I applied the front of my mind to, Darla was at the back of it."

"Head over heels in love, y're saying."

"That's putting it mildly. I completed seminary in spite of myself and we married. I would like to say that meeting Jesus Christ personally was the greatest thing in my life, and it would certainly sound pious, but it would be dishonest. Being married to Darla was greatest, closer heaven than heaven itself. We had nineteen months together. She died in childbirth. Our newborn daughter died twelve hours later."

Samantha closed her burning eyes. Why did such losses never strike scoundrels? Why was it always wonderful people who suffered?

He led her onto the river track. "I mourned her for years. Still do, inwardly. In fact, it never occurred to me that I might get over it—until I found you in a wilted little heap on the track that day. Since then, whatever the front of my mind is doing, you are at the back of it."

Samantha stopped and turned to face him. "Be ye saying 'tis love y're smitten with?"

"I don't know, Samantha. It's been so long, I don't know. And I'm afraid. The last time I loved, I lost." His earnest eyes held hers comfortably. "What if I were to allow myself to love you and something happened? I'm sure it sounds silly, a child's fear, but it's real to me. I'd feel as if I caused another tragedy."

" 'Twas not y'rself sought me out; I came to ye seeking work."

"True. When I left you behind, safe and comfortable in that inn, I told myself you were gone from my life. I had done my Good Samaritan job, and it was over. But I couldn't forget you. And when you walked into my office, out of the blue as it were, the first thing that came to my mind was 'This is a sign from God! He wants this!' "

"Strong words, Reginald."

He smiled and started walking again toward the river. "Not to mention melodramatic. And I'm not normally a melodramatic person. I'm telling you this only to show you my state of mind then. Believe me, the job was yours from the moment you walked in. It was my immense good fortune that you are well organized, efficient, precise, and you can think quickly and clearly. You took care of permits and applications. . . . In a very large way, you made Barmah possible. I couldn't handle all that paperwork and also see to the actual building. It's two full-time jobs. Both of them would have fallen by the way. So, you see, you were indeed a gift from God. I wasn't that far off in my first reaction."

"And now ye dinnae need me anymore."

"So the missions board says."

She patted his hand, suddenly overwhelmed by a mix of—a mix of what? Sympathy? Admiration? Both, and more. "Sure 'n ye'll expand Barmah as time goes on, but y'r essential buildings are nearly complete. 'Tis not the crush of work now that it once was. Ye'll make out fine with Ellen at y'r side."

"Ellen. Yes. She's nearly as big a blessing as you. I've had no prior experience with outback missions, and she grew up in one. Her experience and competence have been invaluable to me. But you, Samantha . . ." He shook his head. "You are unique in my life, not because of your contribution, but because you are you." He smiled at her. "There I am, being melodramatic again."

"And I be speechless."

She had just lied to him, and he a man of God. She was never going to tell him she had lied, for it would profit him nothing to know about Cole Sloan.

Grandmum's quote was no longer true. Cole Sloan had asked her to marry him. Once upon a time he professed his love for her. And he had stolen her heart. But that was another time in another place. He was lost now in the maddening maze of Sydney, and she was just as lost, frying in the empty outback. Never the twain shall meet.

And just as well. Cole Sloan was everything this man beside her was not, and not to his credit. True, Reginald was quite regular-looking and Cole inordinately good-looking. But Reginald was honest and open, Cole crooked and devious. Reginald adhered to a high moral code. Cole openly admitted he didn't mind living in the moral gutter on occasion.

Reginald could be trusted.

Cole could not.

No contest.

Although the air still hung silent and lifeless, it no longer suffocated her. They walked in peace through scattered golden scrub. Somewhere off to the left, the brush rattled as a kangaroo made a hasty exit. Such noises no longer bothered her. Perhaps Samantha was becoming inured to this alien land after all.

Toby shattered the peace by running up the track from the river. "Getcha bag, missy," he grinned as he passed them, heading toward Barmah.

Reginald chuckled. "When perpetual motion machines are perfected, it's Toby they'll have to beat." He sobered. "Speaking of perpetual—"

"Aye?"

"Two things. First, although I admit that my feelings for you are strong, I'm not yet suggesting engagement or marriage or . . . I hope you understand."

"Y'r uncertainty was the first thing ye admitted. Aye, I understand, for I've been victim to fear and indecision meself on many a time."

He smiled. "Of course you understand. You're a wise and understanding woman; one of the nicest things about you. Secondly, I did not press this next issue in the past. I thought you would be in association for quite some time and I could, bit by bit—" He stopped and sighed. Obviously, he was having a great deal of trouble with phrasing.

"Issue?"

"There's nothing to keep you in Echuca, and work is scarce there. You will almost surely move on. I trust and pray we'll remain in correspondence, but this is a matter to be completed face to face, and I no longer have the luxury of time."

"What issue?"

"The matter of a personal relationship with Jesus Christ. I fear you are still eighteen inches away from salvation."

"What?"

"The distance between your head and your heart. Your head knows the catechism and all the words. But you're heart does not yet know the person Christ." He stopped and turned her to himself. "This may be the last time we meet for a while. I cannot let this opportunity pass without begging you to invite Jesus Christ into your life."

"Me, uh, me brother-in-law said essentially the same thing, though he phrased it differently."

"The phrasing is immaterial. The fact of it is all-important. Only the payment Jesus Christ made can give you entry into eternal life, and that you can receive only by receiving Him." He sighed. "I can preach an evangelistic sermon to hundreds. So why do I get all tongue-tied and spout bromides when I look into your eyes?"

"Meself would hardly call it 'tongue-tied.' "

"Tongue-tied! The glory of Jesus is so unspeakable, and all that He can do for you, and all you can do for Him—it all comes tumbling into my mind at once and I can't channel it out to you coherently." He pressed her hands in his. "Very well; perhaps it's best I write a letter, after all. I beg you as a matter of life and death to look favorably on my petition."

"I look forward to receiving it." The intensity of his plea rattled her.

Toby, his skin glistening and his clothes soaked in

sweat, arrived at the wharf about the same time they did. He handed her traveling bag across to Gus the skipper. Reginald bade her farewell and kissed her hands in parting. She heard a loud splash as she stepped aboard the tiny sidewheeler and glanced beyond the stern. Toby, still fully clothed, was bathing.

The little boat proceeded less than half a mile before tying up to a snag for the night. "No moon," explained Captain Runyan with uncharacteristic terseness. Samantha curled up on a lumpy little pallet and slept much more soundly than circumstances would dictate.

A steam sidewheeler, regardless its size, is both dirty and noisy. *Echuca Charlene's* wood-fired boiler spewed soot and rained ashes on the deck. Her piston thudded. She throbbed. Her dual paddle wheels flailed at the brown water and kicked it into a frothy wake. The wheel housing smelled stale and moldy.

And yet, all her quirky little faults aside, she shared the beguiling charm nearly all these riverboats displayed. She glided smoothly, elegantly past forested shores and open fields. She tooted her whistle and rang bells from time to time, sometimes for official reasons and sometimes to greet a farmer in his wagon. She was fun to ride in. Best of all, the flat river met her flat bottom solidly. No pitch, no yaw, no lurching disturbed Samantha's delicate stomach.

By the time *Echuca Charlene* hooted her whistle and reversed her paddles on her approach to the Great Echuca Wharf, Samantha had resigned herself to job seeking. Job seeking? That was the easy part. What about Reginald? That thorny problem defied resolution. Should he actually propose, ought she accept? If not, why not?

Once in a lifetime she might find a strong, sensitive man who loved her. Most women never found such at all, so rare are they. Here was a catch not to let slip away. And yet, she did not return his love.

Nonsense! Love did not sustain marriage. Witness the success of so many arranged weddings. Rather, marriage sustained love. Much overrated, this business of romantic love.

With yanks and jerks and clunks, *Echuca Charlene* was tied up at the east end of the wharf. Samantha picked up her bag and disembarked. Reginald was right. Somehow the summer heat was muted by the river and the trees along the shore.

She stepped in under the wharf and started west along the dusty little path beneath the gargantuan lacework of struts and beams. It could not be called cool under here today, but it was cooler. To her right, half a dozen boys had drawn a circle in the only level bit of dirt under the wharf and were intensely into a game of marbles. Idle stevedores lounged at the river's edge, smoking.

Again Samantha was the only female in this gloomy underworld. Well, that would be no more. Her next job would not give her cause to come down here. Her next job, if she could find one at all, would stuff her into some close little room all day. She suddenly realized what a wonderful job hers had been, taking her out and about and challenging her daily.

With river traffic at a near-standstill, no businessmen prowled these nether regions. Yet a man in a white shirt was approaching, and he looked businesslike. The man stopped dead in his tracks and stared at Samantha.

Samantha's legs ceased moving. Her hand released her bag and let it drop into the dirt. She stared at the man, gaping, frozen in place and time.

Cole Sloan.

Chapter Seven

A Paid Engagement

*Freu - de scho - ner Got - ter-fun-ken,
Got - ter-fun - ken!*

The choir ceased singing as, in frenzied crescendo, the orchestra and the conservatorium's vast organ thundered wildly to the conclusion of Beethoven's Ninth Symphony.

The audience responded with enthusiastic applause. They stood. They cheered. They applauded furiously as the conductor bowed, then the choir director, then a man in the front row of the first violins. The organist, Herr Kugelberg, took a bow. Chris Yorke at the piano and Elizabeth Mapes with her violin bowed along with the rest of the orchestra. Most wondrous of all, Linnet Connolly, ex-maid, present student, bowed along with the rest of the University of Adelaide choir.

Never had Linnet experienced a moment like this. Over six hundred chairs crowded the conservatorium floor, and every one had been filled for this concert. Lining the back and side walls were at least a hundred more music enthusiasts who had paid for standing room only. All those people . . .

Never before had Linnet heard the rich glory of a full orchestra. Never had she sung in such a large choir, and every other voice in it belonged to a professional musician. The heady thrill of it all filled her with overflowing joy.

The choir filed off the stage and melted into the general swarm of musicians and fans. Linnet more or less took steps in place, shoved about by the milling crowd. She had nowhere to go and did not know what to do. The evening had just ended, hours before she wanted it to.

Chris. If she could find Chris, she could at least share her ebullience. Though he was a veteran of many such concerts, the look on his face this evening told her the excitement had not in the least dulled for him.

But Linnet was one of the shorter persons in this vast hall. She could see nothing but formal coats and waistcoats, mostly at shoulder level. She returned her choir robe to its hook in the dressing room and joined the general flow out the side door. Cool night air hit her face and reminded her how hot and stuffy the conservatorium was. Did they ever hold concerts in the open air on summer evenings like these? They ought to.

"There she is!" Three young men were pointing at her as they approached. They looked vaguely familiar, though she could not remember meeting any of them. She paused.

The leader, a rather rakish fellow with his hair parted down the middle, took her hand and kissed the knuckles. How forward! "Miss Connolly, we had a bet going, the three of us. Those two bet that you weren't really a university student; that you were using it as a clever dodge to cadge money in the pubs. I wagered you were the dinkum article. When we spotted you in the choir tonight, I won my bet! Come celebrate with us."

"What. . . ?"

Another piped up, "The Commercial Hotel. Remember? You sang there last week."

"Oh. Of course." These were the rowdies who had teased and jeered; whom the barman had threatened to eject. They seemed decent sorts here, though. Her first impression, obviously, had been an inaccurate one.

The leader purred, "We spotted the lovely tresses right

off. You stand out in any crowd, Miss Connolly, even a crowd of identical choir robes." He reached out impetuously and touched her hair. No doubt some strand had fallen out of place and he was fixing it.

For lack of knowing what else to do, she let herself be led away out across the lawn toward North Terrace. They were probably headed for a pub, these young men's normal habitat, but Linnet was becoming rather accustomed to pubs. She sang in them once or twice a week. Although she had scarce a farthing to her name at the moment, at least her tuition bill had been paid before the deadline. Singing on street corners did not bring her nearly as many donations. Still, she probably ought to curtail her pub activities now that the debt was paid, and limit herself to street concerts.

These young men, laughing and joking, were full of life and good spirits. Obviously the audience had been quite as buoyed up as the performers. The fact that she had contributed to the pleasure of so many people tickled her immensely.

"Linnet!" Chris's voice called.

She wheeled and pushed past the young man bringing up the rear.

Chris came flying across the lawn, wearing his silk top hat and satin-lined opera cape. The cape fluttered and flowed out behind him, casting fascinating shadows from the distant streetlights. He jogged to a halt and seized her arm. "Sorry, gentlemen, but I've been looking all over for her. The vice chancellor wants her at a post-concert soiree and sent me out to find her. Come, Linnet. We mustn't keep Dr. Barlow waiting."

"Here, now!" the leader protested. "She's with us."

"Ah yes!" Chris raised a finger. "Commercial Hotel, a week ago Saturday. Gentlemen, I appreciate your interest in her musical talents, but the school takes precedence. The vice chancellor's word is law. She is a student, you know. G'night."

He hurried her off across the lawn toward the conservatorium. Behind her, Linnet heard the three arguing. One of them complained bitterly about sitting through all that noise for nothing. They were starting to follow, but Chris slipped in among a loose cluster of concert patrons. The young men stopped, still arguing. She glanced at Chris's face. He was livid.

He rushed her through the side door into the choir dressing room and shoved her up against a wall. "Cork! You were raised in Cork, right? Big seaport full of sailors, right? So why, Linnet Connolly, can you not recognize prurient rascals when you meet them?"

"They recognized me, Chris! Sure 'n they singled me out because they remembered me. One of them even made a wa—" She stopped and frowned. "Why be ye so angry?"

The huge dark Greek eyes studied her for the longest moment. "You really don't realize what they were up to, do you?"

"Up to? Me sole intention was to have a cup of tea with them and talk awhile. The night has been so exciting and I fain would have it end."

"It's not *your* intentions I'm worried about. It's theirs. The night would have been exciting, all right. Linnet, they were on the prowl. They were going to—" He stopped. He shook his head. Suddenly he laughed, and it was a welcome change in his demeanor. "Sweet country mouse! Very well, Linnet, I'll leave it at this: You never—I repeat, *never*—mix socially with your audience. Not under any circumstance, no matter how much adulation they shower upon you. Its, uh—unprofessional in concert music circles, and is simply not done. All right?"

" 'Tis clear I've much to learn about this matter of music. What to do and nae do."

"Especially the 'nae do' part." He stepped back and took her hand. "So you don't want the night to end. I agree. Elizabeth says the strings are celebrating over at Westons'.

We pianists shall crash their party. After all, pianos have strings."

She let herself be escorted out into the cool night. " 'Tis hardly like a violin, the piano. In fact, 'tis why ye urged me to take both violin and piano lessons. Piano to train the eye, ye said, for ye can see the notes on a keyboard, and the violin to train the ear. What, then, might the piano be if it nae be strings?"

"Percussion, of all things. Can you envision a noble piano keeping company with a common snare drum? No, Irish rose, the piano is a world unto its own. One per orchestra, and essential to every rehearsal. It can play the notes of any other instrument except certain drums, and usually those of several at once. An aristocrat, the piano. And you, my dear, must learn to associate comfortably with aristocracy." And he led her off into the night.

Chris. Were she to write to her sisters—something she must do soon—how could she explain a man like Chris? Helper. Encourager. Mentor. Free spirit, certainly. Apparently Elizabeth's companion, perhaps even her suitor. Or were they simply friends? No matter how much Linnet watched them together, she could never tell. But then, Linnet was not an expert at reading signs of that sort.

Chris declared the strings party dull and escorted both Linnet and Elizabeth to Herr Kugelberg's house over in East Terrace. Quite as dull. They eventually ended up at Miss Hack's, where they sat around past midnight eating sweet ices and listening to Caruso on a gramophone.

The magnificence of Beethoven's Ninth behind her, Linnet tackled her studies with renewed fervor. She practiced Vaccai daily for the fun of it. She spent half an hour every day on the violin only because Chris wanted her to, and Elizabeth was her teacher. She failed her examination in Latin.

It was the piano she loved most. As she struggled to master Czerny, she thought fondly of Sister Bertrand. That dear and portly old nun would have been a wonderful concert pianist, for she loved the instrument as much as Chris did. Sister Bertrand had, in religious parlance, walked the second mile, providing Linnet with music instruction far beyond that which the school offered.

A small but welcome check from Samantha arrived on Monday morning. In its accompanying letter, Sam described the heat in Echuca as oppressive and asked how it was in Adelaide. She said she was about to embark on a riverboat trip to the outback mission her employer was building. Linnet glanced at the calendar and at the date on the letter. If Sam were staying at this mission for a few days, she would be there now.

The check would put food in her mouth for a week, but where would she get the rent for this tiny garret room? And tuition would be coming again soon. How she hated this hand-to-mouth existence! She had been foolish to give up that job at the professor's—foolish, indeed, to consider university airs in the first place. She ought to quit this nonsense to which she was never born, and return to being what she was—a domestic. She perched her hat on her head and sallied forth to buy groceries.

She detoured to the bank in Rundle Street to cash her check. The greengrocer would be open for several hours yet. Almost on a whim she crossed North Terrace into the university. She could practice for an hour or so and still get the shopping done. She made her way to the lower-level practice room.

Music of all degrees of proficiency leaked out of the tight doors of these little rooms. Each cubicle contained a semituned piano, chairs, and music stands. Beginners set their violins to caterwauling. Beginning voice students did their caterwauling unaided by instruments. And here and there along the way, someone really good was playing, making one want to linger and listen.

Every room was in use. She walked out the other end. She might sit in the stairwell and wait a few minutes. Perhaps someone was nearly finished. She paused, listened, then hastened upstairs to the first floor. This room on the end must be a professor's. Either he himself was playing or he was giving a lesson to an advanced pianist, for the music was beautiful. Tchaikovsky, she was fairly certain. She held her ear near the door and listened, rapt at what a piano can achieve.

The end.

Herr Kugelberg's voice: "Vell. Inaccurate fingering. Ven vill you learn? The phrasing vas poor. Your tempo fluctuated. The whole piece lacks sensitiffity. It's the best you'f ever played it."

"Thank you so much, Herr Doctor," came Chris's voice.

"I am not a doctor, und you vill cease calling me that chust because you are angry vith my criticism. Ve vill take up again tomorrow, ya?"

"Tomorrow, ya."

"I expect marked improofment. So practice, already. Und, Yorke—"

"What?"

"Pay less attention to the ladies, like the Connolly girl, and more to your work. You are not working enuff. You vould be much better."

"G'day, Herr non-doctor." Chris came charging out the door. He spotted Linnet and his face instantly transformed from ferocious to delight. "Just the person I need to see!" He wrapped a long arm across her shoulders and took off down the hall. "How much money do you have?"

"Why?"

"I've got you booked into a concert appearance, but we have to rent a particular gown."

"Uh—wait, Chris." She stopped. "Miss Hack heard about me, uh, singing engagements, and she said dinnae do it. She avers that singing in public houses is demeaning to me art, and I must cease immediately."

"Guli Hack! And I'm sure she's ready to pay your bills for you, too. Never mind Miss Hack. This is not a pub. It's the concert hall in South Terrace by Veale Gardens." He gripped her shoulders, and his eyes absolutely shone. "This one's real, Linn! A paid engagement!"

"Oh, no! Sure'n Miss Hack will say I be nae ready for that yet!"

"Not singing, Linn. Dual pianos. You and me. The main attraction is some bloke from Liverpool who specializes in Bach. We're the opening act. We're paid two pounds apiece!"

"Ye cannae be serious!" She certainly wasn't ready for that, either!

"I've chosen the music. Some of it you already know, and you can handle the rest with no trouble. You'll play second piano and I'll provide the embellishments. You'll be wonderful!"

He pulled her aside into the concert chamber. "This demonstration will be a bit rough, what with the pianos on opposite sides of the room. You can't hear as well. But you'll be amazed. Go sit there," and he waved a finger toward the far concert grand.

He seated himself at the other. He seemed a mile away across the chamber. "The Czerny Etudes you were assigned last week, from the top."

So uncertain was she that her fingers shook. She played the opening bars and tried to listen to what was happening across the room. She was halfway through the piece when she heard his playing depart from the notes she knew. While she held a rest, his fingers were glissading down the keyboard. As she took the arpeggio up the scale he was coming down. This was new! She had always enjoyed piano four hands, but this was infinitely more exciting! She was sorry when it ended.

Rental of the gown cost twelve shillings three with cleaning, fitting, and all. An extra ten shillings rented the hall itself for a few hours in order, Chris said, to get the feel of the place. In this dress rehearsal she made many mistakes.

When the big night arrived, she was so excited she broke into a cold sweat from three in the afternoon on. She could not eat. She donned the gown and Chris declared her ravishingly beautiful. He wore an amazing crushed-velvet formal suit she'd never seen before. He looked quite dashing.

They arrived early and rolled the two pianos into place, belly to belly. They warmed up. Then they waited in the wings, waiting, waiting, waiting. The buzz out in the audience grew from silence to a dull roar. Linnet quelled the urge to peek out at the house. Chris had warned her in advance about the non-professionalism of that.

The stage lights came up. The roar dropped to a rumble. The toastmaster stepped out, his front bright and his back black, to welcome all. Linnet knew he spoke Chris's name and hers, but she could not for the life of her remember him doing it. Chris's hand in hers, they stepped from darkness into brilliance. She felt herself squinting.

Chris had told her over and over to ignore the house and play for her own pleasure. She had no choice. She saw no faces, heard only a few stray coughs and clearings of the throat. All she could see were brilliant footlights. Chris smiled at her as they took their places. He could afford to be relaxed like that. This was nothing new for him. He struck his chords, and they were off.

She only panicked twice in the execution of their repertoire, and on both occasions managed to recover in time and carry on. They completed their program. Enthusiastic applause rose, but the announcer, or whoever he was, stepped out unexpectedly before they could take their bow. Linnet felt cheated. She wanted the applause. She wanted her bow! Then the announcer's words struck cold terror in her heart.

"Ladies and gentlemen, we have received word that Herr Hoffman is unavoidably delayed. Please bear with us, and this incomparable duet, Yorke and Connolly, will entertain you." He bowed as he backed away from the pianos and disappeared in the wings.

No! This incomparable duet had just exhausted their whole repertoire. Linnet knew not a note the audience had not already heard tonight. She could not entertain that coughing, shuffling houseful of music fans. Fear as cold as the wind off the North Sea froze her in place.

Chris was standing beside her. "What a wonderful chance for us all!" he said. How could he say that? "In these final moments before Mr. Hoffman's appearance, I wish to seize the opportunity to introduce you to the world's next great concert soprano. My partner Linnet Connolly here is trained, as are all great voices, in the classical style. But her personal style ranges far beyond the usual program sopranos present."

Sopranos? No, Chris! Linnet thought briefly of that horrid moment when he dragged her in for her first pub concert. This was a thousand times more horrid!

"Ladies and gentlemen, Linnet Connolly!" He was shoving her piano back. Now he was leading her by the hand and placing her beside his instrument. Then, with lovely embellishments, he was rolling out the introductory bars to, of all things, "Brennan on the Moor"!

Linnet laughed suddenly. She faced Chris, with her back to the audience, and for a long moment she could not stop laughing. This was all so ludicrous! The die was cast. Why struggle? She tossed propriety aside and put her heart and soul into "Brennan on the Moor."

Linnet really did enjoy applause! At the close of the piece, Chris explained how Brennan was an actual highwayman from Linnet's native Cork County. Then he asked how many in the audience had used the Vaccai method in their study of voice. "Splendid!" he boomed. "You will recognize this next selection." In her ear he muttered, "Lesson eight, appoggiaturas, both pieces, and go right on to fifteen, riepilogo." He sat down to play.

Singing Vaccai to an audience of music enthusiasts was like showing your penmanship practice page to an expert graphologist. And yet, why not? The tunes were fun, the words delightfully sentimental. Linnet was trapped in an impossible situation created by that impossible young man now playing an introduction. She might as well give it her all.

She put aside the thought that these were vocal exercises. She sang of spring, of flowers and new grass and Cupid. She sang of the sapling by the stream and of fresh new thoughts of love. By the time she sang the final *Compagno e del piacer,* Linnet Connolly was in love with love.

And apparently, the audience was in love with Linnet Connolly. Their response added new dimensions to the word *gratifying.* With two more selections, she exhausted both her vocal repertoire and her voice.

Chris thanked them all, presented her for further applause, and led her offstage.

That night, Linnet received her first curtain call.

Herr Helmut Hoffman, the Bach expert, never did show up.

Chapter Eight

The Wharfmaster's Lackey

"You look much better. How do you feel?" His marvelous dark eyes watched her closely, intently. *Cole Sloan*. Samantha still couldn't quite believe it. *Cole Sloan*. Her mind pronounced the name over and over.

"Much better, thank ye. 'Normal' is stretching it a bit, but 'satisfactory' applies."

He chuckled, from down deep. "The Sam Connolly exactness; I'd almost forgotten about that." He shook his head. "You were the last person in the world I expected to see under that wharf—except maybe the mayor of Perth. And then when you turned from red to white and dropped over, I panicked. Sam, never in my life have I ever panicked, but I did then."

"Sure 'n I'm flattered, sir. And never before has meself ever fainted dead away like that. 'Tis an experience I dinnae wish to repeat."

This was one of her favorite places in town, this little tea garden under a bower, and at the moment it was one of the coolest. Good. No doubt heat had a lot to do with her embarrassing display of fainting fifteen minutes ago. Still, she'd certainly taken surprises in stride before, even the shocking death of Edan, and she burned with shame now for having acted thus in front of Cole Sloan, of all people.

The serving girl brought the scones all smothered in jam and fresh whipped cream. Though not exactly hungry, Samantha was ready for Devonshire tea, that delightful combination of tea with scones and accompaniment. Her hand shook only slightly as she poured for Mr. Sloan and herself.

"You're supposed to be in Melbourne." His baritone rumble was just as pleasant as she remembered it. "Why are you in Echuca, of all places?"

"I obtained temporary work here on me journey south and saw nae reason to go on."

"Temporary? Are you employed at the moment?"

"Nae 't the moment. And what finds y'rself here, a thousand miles from home?"

He smiled. "More like five hundred. I'm looking for a deal. I've been getting heavily into commodities brokerage. As you know, I learn all I can about what I'm doing. I study both the people who are succeeding and the people who fail. People who fail seem to lack contact with their sources. That also seems to be *my* main problem—finding out what goods are available and where to get them. So I've come to the source of wool and timber. I hope to make enough contacts with the producers themselves that I can beat some of the prices the major houses in Sydney offer. An immense business advantage, dealing face-to-face with the producers."

"Meself doubts it's much done. Ye find few city businessmen in Echuca these days, though I'm given to understand that twenty years ago Echuca attracted the best money and business minds in the nation. But, of course, 'twas the Colonies back then." Excellent scone, tasty and fresh. Here was the other reason she so enjoyed this little place. The food.

He leaned back, his mouth pursing out and in. He took

a deep breath. "It's none of my business, but tell me anyway. Have you, uh, found anyone yet? Any swains on your horizon?"

Reginald Otis.

"Nae," she lied. "Nae man me heart feels a-flutter for." That part was true. "And y'rself, since we be prying into each other's affairs?"

He shrugged. "Been seeing a lady named Hilary. I doubt she's the one, so to speak. She's afraid of horses, and she doesn't like to walk in streets that aren't paved."

"Streets that be nae paved. Eh, sure 'n Australia has enough of those."

Endless pink dirt roads through nothing. She owed Reginald Otis her very life. She knew that now.

They talked for another hour. She told him about Linnet's venture into the world of higher learning and he was not nearly so surprised as she expected. He mentioned meeting Pearl and Martin Frobel, Jr., and seemed most anxious to deal in Queensland beef. They exchanged addresses and promised to keep each other informed of any moves. He paid the bill. They shook hands. She further assured him she was quite fine now, thank you. They parted.

The white-bright streets of Echuca turned gray.

She wanted nothing more than to return to her modest rooms and flop on her bed. But she had one chore which, though she had not been instructed to do it, must be done. She left her bag at the tea garden momentarily and walked over to the wharfmaster's office to see if Mr. Drummond was in.

Mr. Drummond was in, but not literally. He sat outside his office door under its little barely stuck-on porch. He leaped to his feet as she approached and waved toward his just-vacated chair. "Miss Connolly! Please sit down." He eyed her worriedly. "My wife and I happened to be walking down by D dock, and I saw it happen—uh, saw you take ill. I do hope it wasn't serious."

"Seriously embarrassing. I'm fine, thank ye." She sat down, simply because he would drive her to distraction hovering over her if she did not. "Mr. Drummond, Mr. Otis received word from his home board that he can nae longer maintain an office in town. From now on ye'll find it necessary to deal with him directly at Barmah."

"Oh." Mr. Drummond seemed to require an extra moment to assimilate this bit of intelligence. "The mission office here is closed completely?"

"It will be, aye. The new arrangement will nae doubt cause inconvenience at times, but nae severe problems, surely." She stood up and offered her hand. "Mr. Drummond, g'day."

"So you'll be working out there, too."

"Nae, Mr. Drummond, I be nae longer associated with the mission. Ye'll be dealing with Mr. Otis himself, or with his assistant, Ellen Fenton." She tried again to leave. "G'day."

"G'day, Miss Connolly. And thank you."

She must also notify the postmaster. She turned, smiling, and walked away. She had not gotten a hundred feet closer the post office before he called her name. She looked back.

He came running up at a waddling, lumbering gait. The hundred-foot dash left him breathless. "Miss Connolly, may I speak with you further?"

"As ye wish." She returned with him to the shade of the little porch and resumed her seat in the wooden chair. He ducked inside. She heard the unmistakable rattle of papers hitting the floor. He brought out a simple straight-backed chair for himself and plopped it down beside her. He sat. Perspiration dripped from his forehead. His face had been dry a moment before.

"Miss Connolly, have you other employment?"

"Nae, sir. I'll look about a bit, but most likely I'll continue on to Melbourne."

"Mmm." He cleared his throat. "In the matter of that shipment of roofing tin and all for Barmah mission: I am much impressed with the way you acted quickly and decisively to solve the problem."

"Eh, sir, much of the credit goes to the captains of the *Echuca Charlene* and the *Etona*. They saved the day, not I."

"You are too modest. At the very least you engaged their instant cooperation, something I find very difficult, as a rule. And the clever way you provided accommodation for Mr. Otis's black crew: most impressive."

"That be more the hand of God, for God be Mr. Otis's ally. The iron bedsteads just happened to be part of the shipment, and that be nae thing meself could have arranged."

"Again, you are too modest. I shall be direct. I wish to employ you as a clerk here on the wharf. You will be an employee of the borough, as am I, and second in rank to myself."

"Sure 'n ye have competent clerks a-plenty, sir. There be more people than jobs in Echuca."

"My last clerk quit several weeks ago. Personal reasons, he said. I suspect family problems of some sort."

"The rate of pay?"

"Double whatever the mission paid you."

Samantha found herself staring. She averted her eyes quickly. From her seat here at the office door she looked across the width of the wharf to the trees beyond the far bank of the Murray. She could see a bit of the water itself, just as the river slipped around a distant bend. Sky, greenery, the worn and weathered patterns of the wharf decking—a lovely view, and it could be hers. She thought about the view behind her, that dustbin of an office. That would be hers, too, were she to accept the job. Twice the pay Mr. Otis could afford, and Linnet in need of money for school . . .

"When could I commence work?"

"This instant; that is, if you feel up to it. When you fell . . ." He shook his roly-poly head. "That bloke coming toward you reached you long before I could, of course—much nearer. He scooped you up in his arms, quite limp, and there he went in that white shirt, up the stairs at very near a run. My wife Martha seemed to think it quite romantic, but I—" Again he shook his unromantic head.

"Be there a budget? For example, I might wish to employ pick-up labor for cleaning. Day work."

"We might squeeze something out. Nothing extravagant, understand."

"I be nae extravagant person, I assure ye. Aye, Mr. Drummond, I would be honored to take the position of clerk, at the rate of pay mentioned. Meself shall bring me latest pay stub around to y'r office to confirm the amount."

"That isn't necessary. I trust your integrity. After all, Mr. Otis is, as you said, a friend of God."

"Nonetheless, I feel far better keeping business on paper, aye?"

"Of course." And he practically beamed. He rose because she did.

She extended her hand. "If ye please, sir, I shall commence me duties first thing tomorrow."

"Splendid! I'll give you a key."

She was on her way five minutes later, a wharf office key in her skirt pocket and a job in hand. Wharfmaster's lackey.

What next?!

If the post office was not closed already, it would be by the time she got there. Instead, she walked down the stairs and under the wharf to the riverbank.

With nearly every boat idled by low water, surely she could hire someone for a minimal sum to scrub and whitewash. But the length of the wharf, as far as she could make out, lay completely vacant. The boys with their game of marbles had vanished. No stevedores lolled. It was near suppertime. Obviously, the world had better things to do than sit around waiting to be hired for a pittance.

Beyond the wharf on the far side, three small Chinese boys played along the river's edge. No, they were fishing. They were the only souls of any sort she saw on the river. She turned to leave.

A piercing soprano scream spun her around. Two small Chinese boys were jumping around on the shore. One of them ran away, thunking up the far stairs two-at-a-time. Samantha found herself running toward the boy still on the bank, although she could not imagine herself moving faster than a stroll through the heat.

The lad was sobbing, his face twisted. A small pillbox hat floated in the greasy brown water perhaps twelve feet offshore. Thinking would waste precious moments. Samantha did not think. She ran out into the tepid river and realized instantly how quickly the bottom fell away. A tiny hand broke the water ahead of her and disappeared. She began swimming. The last time she had swum, she was nine years old, playing in the frigid pond on her uncle's farm behind Cork. This water was warm as a bath.

She kicked something. She folded herself, reaching down, groping, grasping. Foul water filled her mouth and nose and ears, and she remembered now how utterly she abhorred getting her face under water! The inside of her nose caught fire clear to the middle of her head. Her hand touched fabric. She gripped and pulled and began kicking mightily.

Her head broke the surface, but precious little good that did. Her throat was so full of water she could not breathe. Water cascaded down her face from her hair and blinded her. She dragged the child to the surface and kicked wildly, trying to swim one-handed. A foot touched slurpy bottom. She fell forward toward shore and got another foot planted in the mud. Choking and hacking, she pulled the lad ashore with her.

She sat on the bank a brief moment coughing, trying to get enough water out of her tortured lungs that she could breathe. The child lay with his mouth open and his eyes half closed. Only whites showed from behind the slanted lids. She lurched to her feet and draped the limp little fellow in half over one arm. She had no idea what to do. She pounded on his back. She shook him.

He gasped suddenly and vomited all over her skirt. Never would she guess she might welcome such a revolting event, but it was unmistakably a sign of life! She rubbed his back. At length, too spent herself to support him anymore, she lowered him to the ground and sat down beside him.

He himself was coughing now. He struggled a moment. The other boy grabbed him by the shoulders and helped him sit up. Both began to wail lustily. What should she do? One thing she definitely did not want was to listen to this racket. She begged "Hush! Hush!" and gathered the water-soaked lad into her arms. "Hush!" she warned the other.

With sobs deep enough to reach his native China, the dry lad ceased his wailing. She was rather amazed at his self-discipline. The wet lad she held close and rocked, back and forth, back and forth, until his howling abated to a cough-riddled whimper.

The noise, of course, had drawn the attention of many up on the wharf. Men came running down the stairs, now that the excitement was over. The dry lad, still terribly frightened, crowded in against her and eyed the milling swarm of legs.

Samantha chose at random two young men. She asked them to keep onlookers at bay. They seized so earnestly upon their appointed task that they nearly prevented the approach of what were obviously the parents.

The dry lad plastered himself instantly to his mother. Samantha delivered the wet child into her arms and hauled herself to her feet. Suddenly she was so weary she doubted her strength to climb those stairs to street side. In a stroke of genius she mentioned her weariness not to the many asking questions but to the two young men. Eager to bask in reflected glory, they ushered her to the top of the stairs, threatening mayhem to any who blocked her way. Up on the wharf she thanked them profusely, shook their hands, and made her way home. She forgot their names before she reached her door.

She awoke at dawn in her nightgown. She remembered only vaguely peeling out of her foul and sopping clothes the evening before. She had not eaten. She was fully aware of that now. Her job. The key. She pawed through the pile of wet, stinking clothes. Here was the key. Her job was real!

She sat for a few moments at her table, allowing the rest of her aching body to catch up to the day, watching the birds outside. What a time yesterday! The river trip, Cole Sloan, the new job, the near drowning . . . not to mention a marriage proposal and a lost job within the last seventy-two hours. Whatever today brought, it couldn't hold a candle to the last three days.

She washed her hair and dressed. She was just pondering breakfast options in the cupboard when a timid knock came at the door. An hour past dawn? She answered it.

A Chinese man, a Chinese woman, and a small boy stood solemnly in the golden morning light.

Like everyone else in town, Samantha purchased all her milk, eggs, chicken, pork, and vegetables from Chinese market gardeners. They walked up and down the streets with their great handbarrow carts, ever ready to barter. This man was probably also a market gardener, though she did not recognize him as someone with whom she regularly did business.

The three bowed deeply.

Samantha bowed in response and stepped back. "Please come in."

They stepped inside. Her two small rooms here contained no parlor furniture. She pulled out her only chairs, the three lyreback kitchen chairs. "Do be seated. Sorry I've nae started tea."

These people were obviously dressed in their very best. Mother wore a black silk shirt and pants. The shirt, with its erect little collar, was adorned with magnificent silk embroidery in a hundred hues. Birds and chrysanthemums tumbled across her front from shoulder to shoulder. Samantha did not doubt that the back was similarly gorgeous. The father wore a tailored silk version of the cotton outfits the men wore as they peddled produce from their carts. The lad was a miniature of father and mother—a man's suit with delicate embroidery. Even his little silk slippers were beautifully decorated. He and his father removed their pillbox hats.

The mother looked near tears. She sat obediently and her little boy stood close to her side. Samantha recognized the lad at last. This was the child she had pulled from the river! The father stood stoically, watching her. She sat down. He sat down. There was a careful formality to every movement these people made, and yet it was not a nervous or strained politeness.

Samantha smiled at the child. "Ye look none the worse for wear, lad. Meself is delighted y're recovered." She looked at the father. "Be there some way I might serve ye?"

"We are Chinese. My wife, Sun Luk—" She bowed while seated, an interesting skill. "My son, Ah Loo. I am Ah Ching Yet." The father spoke each syllable as if it were a separate word. Oh, that Englishmen would enunciate so clearly! "How do you do?"

"Samantha Connolly. How do you do."

He dipped forward gravely and sat erect again. "You see I have cut off the queue. The pigtail. Still, we hold many of the old ways."

"I'm nae sure I understand."

"Many Chinese come, work, go back home to China. They must keep long hair. No queue, hard to go home. Maybe never go home. Some of us, the hair is short. We will stay here pert—all time. Always."

"Permanently?"

"Yes." The tight mouth almost smiled. Not quite. "In China, if you save the life of a person, you are responsible for that person always. You see, that person would be dead, but he is not dead because of you, so you are responsible."

"I see the logic in that, aye."

"When Ah Lin came running, he said my Ah Loo fell in the river. We came quickly, but I knew—my heart knew—that already we were too late. Too late. Boy dead. River takes him away, gone forever. We came, and our Ah Loo is alive, safe in your arms. Our hearts filled up, poured out joy. With the happiness of the seven heavens now, we give you our son."

One reluctant step after the other, the lad moved from his mother's chair to Samantha. In one stunning moment, Samantha had become a mother.

"The auld ways, aye." She must think. She sat back and took a long, deep breath. "Ye came from China, aye? Ye speak English well."

"Ah Loo, he speaks very well. Much better than I. My wife, not much English."

Samantha nodded. "I am very fortunate. I came from far away also, two years ago. From Erin. But I did nae have to learn another language as did y'rself, for the Irish speak English. Well—" She smiled and shrugged. "After a fashion, as ye see."

Tears welled in the mother's eyes and now the lad looked on the verge of weeping. Think quickly, Samantha!

I don't want this! I don't want any of this! I want the whole three days to just go away. This is too much. I can't! She spoke, past thinking or reasoning. She dipped her head forward. "What wonderful people ye be, to serve honor so faithfully." She laid her arm across the boy's shoulders. "I need a lad. And this boy is strong and brave. But there be a serious problem."

"Problem? I will help."

" 'Tis nae a thing either of us can help. In English society— among the English—only married ladies have children. I have never married. And yet, I can use a strong, bright lad." She frowned deeply.

She let the frown sit a moment, then brightened it to a happy smile. "Ah! There be a way we can serve the auld ways and the English ways as well. If ye please, sir. According to Chinese ways, I accept y'r son. I thank ye ever so much. And now I give him back into y'r keeping, for I cannae keep him. 'Twould nae be proper according to English ways, ye see. He belongs to all of us, aye?"

"You need him, you say?"

"Indeed. So if ye agree, I shall hire him on the spot to work for me when he be nae in school. I just accepted a job down at the wharf. There is much work to do. Might I pay him to work for me down at the wharf?"

"No. He work hard for you. He belong to you. But you do not pay."

"Ah, but if we share in his ownership—rather, our parenthood—sure 'n I must contribute to his upbringing. Meself would be nae good parent if I dinnae give a little something toward his upkeep, aye?"

The father studied the floor in silence, his face impassive. She was not fooling him in the least. She could see that. And the mother had no idea what was happening. The lad beside her, the object of all this, held his peace, but Samantha could practically hear his little body vibrate with nervous hope.

Finally, after half an eternity, the father lifted his eyes to her and spoke. "I salute your wisdom. Yes. I agree. You are sure this is satisfactory, all of it?"

"Aye, most satisfactory for me, if the auld ways are

served well and you are satisfied."

"The old ways are served well. Yes." And now it was he who looked on the brink of tears.

The boy bounded to his mother's side and pressed in close. The mother's face took on the most wondrous look of puzzlement. She had truly and actually prepared herself to surrender her son in the name of tradition. What amazing people!

Why was neither father nor son explaining all this to the mother? *Of course!* Samantha thought. *It is impolite to use a language not known to all present; that must be it.* These people had mastered not only the complex social expectations of their own culture but those of the English as well.

The father stood and bowed. "My son will begin service immediately. You apologized you did not make tea. He is very good at making tea. And I am a launderer. I specialize. I do all, but I do wool very well. Please, I wish to launder the clothes you soiled yesterday in the river."

"Eh, I wouldnae ask ye to undertake such a task. I be certain they're ruined. And the smell from the lad's—" She bit her tongue. "If it please ye, sir, ye may."

The man smiled, the first indication of emotion he had indulged since he arrived. He muttered a few nasal syllables and his wife hastened over to scoop Samantha's wet garments into a compact ball. The lad hurried just as quickly out back to the kitchen, no doubt to start tea. With much nodding and bowing and appropriate pleasantries, the parents made their exit.

Samantha put her chair back by the window and sat down again, absolutely overwhelmed. In this very position less than two hours ago, she had mused that this day could not by any means be as wildly improbable as yesterday.

But this day was not two hours old, and already she had a son!

Chapter Nine

Fantasia on a Pair of Songbirds

November 26, 1906

My dear Samantha,

Just today we received here at Barmah the latest edition of the *Riverine Herald*. I shall be so bold as to assume the *Herald*'s account of your daring rescue is filled with inaccuracies. I've learned from sad experience that newspapers never seem to get it all correct. Yet even with that assumption, your exploits thrill me. The paper mentions, too, that you are now employed on the wharf. If that be true, I rejoice! I have been keeping your employment a matter of earnest prayer. I still feel badly about the shabby manner in which the board handled your situation. You were invaluable to Barmah, Samantha!

Work proceeds well here. We have the donkey engine up and running. Toby is a genius at adapting it to all manner of heavy chores. Invention is no orphan. Necessity may be its mother, but Laziness is the father. The roofs are all on, and I have commenced building an infirmary. The high proportion of elderly blacks among our growing group requires it. The school is closed at the moment for lack of children. Their parents traditionally go elsewhere at this time of year—

off on walkabout—and the families simply disappear. Ellen assures me they will return with the rain. Planning such things as supply orders, not to mention school curricula, is a challenge. How many mouths will we feed next week? One never knows. Fortunately, for I am inadequate to many tasks, I am not the Chief Shepherd, but only an assistant. The Chief Shepherd will see well to the souls and bodies of our sheep. He is adequate to every task.

At our parting I asked to present my Lord's petition in this letter. I thought writing would be easier than speaking. Alas, I find it's nothing of the sort. Please bear with my scratch-outs and mis-phrasings.

The newspaper describes how you saved a small lad. "Saved"—the Christian's favorite word! We tell people, "You must be saved!" Our hearers quickly understand salvation from drowning. But rarely do we adequately explain how to be spiritually saved.

From infancy I have been a member of the church, and for as long as I can remember I have loved to sing. A choirboy, later a soloist at St. Andrew's, I was the perfect Christian lad. Samantha, I might as well have been singing in the town hall next door, for all the good my memorized expressions of faith did my soul. My head knew the facts of Christ's lordship, but I did not act on them. My mouth said the words of the liturgy by rote. I did not possess them in my heart.

I matriculated at age seventeen and as a gift traveled to my uncle's in Scotland. There in Edinburgh I heard the evangelist D. L. Moody and the matchless voice of Ira Sankey. Fifteen years ago almost to the month, I remember it as clearly as yesterday. The words and the music pierced to my heart. I became a true Christian that day.

Samantha, you value honor highly, and that is splendid. You value moral behavior and Christian ethics. Wonderful! But the only ethical, moral, honorable folk who will enter heaven are those who know Jesus Christ personally, in their hearts. I want more than anything else—more than Barmah itself—that you be one of them.

To do that you must first admit your sins—not to human ears but to God. God has decreed the payment is blood, not pious acts; life itself, either yours or His Son's. Pretend you went to pay a fine in court. You lay your pound note on the counter. Jesus lays a pound note down also, to pay your fine for you. You can say "Why, thank you!" and let Him do it, or you can cry "Never!" and pay the fine yourself. Lifeblood is infinitely more precious than a pound note, but you see the picture, I trust.

Accept Jesus' largess. He has already paid your debt, if you will allow it. Accept the gift. Ask His Spirit to enter and dwell in you. Then get to know Him through prayer and His Word.

That is the bare bones of the gospel, but there is so much more! No matter how deeply I plumb its depths, I find no bottom. Its ramifications, its meanings and richness are infinite, and yet a small child can grasp its essence. What an awesome God, to reveal His power in such simplicity!

God bless you richly, dear Samantha, and God bless the lad you rescued!

With enduring affection,
I am your servant in Christ Jesus,
Reginald

December 3, 1906

Dear Reginald,

Your eloquent letter arrived in yesterday's post.

My sister Meg recently married a young preacher named Luke Vinson. In the year prior to their nuptials, Luke addressed both Meg and me on the same subject, namely, salvation not by works but by God's gift.

I understood his allusions and exhortations, but I steadfastly refused to accept that they pertained to my own circumstance. I was born into the church; let the church save my soul. Besides, I lived a good life.

I made moral choices, and was proud of them. Only yesterday did I fully grasp that although I be relatively free of the more dastardly and blatant sins of commission, my sins of omission alone would condemn me. Only yesterday as I read your letter did I realize that you and Meg and Luke are speaking to me—nay, begging me—out of love. You stand to gain nothing from my spiritual state, neither yea nor nay.

When Meg announced to me that she had become a Christian, I did not understand; for she, like I, was raised in a Christian land. So were you. Now, through your testimony, I see.

At last I perceive I am powerless to usher myself into eternity. Neither the church nor good deeds suffice. I now seek to commit myself to Jesus Christ, following earnestly with my heart (as best I may) the path you so carefully laid out, for I know the short span of this life is nothing compared to the expanse of infinity. I am not ashamed of the manner of my walk in this life; I accept God's terms as He offers them that I might walk unashamed in the next.

A few weeks ago, you rescued my physical life from death by thirst. Yesterday you rescued my eternal life from death by stubbornness. I am forever indebted to you.

                In unspeakable gratitude,
                I am yours sincerely,
                Samantha

The railway from Geelong up through Melbourne and the mining country passed through some fairly interesting landscapes. But once past Ballarat and Ararat, Sloan's train droned relentlessly through flat, arid, monotonous wasteland. He was confronting his greatest enemy right here. It whipped by outside the window of his railway car; it pried apart Australia's pockets of civilization and shoved them into remote corners. Distance. Sheer, uncut distance.

Distance so brutally separated supply from demand that it made his job as broker, already a chancy undertaking, nearly impossible. Distance slowed the pace of business to the speed of an outback mail train. Men attacked their enemy distance with rails and roads, bullock trains and camel trains, and noisy little paddle boats on the Murray drainage. Yet distance won the contest handily.

For all the travel Sloan had endured recently, he really hadn't covered much of the nation. Vastness beyond comprehension separated him from Perth, from the pearl fishery at Broome, from the sugar fields of north Queensland that he had once called home. As stultifying as this journey seemed, it was blessedly short when one considered the full enormity of Australia's distance.

A clangor woke him up. It was dawn, or near it, for the light came from behind them. They were lurching and rattling across an iron bridge. Murray Bridge. Adelaide lay fifty-five or sixty miles from here. He was almost there.

Sloan glanced out the window at the narrow stream that was the mighty Murray River in the off season. His mind leaped to the scene of Samantha on the shores of the Murray—she, almost at its headwaters; he, here near its mouth. He remembered the way his heart thumped and his jaw dropped open when he recognized the willowy young woman approaching in the gloom beneath the Great Echuca Wharf. He could not recall ever having been so utterly dumfounded.

It had been months since she worked for him, and she still called him "Mr. Sloan." Would she ever call him "Cole"? Probably not. She had erected a wall like ice between them, and not even this summer heat would melt it down.

Level distance humped and twisted itself into jumbled hills. The nice, straight railway tracks began looping and doubling themselves into a road that would make a snake sick. They were steaming south, the wrong direction, and now west and north, south again, east a bit, north. . . . At last they left the dry and ragged hills behind and rolled up a pleasant valley. At eleven-thirty-five A.M., Sloan stood on the platform of Adelaide's North Terrace railway station and watched uncaring porters toss his trunk off the baggage car.

He inquired about accommodations, had his trunk sent to a hostelry in Franklin Street, sight unseen, and asked directions to the university. "East on this street right here, less than half a mile. A pleasant walk." Cole stepped out into the hot sun, adjusted his hat, and began walking.

The University of Adelaide was not quite so imposing an institution as Sydney's, but considering that South Australia was at best a poor sister to New South Wales (well, anyway, Sloan had always thought so), it looked all right. Here was a huge, pompous building labeled Elder Conservatorium, the sort of structure you'd expect for university blokes who thought a lot of themselves. Sloan had no time for nonsense such as higher education, or for its stuffy fatheads who knew little and said much.

If Linnet were taking a music curriculum, she ought to be in or about this conservatorium. He stood under a gum tree and waited for classes to disperse.

Even before distant church bells chimed the noonday, students materialized all over, streaming everywhere, passing each other, some bewildered, seemingly lost. Many of the young men wore loose, open gowns over their street clothes. More pomposity. Sloan was impressed with the number of women. Scores of young women attended here.

Would he easily recognize Linnet? Surely so; it hadn't been that long. There she was. The red-brown hair was Sam's. The slim figure was Sam's, though not the height. She carried a violin case and folios. Beside her, a dumpy woman with a white cane tapped her way along. They nodded and smiled in animated conversation.

Sloan let them pass. He hastened up behind them, reached down, and hooked a finger in the handle of her violin case.

"Chris!" Linnet blurted peevishly. She turned. The luminous gray-green eyes meeting his were Sam's eyes. Gorgeous! Good thing he was holding on to the case, for she let go and clapped both hands to her face. The shocked surprise brightened to delight. "Mr. Sloan!"

She wrapped her arms around him impetuously, in a bold and happy hug. Propriety quickly got the better of her. She leaped back, self-conscious.

He handed her the violin, and she reached down to gather her scattered pages. "When I greeted your sister, she dropped her bag. So I figured it ran in the family."

She grinned joyously. "What a lovely surprise! Oh! Elizabeth Mapes, Cole Sloan. Libby, Mr. Sloan is the man who brought us over from Ireland to work on his plantation."

Miss Mapes extended a hand. When he took it she gripped firmly, so he did also. "Mr. Sloan, thank you for that. Linnet is a splendid musician, and we're lucky to have her."

"Are ye here for a while, or, uh . . ." Linnet waved a hand.

"In town briefly on business and wanted to look you up. I'd love to take you to luncheon—both of you—if your schedule permits."

"Mine does not, alas. I'd love it, but I have a student in half an hour." Miss Mapes extended her hand again. "Perhaps another time, Mr. Sloan?"

He made the appropriate responses and she did also, as polite and cultured people do; they expressed their mutual pleasure in meeting, and all the while Sloan's mind dwelt on the amazing resemblance between Linnet and Sam. When both were in his employ, he had taken scant note of any similarities. Sam had been the sun, Linnet a pallid moon in comparison. Now he could see how alike they were. There was, however, a towering difference: no wall of ice loomed between Linnet and him.

Sloan took the violin case back. "So where shall we go?"

"There be several nice little places in Gawler Street, if ye wish."

"Lead the way."

As they walked, Linnet described her adventures in the academic world with the same lilting cadences Sam used. Sloan could listen to it forever. Sloan felt younger—that was it, indeed, younger!—with this nubile creature at his side. She positively exuded enthusiasm and innocence. Sam shared that zest for life, and the innocence as well, without the extreme youth. Ten years between them, Sloan recalled.

"Let's see. You've passed your nineteenth birthday now, right?" Sloan led her out across a busy thoroughfare. They angled toward a small north-south street.

"Eh, true, and well nigh me twentieth. Some of the souls here guessed me to be seventeen or eighteen, so I let them have their fancy. 'Tis me feeling they'll be more forgiving of me many blunders if they think I'm younger."

Sloan chuckled. "I daresay that's the closest I've ever seen you come to conniving."

She giggled lightly, brightly, and all the weariness of his long journey drained away. She brought him to a charming, unassuming little sidewalk cafe of the sort university students frequent. And she called him Cole because he asked her to. He noticed with unadorned delight that they were getting farther and farther away from the master-and-serf relationship of the old days at Sugarlea. He admired her flexibility. In the past she was the fawning servant girl when that role was appropriate. Now she wore the cloak of simple friendship quite as comfortably.

They ordered, ate, and lingered over tea in a soothing fog of constant laughter and conversation.

"Be ye still in Sydney?" she asked eventually.

"Basically. I do a lot of traveling, lining up goods, arranging transport at the best rates. For example, I've just been down to the wool stores in Gcelong. Warehouses a block long. Men who can pull a tuft of wool from a bale and tell you the exact nature of that bale's contents. Amazing." This was certainly not the time to mention the heavy frustrations and tensions of trying to arrange sales with precious little in the way of earnest money.

"It sounds to be an exciting life. 'Tis me own fond wish to someday travel far and wide. And me fondest wish: having someone else paying for it."

He grinned. "The only way to go. Musicians travel—opera stars and such."

"Opera." She shook that lovely auburn mane. "Nae opera. Me voice lacks the timbre, so I've been told. But mayhap with the piano, as I improve."

"Or the violin."

"Nae. Never will I master that thing, I fear. 'Tis fine musical training, but 'twould take me a lifetime to build the skill Libby already possesses. We'll let her travel with the violin, aye?" Her luminous eyes went wide. "The time, please?"

He dug out his pocket watch. "Half past two."

"Eh, well, too late now."

"I've caused you to play hooky."

"Aye, me Latin class be past now. Nae much lost; I'll not succeed in Latin this time round. But there's a rehearsal with Chris this afternoon—pianos—for which meself cannot help but be late." Those liquid eyes glowed. "Eh, sure 'n I much prefer being here to being there!"

"And I'm enjoying this interlude so much, I don't feel the least bit guilty about keeping you away from your work." He laid his hand on hers. "In fact, I'll be a total villain and ask you to play hooky tomorrow. I'll be riding out into the Barossa Valley, possibly the Clare—lining up wine shipments. Come along."

"Just skip out of school and come?" A happy smile spread across her face. "Aye, Mr. Sl—I mean, Cole. Let's!"

"There you are!" A wiry, earnest-looking jumping-jack of a young man came bounding up. If he was out to impress someone with his velvet trousers and sleek silk shirt he was succeeding, but the impression was not a favorable one. He eyed Sloan as a duke might look upon a ragpicker.

Sloan stood up and offered a hand. "Cole Sloan. How do you do?"

"Yes. Elizabeth told me. When Linnet failed to appear instantly after her Latin class, I thought you might still be here; this is her favorite place. Come, Linnet. I've booked you for an engagement tomorrow night, and you've much preparation."

"Ye know, Chris, Miss Hack says I be nae ready for any such."

"Miss Hack is not paying your rent. You are. Come quickly, please. We're wasting valuable time." He nodded tersely toward Sloan. "Pleased to meet you. Good day, sir." He snatched Linnet's violin case out from under the table, stuffed her papers into her hands and escorted her off, just like that.

Who in blazes was this boor named Chris? The serving girl appeared at Sloan's side, probably worried about the bill. He paid with the closest coin he had and told her to keep the change.

Linnet and her abductor were halfway up the block already. Sloan closed the distance to a quarter of a block and followed discreetly. For one thing, he enjoyed the ethereal way she rather floated along. Linnet possessed the same grace of movement that made Sam's bearing so elegant. And yet, Linnet lacked the elegance. Curious.

From beside Sloan on the other side of the street, three young larrikins came popping out of the Commercial Hotel. At an eager double-step they crossed the street, moving rapidly ahead of Sloan, and hastened up behind Linnet and her escort. Street noise—the horses' hooves, the buggy wheels, the voices and clinks and rattles—prevented Sloan from discerning words, but their intent was clear. They bailed up Linnet and Chris and engaged them in intense conversation. Linnet was shaking her head and Chris looked worried.

Just as a fellow with his hair parted down the middle laid a hand on Linnet's arm, Sloan arrived at the party. "Linnet!" Every eye turned to Sloan. "Go to your rehearsal. And take your violin along. We wouldn't want it damaged."

Hesitantly she pulled the case from Chris's hand.

"Go."

"No." The larrikin kept a grip on her arm. "She's with us now. And none of this bull wool about the vice chancellor. We invited her and she agreed, days ago. Didn't you, lass?"

Sloan let his tone of voice convey his thoughts, and they were hostile, even murderous thoughts. "Step back."

The larrikin dipped a nod toward Chris. "This dandy's no fighter. Three against one? Leave while you can, stickybeak."

"Linnet, go."

The galah continued to grip her arm tightly.

The fellow had one thing right: Sloan could not expect help from this Chris. There was no black tunic in sight; no help from the police, either. He himself must put them in their place. And the expectation of it tickled him. Suddenly he *wanted* to bash these boozers with their ugly thoughts. He *wanted* to show that no-hoper Chris what a real man was. He wanted Linnet to be able to walk the streets in peace and safety.

He didn't have to think about where the danger lay. The three telegraphed their pugilistic incompetence with their swaggers and sneers. With his left he reached for that hand on Linnet's arm, but it was a feint on his part; his left continued on sideways quickly enough to block the blow coming from the larrikin's companion. He put his full weight behind his right and planted it in the fellow's belly. His knuckles cracked against the lad's belt buckle.

Without slowing he swung on around and grabbed the third drongo by the shirt. With a mighty heave he hauled the flailing man into the first. Both tumbled, and the one larrikin nearly dragged Linnet down with him. The slice in Cole's left arm ripped open again. He could feel it go. But his blood was so hot he didn't care.

A whistle blew upstreet. A helmet and black tunic on a shiny black bicycle came into view, now that the excitement was over. Sloan modulated his voice with considerable difficulty. All three sprawled flat in the street, but he was still ready to fight. He pointed at the jack with the hair parted down the middle. "I never want to see any of you within a hundred feet of Miss Connolly. Understood?"

He stepped back. The cape of the Conquering Hero fit so well, and felt so warm. He had saved the damsel in distress. He dismissed the fact the distress was minimal on a busy street in midafternoon. Distress is distress. And this Chris needed some lessons in manliness, anyway. A smugness, an elation welled up inside Sloan.

After all his recent losses, from the huge setback of Sugarlea's demise to the annoyances of the last few weeks, it was so nice to win one once!

Chapter Ten

Variation on a Christmas Present

Cole Sloan was king of the world. At least, he felt that way. These motor automobiles might as well be called "motor thrones." And Queen Linnet sat on the seat beside him, an expression of pure delight on her face. He regally piloted their shiny black open Tarrant through the little town of Gawler. They had left Adelaide not much more than two hours ago. Thirty-odd miles in a couple of hours, and the mechanical horses still eager to run—what a way to travel! This trip had him absolutely convinced: his next major purchase, once he regained solvency, was going to be a motor car.

They roared along the flat, open track as a dust cloud the size of a merchant ship boiled up behind them. The road was packed hard as a cobbled street now, in the dry season. In the wet, it would be a frustrating morass for any vehicle, motor or horse-drawn.

"Cole? Did ye already know how to operate such doovers as these, or did ye learn last night?"

"Last night when I rented it. Spent an hour with the owner. Apparently he has to give lessons to just about everybody who rents it. Driving a motor car, of course, is never going to be a common thing that everybody knows.

Say, I've been meaning to thank you for being so prompt this morning. As I recall from Sugarlea, you're not always the earliest of risers. I figured we might possibly start out of Adelaide at sunrise if we were lucky; instead, we were on the road more than an hour before sunup."

"Eh, after ye mentioned motor cars meself could barely sleep a wink. Sure 'n I was waiting for ye fifteen minutes before ye pulled up to the door."

Near the crest of some low hills they paused beneath a wattle tree for breakfast. Linnet unpacked the food basket in the back of the motor car as Cole built the fire for tea. After the meal, it took him ten minutes and some anxious moments to crank the auto to life again. They rolled up to the big stone Tanunda Hotel in time for morning tea.

Sloan was ready to sit quietly in the shade awhile. Speedy and efficient though a motor car might be, it jarred one's teeth out and vibrated the hands down to throbbing stumps. Twenty minutes after they were seated inside, his fingers still shook a bit, rattling the teacup.

He watched Linnet sip her tea. "Feel bad you cut class?"

"Nae." She smiled. "People miss class all the time because of illness. Why nae because of happiness, aye?"

"Aye, indeed. On the other hand, I'd hate to see you get into trouble for the sake of a lark."

"And a lovely lark it is!"

Sloan studied the gentle patterns of movement created in his tea. "Who's this Chris lair, anyway?"

She hesitated. Embarrassment? No, apparently not. The hesitation seemed more like uncertainty. "A mentor, I suppose ye'd say. Were it nae for him, I'd be forced to give up me schooling, for I could ne'er afford it depending upon Meg and Sam. And he's a good friend."

"He's a nark."

"Eh, now, I aver he acts like a spoiled brat at times. Our practice yesterday afternoon, after ye left us, was nothing but criticism and impatience. He's a good sort, though. And gentle."

"Gentle!" Sloan snorted and drained his tea. "Ah well. On to business." He escorted her out into the brilliant sun and they began to walk. *Gentle? Bah,* Cole thought. *Gutless. Is she so shook on the blighter that she can't see his true colors?* She didn't seem infatuated or overly fond of him. But then, she was so enthusiastic about everything that you could never tell when something struck her particular fancy.

"We be visiting a winery, aye?"

"Three of Australia's best wine-producing districts lie right close to Adelaide. The Barossa here, the Clare, and the country south of town. I intend to hit them all within the next few days."

"Quite a lot of wine to be tasting."

He chuckled. "You don't have to taste it all to know whether it's good stuff or lunatic soup. We'll start here with Basedows."

Although some brokerages dealt with one wine-producing area or another, and often with one vintner alone, Sloan would pick and choose from among the whole lot, a batch from here and a batch from there. He would provide New South Wales and the world with the bounty of South Australian wines.

But he would, in effect, be providing coal to Newcastle. Face it. Excellent vintners called New South Wales home, and the world had plenty of quality wines already. If Sloan were to cut an edge at all, that edge would be price.

A block or so from the Tanunda Hotel and across the railway tracks, he escorted Linnet into what was obviously her first wine cellar. They descended from summer heat into endless and uniform cool. Her large eyes flitted about, dancing across the many racks of bottles, the ornately carved tasting bar, the hundreds of twinkling glasses hung by their heels from ceiling racks. She craned her neck to see through an opened door into a dark aging room beyond, where stack upon stack of wooden casks sat brooding in the gloom, undisturbed.

Half a dozen men and a few women stood about at the bar or surveyed the racks. Whether they were patrons or escapees from the heat, Sloan did not know.

Sloan introduced himself to the young man behind the bar, and the fellow trotted off to summon the manager. The manager was not at all what Sloan would expect a wine maker to be, for here came a very short, dark, Turkish-looking fellow. He was wide and square, yet lean. Muscular.

He extended a stubby, powerful hand. "Herbert Ajanian, Mr. Sloan. Welcome to Basedows." His eyes flicked to Linnet and stared. "Why . . . indeed, it is! Miss Connolly! Linnet Connolly, is that correct?"

She looked at him blankly. "Aye, sir. How do ye do."

"Miss Connolly, I'm honored! My wife and I traveled down to the city for Helmut Hoffman's Bach presentation. You were splendid! What a sweet voice!"

"Y're too gracious, sir. Thank ye." Her cheeks flushed.

Sloan realized he himself was staring. He was almost certain Linnet had never been through the Barossa before. Yet here they were over forty miles from civilization and this total stranger, obviously a patron of the arts, recognized Linnet on sight.

He commenced a business discussion with Ajanian, sniffing this wine, carefully tasting that one, arranging for shipments by the case. And all the time, a discordance rang at the back of his head. That Chris bloke—what sort of mysterious power did he wield over the gentle Linnet? What precisely was the nature of his financial aid to which she alluded? And now, to have this Ajanian pick her out of nowhere. . . .

Mrs. Ajanian appeared, obviously his wife even before her husband introduced her. She was framed along the same short, solid lines as he. As she greeted Sloan and crowed rapturously over Linnet, their hired man brought in two big boxes.

"Christmas decorations." She smiled, almost embarrassed. "I realize the first week into December is a bit early, but I do love the season so."

Linnet looked misty-eyed. "I've naething to do while Mr. Sloan completes his business. Might I help?"

"By all means!"

While Sloan haggled and calculated, Linnet hung garlands. In Sloan's youth, decorating had fallen primarily to the servants. Pity. It rather looked like fun.

"Miss Connolly, do you not think we might sing carols as we work?" Mrs. Ajanian handed Linnet one end of a coarse pine-bough swag and trotted nimbly up a small ladder.

"Aye, the very thing!" And she plunged instantly into song.

"God rest ye merry, gentlemen, let naething ye dismay.
Remember Christ our Savior was born on Christmas Day,
T' save us all from Satan's power when we were gone astray. . . ."

All discussion of wines had ceased. Everyone stood about rapt, engrossed in the impromptu concert. About half the voices in the low, echoing room joined her for the chorus.

" . . . O-oh, tidings of comfort and joy, comfort and joy;
O-oh tidings of comfort and joy!"

Sweet, rich, melodious—what a glorious voice! Sloan was a man not easily impressed by artsy sorts of things, but he stood there agape, quite as taken over as every other person in the room.

To save us all from Satan's power when we had gone astray. Astray. Sloan was ofttimes accused of straying. Hardly! He smiled to himself. He was not astray. *Astray* suggests wandering. Sloan seized the moment whenever opportunity appeared. He was blasting through life with grit and determination. He had locked horns with fate, and he wasn't about to let fate win. By no stretch of the imagination could that be called wandering.

He wrenched his thoughts back to Ajanian and the business at hand. "I understand you make an excellent red. What have you available in the reds?"

"For you, nothing." Ajanian smiled apologetically and waved a hand. "My reds are spoken for."

"Then let me bid on next year's pressing."

"I'm sorry; I was unclear. My reds are committed to another brokerage. They take all I produce under exclusive contract. Except, of course, for the few bottles I sell at the cellar door."

"When does the current contract expire?"

"It is, ah, an ongoing understanding. My reds are not available at wholesale. I'm sorry."

"I see." Indeed, Sloan saw quite a bit more than he wanted to see. He was the new chum; his rivals were well established. He would no doubt be forced to wait years to gain the sort of entree the older brokerages expected as a matter of course. How many more exclusive contracts was he going to slam into today? He hated to think about it.

With difficulty he pried Linnet loose from the admiring Ajanians and hit the road again. Saltrams sold to several purveyors—all under exclusive contract, of course—and none of them was Sloan. Except for a few of Basedow's common whites, Sloan was scoring zero so far. Henschke down in Keyneton had committed their good stuff, the Mt. Edelstone and Hill of Grace reds, but Sloan managed to consign for himself a number of cases of their dry whites.

By the time they reached Hamilton's down in Springton, Linnet's bounce had flattened out. She no longer glided from place to place. She slogged. To be sure, it was a smooth and delicate slog, but a one-foot-in-front-of-the-other slog, nonetheless. She was getting sun-dried, too. Sloan watched Linnet's nose turn red and thought of poor old Sam's ever-peeling nose. Linnet did not take sun well, but Sam took it far worse.

The Hamilton winery, built of big, honest blocks of bluestone, provided welcome relief from the heat of the waning day. Sloan settled his wilted songbird at a table in the coolest corner of the tasting room, asked the lad on duty to provide whatever she requested, then sat down face-to-face with the manager, a man by the name of Geoffreys. The fellow looked and acted cynical enough that perhaps Sloan at last could arrange some business. The day so far had been pretty much a total loss.

Geoffreys nodded toward the corner table and wiggled his massive black brows. "Bonzer sheila to smoodge up to, eh?"

Sloan's success now depended upon how accurately he read this leering lout, and how well he played upon what he read. He tightened both his face and voice. "Sister of a good friend. And innocent, so I take idle comments about her very seriously, and so does the friend. Now you can ogle some sheila you don't know, or talk business that can make us both a few quid. What'll it be?"

The eyes beneath those beetling brows narrowed. Suddenly he laughed. "Let's talk business, mate."

"I'm interested in whites."

Geoffreys flagged his barboy and with one finger tapped a bottle behind him. The lad nodded and disappeared into the back room. The man studied the tabletop a moment. "Dessert wines?"

"If the deal is as sweet. I'm looking more to table wines."

"Whites. Fix you up with some sauterne in quantity, and chablis. Sure you can't use reds?"

Sloan shrugged casually. "Such as—?"

"Burgundies, clarets, perhaps rosés, if you're willing to move smaller quantities."

"I'm out to build a reputation as a broker, not peddle red ned."

"Good stuff. I'll show you."

This ratbag was beginning to irritate Sloan immensely.

His manner grated, especially his clumsy attempts at superiority. Superiority? Without even trying, Sloan had him pitching the one sort Sloan really needed—the reds—and the drongo hadn't the slightest notion he'd just been played.

The barboy had returned from the back room and was serving Linnet a glass of something dark. Port? She had not tasted wine at all yet today. Apparently she had changed her mind, for Sloan had told her to ask for whatever she wanted.

"Beetle Brows" poured a claret. "Now this stuff is supposed to be consigned, but the price isn't no picnic. If you can better it, I'd like to let you have it." The bushy head wagged. "Don't want to offend the blokes, though, by going behind their backs. Don't know how to ship it, ah, inconspicuously. Know what I mean?"

"How's it go out now? Tanunda to Adelaide and east?"

"Yair."

"The Murray's not fifty miles east. By the time you hauled it up to Tanunda, you're halfway to the river. Put it on a boat at Mannum, ship it upriver, and send it by rail from Echuca. New shippers, cellars to shops. No nasty rumors about what's going to whom."

Geoffreys nodded. "You sign for me that you'll ship it by river, and you've got a deal."

In a superb display of acting prowess, Sloan hid his glee as he signed on for the reds he needed so desperately. He'd work some kind of arrangement at Echuca and score a big win back in Sydney. He'd been right. There was no substitute for getting out in the field yourself and gathering the goods.

He walked over to Linnet's table. She smiled at him somewhat glassy-eyed. He frowned and lifted her empty glass. "How many of these have you had?"

"Three. Meself be very thirsty, Cole. Dry day, aye?"

"Don't you know wine won't quench thirst?"

"Eh, he said it would." She waved a hand toward the barboy.

Geoffreys appeared at Sloan's elbow. "My orders; the lad knows what to do. Thought I'd soften her up for you, know what I mean? Just a little favor of the house."

Never in his life had Cole Sloan resorted to alcohol to soften up some sheila. He didn't have to, and the mere suggestion that a little wine might be needed impugned his manhood. If he wanted Linnet, he'd win Linnet, and without resort to booze or gimmicks.

He turned on Geoffreys and started walking, forcing the hairy drongo clear across the room, backing him up against the wall. He stopped when his nose was six inches from Geoffreys'. "Don't you ever presume to do me a favor again. My only restraint from strangling you is my need to do business with you. So help me, I'd kill you right here if it weren't for that."

The literal fear of death flashed across Geoffreys' face for a moment. He drew a deep, shuddering breath. "Ye can count on it." He paused a moment, almost as if waiting for some axe to fall. He forced a smile. "Still business mates?"

Sloan backed off. He did not offer his hand. "Only because we can use each other."

Geoffreys nodded. "Good honest reason. Appreciate working with a man who puts it right up front."

Sloan turned his attention to Linnet. How shickered was she? She seemed a little unsteady on her walk out to the motor car. She giggled, but then Linnet did that anyway. Maybe it would wear off by the time they got home.

It didn't. Rather than return to Tanunda, Sloan cut straight across to the west, along a tired, rutted little track that wound gracelessly between low hills. He drove into Adelaide just after dark. As they chugged south down King William Road, Linnet was still quite obviously inebriated.

Now what should he do with her? If he sent her up to her room like this, and her priggish school learned about it from the landlord, she could find herself in deep trouble, trouble not of her own doing. Letting her sleep it off in his hotel room would be far worse; that would guarantee her expulsion, should it become known.

He pulled up to the house where she stayed. Its doorway, shrouded in darkness, looked half a mile distant, though it was only a few yards beyond the hedges and plantings. He would have to send her up to her room and hope she didn't slam into walls. That was best.

He gave her a hand down. "Watch your step, luv. There you go."

She melted against him. "This was such a beaut day, Cole! Meshelf enjoyed the holiday immenshly. I feel so good."

"I'm sure you do." *But just wait 'til morning, and the headache . . .* He hesitated. *Taking unfair advantage is one thing; taking what's due you is another,* he thought. *A good-night kiss will not be out of line in the least.* She responded to his kiss freely, comfortably, the way she responded in everything—with no guard, no reservation.

And in that sweet, gentle good-night kiss, Sloan learned again the lesson he already knew: Linnet was not Sam. No matter how closely the sisters resembled one another in some respects, it just wasn't the same.

At Sugarlea, Sam had attracted him; Linnet had not. He could not manufacture that attraction now, no matter how hard he tried. Still, a girl like Linnet was superior to, say, Hilary.

He escorted her toward the door as she tried simultaneously to walk and to grub her key out of her handbag. She couldn't do either one adequately, let alone together.

"Don't bother, Linn. I've a key here." Chris was perched on her front stoop! He stood up, his silk shirt gleaming in the light of distant streetlamps. "I cadged a spare from the landlord; told him you mislaid yours."

Linnet lit up like fireworks. If Sloan doubted before

where her heart lay, he doubted no more. "Chris!" she beamed. "We went on such a lovely excursion. 'Tis lovely country, with the vineyards and the lovely stone wine cellars."

"We had an engagement to play for a banquet tonight, or did you forget why we practiced all afternoon yesterday?"

"I'm sorry, Chris." And her tone of voice echoed the sentiment. *Sorry. I really am.*

"It was more my fault than hers," Sloan cut in. "I led her astray."

"You certainly did!" Chris snorted. He wrenched his key in the lock and shoved the door open. "Do try to make it to class in the morning, Linn. Good night." He gripped her elbow, thrust her through the door and locked it again. Without a glance at Sloan he walked out to the street and disappeared beyond the hedges.

So that was how the wind lay. This Chris, remarkably protective for a mere friend, agreed that Sloan was leading Linnet astray. Why not? It seemed that way to all external appearances. Astray. There it was again. *Remember Christ our savior was born on Christmas Day, to save us all from Satan's power when we were gone astray.* That wasn't Satan, it was Geoffreys. Despite Milton's opinion in *Paradise Lost* of what constitutes evil, Geoffreys wasn't smart enough to be Satan.

Sloan started back to his motor car. He'd have to purchase more fuel tomorrow before heading north into the Clare Valley. Or perhaps he'd just skip the Clare completely. He'd heard of the Reynell vineyards to the south, one of the oldest wineries in South Australia. He might just dabble down south and search out a bargain or two there.

A shadow stepped out of the hedges beside him. "S'cuse me, mate. Got a light?"

"No, I don't. Sorry."

Then the world exploded. He was on the ground behind

the hedges, unable to breathe or cry out. Something smashed him in the side of the face. A boot kicked him in the belly, and it was flying at him again. He grabbed it frantically and twisted. The fellow crashed into the hedge. But there were other boots and fists—too many to fend off.

"Early Christmas present, blighter," an unknown voice crowed gleefully.

And suddenly he was enraged—enraged at that spineless Chris for arranging this and probably participating, enraged at himself for not being on his guard, for letting this happen. Most of all he was enraged by the thought of losing. Never in his life had he lost a hand-to-hand fight, but he didn't have Buckley's chance with this one—not when he was down and unable to get his breath.

Rage and consciousness faded together into ignominious defeat.

Chapter Eleven

Intermezzo With Old Friends

Samantha stood in the office doorway and surveyed the effect. Washing the windows and whitewashing the walls did indeed achieve miracles of brightness. But the floor—that sad floor. No amount of scrubbing seemed to help. Its planks remained much the same color as the weathered dock outside. Should she cover it with something? No. She had neither money nor brilliant ideas at the moment. It was clean; that would be enough.

"Ah Loo, we'll bring the desk in first and place it by the window there."

Her Man Friday jogged outside and had removed the drawers by the time she got there. The desk was fashioned from red gum, too heavy to move with the drawers in. They positioned the big wooden file cabinets *sans* drawers and the straight-backed chair and empty side table. They polished the brass postal scale and cleaned the oil lamps. They removed the shade from the one electric fixture and dumped its load of dead insects outside. Then they spent several minutes oohing and awing over this bright creature and that. Wonderful things, insects, so long as they're dead. Finally they brought in all the drawers full of papers as well as the many boxes and piles of papers, stacking them in the one remaining corner.

Samantha dug into her beaded reticule. "Y'r day's pay, Ah Loo. Well done! I could nae have managed without ye."

He grinned. "It was fun. This place looks so much better. I liked the whitewashing especially. It's fun when you can see a big difference, huh?"

"Absolutely! G'day now."

"G'day, mum!" He looked for the first time at the coins in his hand and his eyes grew large. "Thank ye, mum!" and he was off.

He almost collided with Mr. Drummond on his way out. Drummond scowled after the lad. "How much did you give him, anyway?"

"He earned a man's pay, for he did a man's work this day."

"Absurd! He's what—nine years old at the most."

"True enough. But ye'll notice, sir, that the whole task be finished in a single day. Often 'tis a great saving if ye can somehow complete the work quickly and smartly." She led the way to the stack of drawers and papers. "Meself wishes to dispose of all records more than seven years auld, and store those older than three years. As is, ye've more paper here than the room can hold."

"Yes. But, ah, if you're going to store some, store all. Uh, where did you intend to put them?"

"The vacant warehouse next to us. Records show it belongs to the wharf, despite that several wool brokers use it seasonally, apparently rent free."

"Certainly! Oh, and Miss Connolly, I'll not be in until late tomorrow morning. There's a commissioners' meeting."

"Aye, sir." That suited her well enough. If he wasn't around, he wouldn't be trying to help sort through this rats' nest. He went his way, and she carried the first of many drawers over to her desk. What a mess!

Twenty-four hours later Ah Loo had trundled away thirteen fruit crates of paper on his little dock dolly. He had been paid and dismissed. Samantha sat back in her chair by the office window and stared awhile at what remained. It had melted down to a tiny pile, praise God, and tomorrow—perhaps even tonight—it would disappear completely. Praise God. Yes. Samantha could do that now, though the reality of God's presence still startled her somewhat. It was very new.

She looked around the room. All relevant and necessary papers were tucked into their appropriate cabinets. The stationery and postal necessities rested in a place of their own in her desk drawers. Incoming mail and business had its place, easily found, and the outgoing mail sat in the little basket on the corner of her desk. The typewriter was off the floor at last and back on its proper typewriter table. It must have been deposed years ago, for none of the papers she had taken off the little table was dated 1905 or later.

Samantha stood up suddenly and pulled her purse off the hatrack. She had been at this onerous task two full days, and then some. Mr. Drummond was already gone for the day. There was nothing so urgent that she should work into the evening. She felt a strong compulsion to go home.

She strolled down High Street in no real hurry and thought of the evenings back in Cork, so cool, even damp. This evening, with its waning golden sun, was nearly as torrid as midday. Echuca never cooled off; it was only more or less hot.

As she turned the corner into her street she heard footsteps behind her. "Excuse me, mum, can you spare a coin? I'm penniless."

That voice! She wheeled. It was! And look at him!

She clapped her hand to her mouth, stunned. "Mr. Sloan! Whatever happened to ye?!"

One of three large bruises on the sides of his face had swelled his left eye nearly shut. A bit of plaster covered a cut over his right eye. Worst of all, he looked—well, he looked beaten. Defeated.

He extended a hand, and when she offered hers he held it a moment and kissed it, ever courtly. "I'm delighted to see you looking fit and well despite the heat."

"Ye did nae answer me question."

"Nor did you answer mine."

She frowned. His question?

"Can you spare a coin?" he repeated.

"I'll wager y're in need of far more than a coin, but let us start there. When last we met, ye treated me to tea at the garden. Might I reciprocate today?"

"I accept with pleasure and as much dignity as the circumstance will permit." He took her arm in his and headed back down the street with her. "Which isn't much. I haven't let the lady pay my way since I was a lad asking Mum for a penny to buy candy." He walked stiffly, almost with a limp. "You are looking well, Sam. I'm glad. I know you and heat don't get along."

"Me son tells me the rains will return come March, and then I'll be enjoying glorious weather. Now ye must stop evading the obvious question. Whatever befell ye?"

"Ruffians robbed me in Adelaide. They stole my hotel key along with everything else and cleaned out my room before I returned to it. I wasn't joking a moment ago; I really am penniless. I accepted a loan from a friendly police officer for the train ticket this far. Very nice police in South Australia. Polite, considerate."

"Adelaide! Have ye visited Linnet at all?"

"She sends her warmest greetings. She's doing very well and succeeding brilliantly with her music. She was hoping to come to Echuca for the holiday, but a friend of hers is booking her for a number of engagements. Christmas concerts and the like. She'll be paid for some of them, apparently."

"Meself be pleased to hear it. She never writes, and I do wonder sometimes how it goes with her." Ruffians! Ever so briefly she thought of this stalwart and handsome man being pounded into the ground by bullies. A chill ran down her back despite the heat. Beaten and robbed. It could happen to anybody. But to him . . . to someone so proud . . .

If he were robbed blind, why did he not request a loan of Linnet? Silly Samantha! Linnet had no money.

Here they were at the tea garden. The proprietress tried to hide her shock with a smile. It didn't work. She seated them in the cool of the bower and hastened off to bring tea.

Samantha held his hand a moment, surveying the poor scuffed knuckles. "In a perverse way, I be pleased to see ye did nae go peacefully. 'Twould nae be the Cole Sloan I know if ye did nae give near as good as ye got."

"Nowhere near as good as I got. But I tried. I was hoping against hope you were still at the address you gave me, and hadn't gone off to Melbourne looking for work. May I take it you've found a good position here?"

"Aye. Assistant to the wharfmaster. And what a job! I learned lately that the wharfmaster himself, Mr. Drummond, was hired less than a month ago, replacing a man who apparently was incompetent. And the clerk quit a week before that. So neither Mr. Drummond nor meself knows anything of the working of the place, nor of the paper work. We're starting at the beginning, if ye will. Praise be, 'tis between seasons until the rains fill the river again. We need nae leap into the midst of something."

"All the abandoned buildings, the collapsing sheds—if I didn't know already that Echuca's in eclipse, I'd learn it by walking down her streets. The wharfmaster's position can't be too taxing these days."

She giggled. "Clever choice of words, Mr. Sloan—'taxing.' Ye see, before—"

"Sam? Would you do me a very big favor?"

"Aye, sir, if I can."

"It's Cole. Not Mr. Sloan."

"Cole." This would be very difficult. He was Mr. Sloan. He'd always been Mr. Sloan. And yet, she was no longer in his employ. And there was not *that* much a gap between their ages that she should show him some sort of deference. "Ye see, before federation, Victoria here and New South Wales across the river each levied customs duties on all the goods entering their borders. And of course, the border was the river."

"I'm well familiar with the customs houses in the designated border towns. They were a royal pain, until federation and Free Trade."

"Eh, and what a mountain of paper! Every item landing on the wharf here in Echuca had to have the proper papers and be checked against the manifests, boat and train alike. The wharf kept records of all that went into the bonded store. We've records nae even Shackell's Bonded stores bothered to keep. They were all in the office, filling every cranny. Every tax and duty receipt ever generated by the wharf, so far as we can tell. I could scarce believe the extent of the mess."

"You're not one to tolerate disorder."

"And well I suffered for over a fortnight, going about me meager duties and planning how to change everything around. Mr. Drummond had nae objection. So yesterday, when I could stand it nae longer, meself bundled up the lot and stuffed it into some unused space next door. Sure'n Mr. Drummond had nae idea what color the top of his desk might be until today. But we're ready for trade now, or nearly so. Tomorrow I'll complete me task."

He was studying her thoughtfully, steadily, with his one good eye. "It sounds as if this Drummond is giving you carte blanche. Whatever you wish, do it."

"Eh, nae, I dinnae mean to give that impression. He handles the, ah, personal relations; he attends meetings, and talks to councilmen and shakes hands. Meself takes care of correspondence and day-by-day affairs in the office.

It suits me well. I dinnae enjoy politics, and he thrives on it."

The tea and scones arrived. Mr. Sloan—no, Cole—took over as mother of the pot.

"This be on me tab, please," Samantha told the proprietress, and she nodded as she left.

Cole was pouring when a familiar soprano voice pealed out from street side. "There she is!"

Samantha's son came running up. He bowed respectfully and even managed to avoid staring at Cole's bruised face.

"I present me son, Ah Loo. Ah Loo, this is Mr. Sloan. And behind Ah Loo is coming his uncle, Ah Sai Guy."

The ancient uncle, seller of the best produce in Victoria, left his greengrocer's cart outside the garden and bowed low by her table. Cole rose and gravely shook the man's hand. Samantha was flabbergasted. This was the sugar planter who repeatedly found himself in trouble for using Kanakas, the South Sea islanders, as illegal labor. This man held any race save his own in extremely low regard, and didn't rate his own too highly in selected instances. Was this a new Cole Sloan, or did he see some advantage to be gained?

Cole sat down again. "You said 'son' before, but I thought I heard you wrong. I can't wait to get *this* story."

Samantha smiled at Ah Loo. "What might I do for ye?"

"It is the close of day and my uncle still has some very fine tomatoes. He would like to give them to you."

"Thank ye." Samantha nodded at Ah Sai Guy. "Thank ye."

The old gentleman was staring at Cole's eye, and yet it was not an impolite sort of stare. He raised a finger. "Have just the thing. Excuse, please." He bowed and hastened off.

Ah Loo licked his lips. "My uncle is well known among the Chinese for his herbs and medicines. I think he's going to give you something for, uh, that." He glanced at Cole.

"If it works, I'll take it." Perhaps it was indeed a new Cole Sloan.

Ah Loo grinned. "When Uncle and I stopped by your house and you weren't there, I said, 'I bet I know where she is.' " He snapped his fingers.

"And glad I am ye found me. Not just for the tomatoes; I've decided I will nae need ye on the morrow. Stop by again on Friday, if ye will."

The uncle came jogging up at that shuffling trot. He did not trust his recipe to his limited command of English. He explained his handful of weeds to Ah Loo.

The boy translated. "The gentleman is to pound these together in a—you know, one of those—" He made mortar-and-pestle motions. "And make a—you know, like a pillow—"

"A poultice? A pack?"

"That's it. Keep it moist with cool water. It will bring the swelling down so he can see."

There followed a nearly endless flurry of thanks, nods, bows, leave-taking and hand-shaking. Ah Loo and Ah Sai Guy retreated, and Samantha sipped her tea, wearied by the frantic spate of politeness.

She glanced at Cole. If she felt wearied, he looked it, immensely so. She pondered options. It didn't take her long; there weren't that many. "Bank of New South Wales?"

He nodded.

"Over in Moama across the bridge. Even if ye be waiting at the door when it opens, ye'll not make it back to the railway station in time to catch the train. So y're here at least another day."

"That's no good anyway. I've no identification and nothing the bank wants to see to prove I'm a depositor."

"I'll sign for ye; I've a permanent address here and an account in the Bank of Victoria." Why was she doing this? There was no chance of an intensified relationship with this man. She could not trust him before; she could trust him no better now. She should see him on his way as quickly as possible. Having him near and yet unavailable hurt, she suddenly recognized. Why twist the knife?

Pity. That was it. Here was a man beaten by life, virtually friendless, stranded, in need of rest, of succor. This was the least she could do. A Christian duty, if you will. "Forgive me boldness. But if ye've naething calling ye immediately to Sydney, perhaps ye'd like to spend the holiday here in the Riverina and return home after the New Year. 'Twould give ye a much-needed rest. And ye would nae be going back to the city looking as if ye were trampled by a camel train."

"There," he smiled wryly. "There's the difference between you and Hilary. Hilary would refuse to be seen with me until I healed up. You take me out to tea in the middle of town." He nodded. "Maybe it would be good to just relax here awhile. Since Sugarlea, I haven't stopped running. I am tired."

Why did she feel so happy with this decision? It was bound to lead to nothing but pain and trouble. She knew that even as she said, "Splendid! We'll secure ye a room; the Esplanade or perhaps the Bridge—both be good hotels; and mayhap spend a quiet evening at me house creating poultices. Eh, y'r poor eye!"

Ever since it was delicensed ten years ago, the Esplanade maintained a sly-grog shop in its basement, where men bent upon drinking something virtually poisonous could sneak down and do it. There was even a little passageway out the back and to the surface that those same men might elude police during the occasional raids. Everyone, including the police, knew about it. Samantha signed for a room for Cole at the Esplanade anyway, because the Bridge down the street maintained several rooms of ill repute. And these were two of the better accommodations.

And then Samantha Connolly did what she had never

done before; she invited an unattached male into her home. The circumstance was certainly harmless, and yet she felt oddly uncomfortable doing it. She left him at the dining table and retired to the kitchen out back to prepare a light supper. Cole turned chemist, pounding his mysterious herbs to a paste in a crockery bowl with a wooden spoon. By the time she was ready to serve chicken with rice, biscuits and tomatoes, he had built a serviceable poultice out of a linen towel and had fallen asleep on her bed with the green blob lying on his face.

Should she wake him or let him nap? A difficult choice—he badly needed both rest and sustenance. Indeed, he could use the poultice, too. She left the question momentarily unresolved by leaning in the bedroom doorway several minutes simply watching him.

Handsome, well built, strong and healthy. There was nothing about him physically that would not recommend him. He knew her well and seemed to accept her as she was. He had professed love for her once upon a time. But he had his dark side, too—his lack of scruples. Was she being too choosy? All men had flaws, even Meg's preacherman Luke Vinson, and yet women happily married them.

So many of her friends were introduced to some gentleman, were courted properly, fell in love, accepted the man's proposal, and wedded—the end of singleness, the beginning of marriage and motherhood, the roles a woman was born to. Meg had met and married without trauma or difficulty, a straightforward courtship. What was wrong with Samantha that she could not? Why did every position she accepted disappear out from under her for one reason or another? Why did this new decision of hers to accept Jesus Christ fully bring with it so many questions, mostly unanswered? She yearned for a bit of simplicity in her life, for black and white answers to honest questions. She despised uncertainty, and she was plagued with it.

Someone knocked. Ah Loo again? Cole stirred and

reached absently for the glob on his face. That solved that problem. He'd be awake now. Might as well feed him. She crossed to the door and opened it.

On her doorstep a cheerful smile divided a neat, trimmed brown beard. He carried a large, elaborately wrapped Christmas gift. "Good evening, Samantha. Sorry to just pop in on you like this. For a number of reasons I decided to come into town over the holiday. Is this a good time to call?"

Frankly, it's a terrible time to call.

"Yes, certainly, Reginald. Good to see ye."

Chapter Twelve

Recitative on Love and Handel

"A— — — —men." *Pause; watch the conductor.* "A—men. A—men."

Silence.

Applause erupted. "Bravos" shot like firecrackers all over the hall. The hubbub ignited Linnet's cheeks and heart together. Why did she always blush when applauded? Chris said it was one of the most charming things about her. But she found it excruciatingly embarrassing.

Although Handel mounted the first performance of his *Messiah* in Linnet's own Dublin, she had never before heard it performed. Chopping out the various parts for practice, much less the constant rabbit-like starts and stops of rehearsals, in no way came close to this awesome full performance.

The tenor took her hand in his and led her forward for a bow. She dipped in a curtsy until the lights blinded her. She stepped back with one arm raised and could not contain the grin on her face. From the darkness in the wings—from nowhere—a page thrust a huge bouquet into her arms. Chris had rehearsed her about this, though at the time she did not believe it would ever happen. She plucked a rose from her bouquet and handed it to the tenor.

Continuous applause. Another bow. And more . . .

There stood Chris beside the orchestra piano, barely visible in the gloom beyond the lights, beaming at her and clapping. She could make out no one else in the orchestra—only Chris.

Finally they left the stage, returned once more to applause, then left for good.

Mr. Giambone, the voluminous tenor, kissed her hand before releasing it. "My dear, you saw it through like a seasoned trooper. I must admit I worried a bit, learning this was your first *Messiah* performance, solo or chorus. You've a wonderful gift. I was pleased to sing with you."

She curtsied. "I'm honored, sir. Y're so . . . y're very . . . Sure'n I'm honored. Thank ye, sir." This professional singer, brought over from Sydney for the occasion, was praising her! What a glorious, wonderful night!

Guli Hack, an acre of hat perched on her head, loomed beside Linnet. Almost manly with those dark eyebrows and firm jaw, her face looked nearly ready to smile. Not quite. "You did well, Miss Connolly. I knew you would. Tomorrow remind me: we'll work on your apoggiaturas. You got quite sloppy with them in *How Beautiful Are the Feet*." She handed Linnet a check.

"Thank ye, mum." Linnet curtsied.

The dark face eyed her gravely. "Miss Connolly, I—yes, I will say it. You should know, or perhaps you do already. You are no student. I believe you realize that. You are bound to fail your examinations in everything save your music, and in that you excel. Did you not excel, you would have been dismissed from the program weeks ago. We're keeping you simply because we want the university's name associated with your musical training."

From behind her Chris spoke. Linnet hadn't seen him approach. "Does that mean, Miss Hack, that you and the other decision-makers in this brain factory think she's going to achieve a name for herself?"

"If she doesn't do something foolish, like marry or become involved with some man so as to give up her career." She glared at Linnet. "Do you understand my meaning?"

"Aye, mum." Linnet curtsied again.

Miss Hack moved just enough to present her back to Chris. "There are many fine sopranos in the program, Miss Connolly—girls from upper forms with seniority. We chose you, a beginner, as soloist only because of the quality of your voice. You still have much to learn."

"Aye, mum."

The brooding Miss Hack turned away to other students. A crowd of well-wishers and congratulators occupied Linnet for the next half hour. She clung to her bouquet, her marvelous bouquet, curtsying and murmuring "Thank ye" to everyone around. Her throat was getting a bit rough with all this. All along the way Chris hovered at her shoulder, fending off the crush, strengthening her simply by being there.

She wished Mr. Sloan could have remained in town long enough to see this performance. Of course, it was now that she wished him here; during rehearsals, when she so feared making a fool of herself, she had been glad business had called him away. She did wish, though, that he could have said goodbye in person, rather than with a simple note delivered by a page. Where was he now? Back in Sydney, probably. Thoughts of his kiss flitted in and out of her mind.

At long last the excitement waned. Weariness and exhilaration fought each other inside her and wearied her further. Handel's *Messiah*. What a thing! She changed from the rented concert gown to her plain black skirt. Chris led her out of the conservatorium into the close and muggy night.

"There she is!" Mr. Giambone's booming voice vibrated through the darkness. Not only could his ringing tenor fill the concert hall, it filled South Australia. Chris and Linnet stopped and turned to watch him come.

He approached accompanied by a man half his size. The other fellow appeared quite ordinary in his lightweight suit and bowler hat. Mr. Giambone himself had shed the cutaway coat and stiffly starched collar. His ruffled white shirt nearly glowed in the dark, for the streetlamps cast little light into this area of the conservatorium lawn.

He was puffing slightly. "My business manager, Mr. Osgood Dwyer, Miss Connolly."

"How d'ye do, sir."

Mr. Dwyer dipped his head. "Miss Connolly, I apologize for being so abrupt and hasty, but we've a train to catch. Tell me, do you have representation?"

Linnet had no idea what he meant. Since she probably would at least know what it meant if she had any, she was about to say no.

Chris stepped forward. "She does. Esmond Christenikos Yorke, at your service, sir."

The men shook hands all around, stiffly, formally. So Chris was her representative! What did that mean?

Mr. Dwyer offered his business card both to Chris and to her. "Mr. Yorke, we are mounting the *Messiah* as an Easter presentation in Sydney next year. I wish to sign your soprano here for the solo. Thirty pounds plus direct expenses. The production will be staged March 28, 30 and 31—31 being Easter, of course—with rehearsals the two weeks preceding."

Chris nodded. "Two items. One, I always accompany Miss Connolly on the road, for I am her rehearsal pianist and coach as well as agent. I would expect my immediate expenses to be covered as well. Second, I would like to know the circumstances of the dismissal of your original soprano soloist, since I'm certain you would have signed one by this late date."

Mr. Giambone emitted a high-pitched laugh, nothing

short of a giggle; Mr. Dwyer smirked. "Very simple. She is with child, a condition no one foresaw when she signed the contract. We learned the week we left Sydney to come here."

Chris nodded. "Write the contract as we've discussed here and we'll gladly sign. Miss Connolly's career will benefit from exposure beyond her current environs."

As the gentlemen hurried through their formalities of handshaking and parting, Linnet tried to sort out what had just happened. Thirty pounds? Was she to be paid that extravagant sum simply to perform a work she already knew? Direct expenses: travel costs and all that? Surely she couldn't be interpreting this scene correctly. No one would buy a servant girl's voice for that much. She looked at the modest check in her hand—only soloists were paid for university performances—and at her magnificent bouquet on her arm. A lot of things were happening very quickly.

Sydney? Mr. Sloan lived in Sydney. Perhaps he would hear her sing in concert. Lovely thought!

Giambone and Dwyer hastened off toward their waiting cab. Chris took her arm and recommenced walking casually. The cab rattled away to the west beyond the buildings, out of sight.

Chris grabbed her arms and danced her in circles. "Sydney! Less than three months from now—Sydney! We're on our way, Linn!" He wrapped his arms around her in a tight hug that nearly squashed her lovely flowers; then he kissed her—impetuously, firmly, delightfully.

With the most unusual expression on his face, he backed her off to arms' length as if he were looking at a stranger.

"Chris, ye needs control y'rself a bit more decorously in public, aye?"

He laughed suddenly. The spell, whatever it was, had broken. "What? And live a dull life?" He swooped her off across the lawn toward North Terrace. "Linn, we're on our way!"

"So ye've said. But where?"

"The sky, the stars, the world. Wherever you wish to go." He put a lean arm across her shoulders and pulled her in close. Suddenly he moved away, stopped, and turned. "And in keeping with your emerging importance in the world of music, you need lessons in deportment." He adjusted his cape as he walked off ten paces. He wheeled. "All right. I'm the mayor of Sydney. I come up to you backstage."

Linnet nodded and licked her lips.

Before her eyes, Chris changed from a bouncing, lilting artist into a pompous politician. He stood taller. His chest puffed out as his nose tipped up. Magisterially, he strode across the grass to her. As he took her hand in his and grandly kissed it, his voice rumbled, "My dear, you were marvelous."

He *was* the mayor! Abashed, Linnet curtsied deeply. "Thank ye, m'lord."

"*No!* No, no, no!"

She cringed. *Now* what had she done?

"You curtsy to the king. You curtsy to the archbishop. To everyone else in the world, except maybe the prime minister, you dip your head in a single nod, like this, and close your wonderful eyes so that when you raise your head and open them again—like this—they simply engulf the man."

"I dinnae curtsy to the Lord High Mayor?"

"No. It's servile."

"I *am* a servant, Chris. A domestic."

"*You are not!*" His ringing tenor vibrated to the stars. He must have seen the fear in her eyes, for he lowered his voice a few decibels. "You must retrain your mind, Linnet. You must understand that you are no longer a servant. You are an artist. And more! You are an exceptionally talented world-class artist."

"Oh, really now! I—"

He laid both hands on her shoulders; his black eyes penetrated her whole being. "You curtsy to the king because you are his subject. You are *not* his inferior. You curtsy to the archbishop because he's the top rung of divine representation. You may curtsy to the pope also, if you wish. But you are Linnet Connolly, consummate artist. You have earned your position of honor, and you will assume it."

"Honestly, Chris."

"Assume it! Not presume it. This is not presumptuous, don't you see? You are worthy of honor! The gifts you were born with make you the equal of men and women who were born to their positions. Now step into the role God ordained for you."

He released her and stepped back. "We'll do it again."

The "mayor" came striding toward her, magnificent in his power. Again he praised her. To her dip of the head she added the slightest of bows, a tiny movement of the shoulders. She raised her head and took care to open her eyes slowly.

His dark face lit up like the sun. "Pure elegance!" He stood staring at her a moment, and the look in his eyes was almost one of awe. He took a deep breath. "Good. Next we'll work on how you'll handle the ugly, suggestive little notes that are going to be slipped under your door."

Reginald Otis, while certainly no Notre Dame hunchback, was not an exceedingly handsome man. Because God had given him important other gifts far more beneficial and enduring, he accepted his rather ordinary appearance gladly—until now. Now, despite his best intentions, he felt a pang of envy.

Across the table from him sat a darkly handsome man, the kind of man to turn a lady's head. And at the table to his right sat Samantha. She was as sensible a young woman as you'll find, but her head was surely turn-able. Samantha and this Mr. Sloan, her former employer, shared an easy sort of comfort. When Sloan addressed her as "Sam," he sounded like a brother. Yet, deep inside Reginald, a tiny green-eyed demon poked at his heart with the trident of jealousy.

In spite of himself, Reginald found himself counting out the strokes against him. Stroke one: beauty attracts beauty. Stroke two: Sloan's injuries could not help but invoke sympathy and warm feelings from a lady as tenderhearted as Samantha. Stroke three: they knew each other well, and obviously liked each other well. Worst of all, four, Sloan was here—*here*—with time on his hands. Reginald's days would be stuffed full with business during most of his stay in town. He would have to make at least two trips to Melbourne. And as he dashed about preoccupied, trying to do the Lord's work with—financially speaking—one hand tied behind his back, Sloan would be wandering free.

Free to do what? To court Samantha? If he had even half an eye for quality, he'd be doing everything in his power to win her.

In Samantha's presence Reginald lost twenty years of sophistication and fumbled about like a schoolboy. His mouth said things without first consulting his mind—too frequently, disastrous things. She filled his thoughts whether he was in her presence or not. *Reginald Otis, you silly goose; you're in love worse than when you courted Darla.*

Samantha passed the dish of chicken with rice. "Gentlemen, do try to finish it. I'd much prefer starting anew tomorrow."

Sloan shook his head *no* and raised a hand. "But I'm glad this high-powered executive job of yours didn't take the edge off your splendid cooking."

She smiled modestly. Reginald knew the modesty was

genuine, and from her it was so fetching. Were it just he and she, he would take a second helping. She excelled indeed as a cook. But Sloan had refused, and Reginald must not appear self-indulgent and greedy.

Schoolboy thinking! he reprimanded himself. Reginald held out his hand. "I'd like just a tad more, please. It's too good to pass up." With thirty-two years to grow up in, he ought to be in firmer command of himself. Honestly.

Sloan began to wilt visibly as they finished with tea. He would surely excuse himself any minute now and return to the hotel. Time ticked on.

Samantha set down her empty cup. She studied Sloan intently. She drew a deep breath. "Now I shall be an absolutely boorish hostess, undeserving of ever receiving a kind word again. Meself will freshen y'r poultice, Cole, and then I'm sending ye home to sleep. Sure'n I ken y're being polite in y'r after-dinner company, but ye need the rest."

Sloan chuckled. "The day you're boorish, Sam, the Coral Sea will freeze over. I appreciate your care. Thank you."

She nodded and stood up. Reginald and Sloan rose as one. She glided away, scooping up the poultice on her way out to the kitchen.

Reginald sat down again. "Where are you staying?"

"Esplanade."

"I'll accompany you, if you don't mind. I'm there also."

"I welcome your company." Was there an edge of irony in Sloan's reply, or was Reginald's imagination running away with him?

Samantha returned presently. She handed Sloan the stained green cheesecloth bundle. They all said their goodbyes and Samantha's door closed, she on the inside of it and the men outside. Almost before he knew it, Reginald was where he didn't want to be. He wanted to be in the stuffy little cottage absorbing Sam's good company. He didn't want to be out in these hot, dark streets. Ah, well.

The two strolled casually through dappled blackness. They emerged from under the red gums into the treeless main thoroughfare and the world brightened to silver. The first-quarter moon was just now pulling itself high enough to make its presence felt.

Reginald suddenly realized he was walking not upstreet toward the hotel but at an angle toward the river. He continued in that direction, though, for Sloan seemed similarly inclined, as if drawn to the water. Without speaking they ambled through the moonlight, out onto the Great Echuca Wharf.

The sluggish summer remnant of the Murray River wound out around its S-curve, white in the light. Huge black globs of red gums on the far shore contrasted sharply with the bright water. Would that life were as black and white as this tranquil scene! Sloan's baritone purred in the darkness. "I'm glad she's found something better than housemaid work. She's too intelligent for scullery."

Reginald nodded. "You can't begin to know how efficient she was in keeping all my affairs in order. I'd scrawl a hasty little note telling what I needed, and instantly a boat would come pulling up to the dock with as many items as she could ferret out. We can never get everything we need; some things are nonexistent, some too costly. But she worked miracles, and I don't use the term lightly."

Sloan was looking at him. *Smirking at him,* in fact. "You deal in miracles, too, don't you? Another preacher."

"Another preacher?"

"Bible bashers. Luke Vinson. The only preacher north of Innisfail, and he had to set up housekeeping in my very dooryard. Here you are, supposed to be wandering out beyond the black stump and you're right here under my nose. That backblocker Frobel telling me what's divine providence and what isn't. I can't get away from them."

Reginald smiled. "Could be God is trying to tell you something."

"God's never done me any favors."

"None you'll admit to, you mean."

Sloan glared at him. Either Sloan was about to start laughing, or Reginald was about to get thrown off the wharf into the Murray.

Reginald risked the Murray option and pressed on. "You're a highly intelligent man, Sloan, modern in your outlook. It's the fashion among modern thinkers to dismiss the Bible. That's fatal, and a little logic will tell you it's fatal. Exodus, written two thousand B.C., described the Lamb to be sacrificed for sins. John the Baptist saw Jesus and cried out, 'Behold the Lamb of God, who takes away the sins of the world.' We're the world, Sloan."

"This discussion isn't doing my headache a lot of good."

"Then in Revelation Jesus appears again as the Lamb. Isaiah said, 'All we like sheep have gone astray,' and Jesus said, 'I am the Good Shepherd.' It's a multiple reference; Ezekiel prophesied against the false shepherds of Israel—the heartless and uncaring priesthood. Bad shepherds, Good Shepherd."

He watched Sloan a moment; no overt rejection. He went on. "David, a thousand years before Christ, described crucifixion in detail, a means of execution he himself never knew about because it wasn't invented yet. Deuteronomy promised that a man hanged from a tree is accursed; and when Christ was crucified, He cried out to his Father, 'Why have you forsaken me?' "

Reginald raised his hands in illustration, and laced his fingers together. "It all fits, Sloan. Dovetails together, you might say. A book that was written across a span of two thousand years fits together perfectly, theme to theme, passage to passage, as firmly knit together as a Shelley poem. You discount it at your peril."

"What makes you think I discount it?"

"What reason would I have not to think so?"

Sloan stared at him a moment and laughed loudly,

mirthlessly. At least he wasn't tossing Reginald into the drink. The laugh faded into the darkness. "Did Sam tell you I indentured her and her sisters because I couldn't afford to pay them a decent wage? And the courts nullified the arrangement?"

"She's never mentioned you. Indentured, like the Kanakas?"

"You might say so."

Reginald nodded. "I understand they're sending the Kanakas home and bringing in Italians for the labor."

"So I heard." A pause. "Then you wouldn't know I killed a man while Sam watched. The official determination was self-defense. She thinks I did it on purpose."

"Did you?"

Silence.

A frogmouth flitted by, its wing feathers, barely audible, whispering, *wshwshwshwsh*.

Sloan stood awhile in the moonlight examining infinity. "What are you looking for, Otis? I mean, in life."

"I don't think you're going to like the answer: the soon return of Jesus Christ. Then joy and glory will replace misery." He shrugged. "Until then, I'm looking for some way to keep Barmah mission afloat."

"That's the kind of thing bronzewings and silvertails like to put their money into. Makes them look charitable. You should have plenty to work with. What would sink it?"

"Not enough bronzewings and silvertails who care. An entrenched bureaucracy half a world away. A thousand random factors working against me."

"I see. In other words, you're looking for glory at the end of it. Maybe a few pounds to sweeten the prestige. If your mission flops, no glory."

Reginald felt his ire rise; it took him a few moments to beat it down. "I suppose that's what it looks like from the outside."

"Outside of what?"

"Outside the fold. You're outside the peace and safety of the Good Shepherd's sheepfold."

Sloan scowled into the darkness. "Let's quit the talk about stray sheep, all right?"

"It's the most important conversation you can ever engage in, but I agree. For now, let's let sleeping sheepdogs lie, enjoy the night, and return to our beds. I'm very weary."

"That's about the first thing we agree on."

They turned their backs to the silver water and black trees and walked out into the street, hotel bound. Beyond the handsome face and weary body, what was this man beside Reginald? He obviously possessed a full measure of self-confidence and then some.

And suddenly Reginald realized his dilemma, a conundrum he never anticipated when he knocked at Samantha's door this evening. There is a teaching among some, an interpretation of Second Corinthians, that a Christian should not yoke up in marriage with an unbeliever, with anyone not wholly given over to the Lord. Samantha, though quite new, had espoused the faith. Sloan opposed it. Sloan therefore was, in the spiritual sense, unsuitable as a prospective mate for a woman in Christ.

But Reginald's duty as a servant of Christ was to present the gospel to this lost soul. If by some miracle (and all salvations are miracles) Sloan came into the fold, Reginald could count still another stroke against himself, quite possibly a killing stroke: Sloan would become as handsome a man spiritually as physically. He would appear even more attractive to that fair Irish woman, and Reginald, plain Reginald, would be left further back in the ranks of desirability.

The soul of Reginald Otis, pillar of the Barmah Mission, cried out to God as it had cried out more than once in years past: *Why, God?! Why me?*

Chapter Thirteen

Cutting Deals

Silence. Hot, heavy silence. Still-as-death silence. Samantha took a few steps more just to hear the sound of her feet in the dry duff. So this was Barmah Forest. Samantha Connolly was no authority on forests. But she'd walked through two of them now—the rain forest of Queensland and this one—and the only thing they shared was the word *forest*.

In the darkness of Queensland's coastal forest, birds flitted far aloft in the warm, humid air. Unseen creatures rustled. Strangler vines tied the dense canopy to the fern-covered floor. And though it was tropical, the Queensland forest did not force its warmth upon you. Shade muted the sun's heat and brilliance.

Not so this place. Nothing stirred—no living things, not even a gentle breeze. The legendary red gums did not crowd together here as did the many kinds of rain forest trees in distant Queensland. Instead, they maintained a discreet distance from each other, like polite butlers, and let the torrid summer sun beat down.

Which way lay the river? She shouldn't have wandered off. How could she find her way back? Every direction looked the same. The sun burned precisely overhead, casting no slanted shadow, permitting no hints regarding north or south. Even in this heat, the chill hand of panic seized Samantha's heart and squeezed.

Wait! She no longer belonged to herself. As Reginald explained it, she had given Jesus Christ permission to purchase her with His very lifeblood. From somewhere in her past, the line *a very present help in time of trouble*—or something like that—nudged into her consciousness. Was her Owner truly present? Might the Lamb who redeemed her soul possibly do her body a favor as well?

Once upon a time, Cole Sloan had purchased her services through indenture, a prelude to this most recent acquisition when Jesus Christ purchased her completely. Cole took care of his own. Surely Jesus would do no less. Samantha sat down on a gray stump, suddenly overcome with a remarkable sense of confidence. Peace. That was it. Peace. Never before had she tasted peace. Never had she experienced the likes of this amazing victory over fear and uncertainty. She would be cared for. And were she to die this day, she would be cared for all the same.

She closed her eyes and tried to address God simply, without the thees and thous of formal prayer. Luke Vinson talked one-to-one with God. So did Reginald. So might she.

But it was a far more difficult thing than she had imagined. How do you engage in conversation a divine person who is completely beyond your senses? Besides, God knew her situation. Nothing she told Him would be news. At a loss for words, she shifted her prayer efforts to thinking about how wonderful God was; the Creator of the universe—of this sultry forest—cared enough for a simple servant girl that He would sacrifice His very Son. Inconceivable. The heat was penetrating to the quick despite her broad straw hat. She should ask God to send someone soon, for she had no idea which way to turn.

Huuuuuuuuuuhhhnnn!

That was *Echuca Charlene*'s steam whistle! It came from her left. She had become completely twisted about in this senseless maze of open wood. She leaped up, turned to face the sound and began walking.

Huuuuuuuhhhhhnnnn!

Certain now of her course, she increased her pace through the dry, crackling duff.

"Sam! Over here!" Cole's white shirt shone in the distance, a beacon in the gray-green-brown vastness. She hastened to him, not caring that dry, scratchy bits of leaves were working down into her shoes.

Cole was smiling, and that old elan was back. It was the first time she'd seen the spark since he returned from Adelaide. He shook hands vigorously with an unkempt, grizzled, weather-worn gentleman. The men exchanged parting pleasantries. Cole took her arm and led her off in what seemed a random direction.

"Next time stay by the boat," he said.

"Thank ye for coming," she replied.

As they passed a group of trees, he slapped a tree trunk. "Do you realize how many board feet are in one of these? And what price it would bring in Sydney? I've just cut a bonzer deal with that bloke with the beard. He looks a little rough, and acts a little snaky, but he's the chief timber harvester in this section."

"May I take it, then, that your business trip is a success?"

"You may." He squeezed her arm. "And you helped make it so. Loaning me money until I could send for a bank draft from Sydney was part, of course. But bringing me down to meet riverboat skippers was the biggest help. I had no idea what rocks to look under. I'd never have found the men I needed to deal with."

She laughed. "Apparently nearly all of them simply run their boats up on the bank during this low water and wait for the river to rise again. Temporary abandonment. Sure'n I've just begun to learn their off-season haunts meself. Quite a motley assortment, aye? I've new appreciation for the word 'roughhewn.' "

"Good businessmen, though, it seems. Sensible. Certainly know their trade." He took a deep breath that almost came back out as a sigh. "I've suffered several setbacks recently, not to mention some highly peculiar incidents. I have to succeed quickly in order to stay afloat, but I'm the newcomer in this business. Amenities the established brokers take for granted, I must earn. I need an edge, and I think that edge will be transportation. The doors you're opening for me are vital to me. And I thank you."

That wonderful boat whistle hooted again just ahead. They were walking in the right direction. Cole chuckled. "Gus is anxious to get going."

Samantha buried herself in thought. Was it divine providence that the boat whistle led her out of the forest? Or was it happenstance, a result of Captain Runyan's impatience? Perhaps both? Neither? Her new-found awareness of God was no black-and-white thing!

Echuca Charlene vibrated impatiently at her temporary wharf as wood smoke boiled out of the smokestacks. Her side-wheel paddles began churning even before Cole stepped aboard. Like all the other little paddle steamers on this river, *Echuca Charlene* was essentially a self-propelled raft, for she possessed no deck furniture beyond the bare necessities. Between her two side-wheels, an on-deck shed provided storage for firewood. On the shed's roof perched the wheelhouse. A few feet below her inches-high gunwales, the muddy Murray coursed past at a whisper. No rails, no protection. Samantha missed a forward rail upon which to lean.

So low and narrow was the river that several times on the brief voyage from the forest wharf to the Barmah Mission dock, one wheelhousing or the other would brush the shore. When the paddle blades hit bottom, the little boat jumped up and down violently enough to throw Samantha to her knees. Low water turned this most innocent of trips into a nerve-wracking adventure.

Cole and Samantha were simply standing near the bow, waiting for the Barmah Mission wharf to appear around some bend, when Captain Runyan came down out of his wheelhouse.

Ragged as a sheepdog with summer mange, he stood beside them and rolled himself a cigarette. "Now I wish to employ the charitable services of the both of you in the next ten minutes. We dock at Barmah Mission inside the quarter hour, barring any catastrophe. You, fair Irish lass, are well known to Toby already. Your task, and a task you fulfill admirably under any circumstance, I might add, will be to stand about looking beautiful. You will represent the corporate interests of Echuca, the largest town known to these locals, should the need arise, though I doubt it will. I would also be well pleased if you would clap and cheer or otherwise express approval when the moment requires."

The rough-cut captain dug about in his pockets, seeking a match. "You, Sloan, possess the three requisites for our business here: impressive physical stature, an apparent flair for the dramatic, and a visage, however battered it may be, unknown to the principals of our unfolding melodrama."

Cole's eyebrow rose, a gesture of bemusement Samantha rarely saw in him. "One of us here isn't speaking English."

"Ah. Permit me to elaborate. Miss Connolly, fair rose of Erin, you well know Toby, the overzealous factotum of our devoted Mr. Otis. Toby, I am pleased to report, has been pierced by cupid's arrows. Absolutely smitten." He found a match.

"Eh, Captain Runyan, I be very happy for him."

"As would I under the dictates of normal circumstance. However, it seems he recently learned that the heathen totems of his clan and the bride elect's are not compatible. Details of the embroglio escape me, but the end of it is, their romance is all at crossed tracks, lying in tatters beneath the evil feet of pagan practice."

Cole frowned. "In other words, they can't get married."

"So it would seem." The captain turned his back to the bow to light up. "In recent correspondence with Ellen Fenton, in whose capable hands Barmah Mission rests during Otis's absence, I was apprised of the situation and requested to possibly offer some recourse. The scheme I have promulgated should ease the situation to the point of smoothing the course of true love right up to the altar. Sloan, I shall rehearse you as to your part in this sweet and gentle deceit. You shall play the role of seneschal, dispensing justice for none other than King Edward himself, before whom petition was made on Toby and Polly's behalf." His rather lumpy cigarette dangling dangerously near his beard, he jogged over to blow his steam whistle.

When *Echuca Charlene* docked at the mission wharf ten minutes later, Samantha was greeted by a Toby she did not know. Here slouched a despondent man, beaten, defeated by the unseen forces of his ancestry. The verve had disappeared.

Nearly a dozen blacks, all but three of them aged, sat about on the riverbank. Some had brought large baskets. Samantha recognized most of the faces and could recall at most two names. Ellen Fenton came running down the path to shore as Toby threw *Echuca Charlene*'s hawses over the pier posts. She stopped cold to look at Samantha, at Cole, and back at Samantha.

Captain Runyan pointed a burly finger at Toby. "You. Come aboard. Where's Polly? You, too, lass."

Samantha could easily tell which girl was Polly; it was the pretty young lady with the sudden fear on her face. Cautiously, even reluctantly, she climbed to her feet, threaded her way among her companions on the riverbank, and ventured aboard.

Cole stepped forward, magnificent in his power, and unrolled the large foolscap scroll Captain Runyan had provided. He read from it in stentorian tones. "A proclamation. Whereas, Toby loves Polly and Polly loves Toby; and whereas, this situation has come to the attention of his Royal Highness; Edward King of England, protector of the faith, hereby decrees that Toby and Polly should be instantly married. His Highness further declares that laws about totems and such are all null and void."

Cole glared at the skipper. "Are you, Captain August Runyan, empowered by the state of New South Wales to perform weddings?"

"I am," boasted the captain in tones equally stentorian. He whipped out a book of common prayer, his finger already holding the appropriate place. As the steersman pumped out "God Save the King" on a battered concertina, the wedding rite commenced on the spot.

His part completed, Cole moved back to Samantha's side and smugly, casually folded his arms.

She murmured above the din of concertina and celebrant. "Sure 'n ye look dazzlingly pleased with y'rself for a man who just lied about the king. 'Tis treason, ye know. And be this wedding nae but a mockery before God himself?"

He shook his vainglorious head. "It's legal."

Ellen had come aboard. She stood by the gangplank looking totally delighted. Her eyes flicked to Samantha, and her brown face hardened instantly. What was this?

The ceremony completed, Samantha joined in the clapping and cheering. Cole, the king's emissary, limited himself to sedate applause. The wedding party came scrambling aboard with their baskets, and amid laughter and gay banter, they commenced unloading.

Ellen had arranged her face to a softer, more pleasant expression. As Samantha greeted her and introduced Cole, she watched for some hint, for the slightest indication, of what might be bothering the slim girl. Nothing.

Ellen smiled at Cole. "Thank you very much for your

part. They do so care about each other. It was a lovely device, and it's working perfectly."

"Unless someone notices that the royal proclamation is written out in pencil. I'm pleased to meet you, Miss Fenton."

Samantha nodded toward the parade of porters hauling large sacks and boxes from the stern. "Seems an interesting reversal, aye? Previously Reginald worked here while I arranged supplies in town. Now he's in town sending supplies out to y'rself, and ye be filling his shoes here."

"He sent word this would be coming, the flour and shortening especially, but he didn't mention that you would be along."

Samantha smiled in a vain effort to melt the iceberg that stood between Ellen and her. "Mr. Sloan here wanted to meet certain rivermen, as well as some primary suppliers. Since *Echuca Charlene* was bound this way, we came along. We've nae association with the mission shipment."

Ellen studied her oddly, as if weighing her words against some secret knowledge. Quietly she turned and led the way ashore.

Cole stepped aside to make way for the line of porters with their burdens. "I should think you'd have bullock carts or wagons for this sort of thing."

Ellen shook her head. "The bullocks are working the back section putting in fence. We've a team of horses, but one is lame."

"Which one?" Samantha frowned. She still vividly remembered the first time she saw Reginald's horses on that infamous southbound track. So long ago, it seemed.

"The roan."

Cole echoed Samantha's thoughts: "I'd like to see him, if I may."

"Certainly, as you wish."

Like Reginald, Cole seemed inured to this heat. When

they arrived at the mission station, he still had not removed his jacket. Ellen led them straightway to the stables. When first she visited here, Samantha had seen buildings without roofs. Now the roan stood listlessly beneath a roof without walls; four poles supported a few sheets of that ubiquitous tin roofing.

One ragged ear flicked toward them, but the roan hardly raised its head. It stood with one hind leg cocked, its backside tilted and sagging. The near front foot was the injured one, however—just above the hoof. The exact nature of the injury Samantha could not tell, for a solid black mass of flies covered it.

Without hesitation Cole slipped between the loose strands of barbed wire fencing. He spoke to the horse, stroked its neck, patted its shoulder, and casually picked up the foot. The fly swarm lifted away quickly. A jagged rip zigzagged across the pastern, oozing black oiliness down the hoof. Yellow pus and swollen flesh had wedged the wound open. An odor somewhat akin to dirty, sweaty feet pervaded the hot and torpid little shelter. What a hideous, seeping mess!

Cole poked about with his thumbs a few moments, brushing at the persistent flies as the roan jerked and tossed its head. He let the foot down and stood erect.

Ellen licked her lips. "He cut himself on roofing tin. No one here knows quite what to do. Neither does Reginald."

Cole stood erect. "May I?"

"Please."

With Samantha's help, Cole cleaned the injury thoroughly until the raw flesh oozed clear pink and red. He called for disinfectant. Carbolic? No. Alcohol? No. Peroxide? No. Whiskey? Silence. Sly-grog perhaps? Toby's friends, as affectionate toward horses as they were toward Toby, provided a bottle of wedding libation to be used medicinally on the roan's foot.

Cole demonstrated how to bind the roan's foot as protection from the dirt and flies. He talked Ellen through what would be the daily regimen of unwrapping, clearing out the wound, disinfecting, and rewrapping. Finally, on behalf of King Edward, he wished Toby all the best and sent the joy-filled groom on his way.

During that hour, Samantha felt a prickling wall growing between her and Ellen. Ellen had once treated her so warmly. Why the change? *Sometimes the best way to approach something is directly,* she thought. *Face to face.*

The porters were returning with another load. As lightly as they were laden, that was probably the last of it. Time to go. Captain Runyan no doubt would be snorting impatiently soon. Samantha must seize the bull by the horns now or never.

"Miss Fenton, might I speak with ye privately a moment?"

Ellen eyed her guardedly, as a postal carrier might watch a belligerent dog. "As you wish, Miss Connolly."

Samantha fell in beside the girl and started for the track to the river. "Meself desires to know if I've given offense or in some way hurt y'r feelings."

Ellen drew in a deep breath of hot, dry air. "I'm sorry, Miss Connolly. This is not a Christian attitude, and it's not Christian behavior. No. It's nothing you've done."

"Eh, then what is it, might I ask?"

"I'd rather not discuss it."

"As ye wish. I've learned, though, that such things fester—nae less than that poor roan's foot—when left in the dark to themselves."

Ellen nodded. Her lovely black eyes looked on the verge of tears. "You're aware of Reginald's feelings toward you, I trust."

"Aye. He's voiced them."

"They're the same feelings I have for him. You see—" Her voice nearly broke. "You see, at Ebenezer we celebrated Christmas. It was the one time of year that was truly festive and bright. Gifts, lights. Roast fowl, even if it was bustard."

"Eh, so in Erin, too."

"He won't be here. He'll be in Echuca, with you. I—I'm sorry. I look at you and see you with everything I yearn for. And that includes being white—being the same race he is, so I'd be more desirable. This jealousy is wrong. I know it's wrong and I can't rid myself of it. I pray, I fast . . . nothing. I'm so sorry. But I can't look at you without this jealousy and hatred leaping into my heart."

"Do ye ken how much he cares for ye?"

"You mean 'Dear, practical Ellen! I couldn't handle this place without you'? Wonderful. I'm first in his head. You're first in his heart."

They were slipping in among the scattered trees now, from splotchy bits of shade, to sun, to shade.

"I dinnae know what to say to ease y'r mind. Perhaps there be nae answer."

"I don't know either."

They walked in heavy silence through the stifling woods. Samantha suddenly felt the old homesickness she thought had been vanquished months ago. Christmas means family and friends, warm toasts, a Yule log, roast goose, holly and church bells, and cold, absolutely miserable weather that you love to complain about. Christmas is dark winter solstice with its unspoken promise of renewal three months hence. None of the things in this hot, brilliant alien summer—not a single thing—was Christmas. Samantha was being robbed of the one holiday that truly sings to the heart.

Echuca Charlene hooted somewhere ahead.

Samantha stopped and turned to the unhappy girl beside her. "God bless ye, Ellen Fenton. Goodbye."

Ellen could not meet her eyes. "God bless you," she mumbled. She hastened back up the track toward the mission.

Cole hurried aboard less than a minute after Samantha

arrived at the boat. Captain Runyan's steersman came aboard lugging what was no doubt the last of a load of firewood. With a hoot and a shudder, *Echuca Charlene* eased out into the narrow channel and commenced her run home.

Samantha yearned more than ever for a rail to lean against, for leaning on a boat's rail invites clear thinking. For lack of a rail she simply stood about idly on the foredeck and watched the flaccid water disappear under *Echuca Charlene*'s prow. So many wayward thoughts clamored for attention. Jealousy. True love. Cole Sloan. Head versus heart. Christmas. The poor roan. Cole Sloan. Reginald. Answers to prayer and the complexities of divine providence. Ellen's anguish. The handsome man with the beat-up face who had just spread his coat across a rank of firewood and was stretching out upon it. He yawned mightily, settled himself to repose, and closed his eyes.

The boat's paddle-wheel housing brushed the shore on an outside curve; the whole craft lurched and shook. Samantha heard ungentlemanly comments from the wheelhouse. In florid prose, Captain Runyan upbraided himself for venturing out upon such low water. He cursed the filthy lucre this trip was earning him. His steersman yelled something.

With a rasping roar, the boat jerked to an instantaneous halt. Samantha cried out as she flew forward. She grabbed at a mooring post and missed. For an endless moment she stared at the tired, dirty water; then it sucked her under.

She surfaced coughing. Inches from her face a paddle wheel flogged the river helplessly. In her own flailing, she kicked bottom. Cole must have heard her cry, for he started toward her. No rescue heroics were needed, though. She gained her feet and stood erect in the mud; the water was less than a yard deep.

Echuca Charlene's engine strained and screamed.

Sooty steam billowed from the stack. The paddles surged; they backed. She sat immovable, high-centered on some sort of bar or snag beneath the surface.

Cole Sloan stood all clean and dry on the deck, arms akimbo, and laughed. He laughed!

Captain Runyan, swearing like—well, like a riverman— came boiling down onto the deck. He glared at Cole, who was quite obviously the source of all his troubles. "We're a mile from the Goulburn mouth, and that's seven miles east of town. You can walk to town if you want to get there by Christmas, or you can sit on this bleeping boat until the water comes. Have your choice. I'm shutting the engine down and going home." He stared at Samantha. "Next time sit down when the boat's moving." He turned on his heel and disappeared into the wheelhouse.

Samantha used both hands to push her waterlogged hair out of her face. Here she was, absolutely drenched again with the filthiest water on the continent.

Still sporting a fiendish grin, Cole offered her a hand. "Is this your holiday bath, Sam?"

She was going to cry. She could feel it coming. She would not be able to stop the tears shed for home, for lost simplicity, for life's cruel twists. And there the nong stood, grinning.

She accepted his hand, planted a foot firmly on the gunwale and yanked. In wide-eyed shock he flew past her. She heard the splash behind as she pulled herself onto the deck. New South Wales was the closest shore. She'd walk home on the north side and cross the bridge into Echuca. Eight miles. Three hours, at least, for she would not make good time weeping as she went.

She shot one final glance at the bedraggled Mr. Sloan before beginning her trek. "Merry Christmas, mate."

Chapter Fourteen

Air on a Shoestring

In like a lion, out like a lamb. Beware the ides of March. Mad as a March hare. Creators of bromides did not live in this topsy-turvy world. *MARCH—TIME TO SEE TO YOUR AUTUMN WARDROBE* proclaimed the advertising sign in the window. Linnet stood before a charming little draper's shop in Divett Street across from the National Bank. Although full of warehouses and chandleries and such, Port Adelaide had few shops, for bustling Adelaide proper lay not much more than half an hour to the south by railway. Ah, but the shops it did have! Just look at that lovely fashion in black crepe silk!

Chris came across the street, dodging carts and wagons. He charged up and halted beside her, giving the shop-window the barest of glances. "Don't go spending money before you've made it, Linn girl. Our trunk's aboard, and it's nearing time to sail."

" 'Tis a fine deal ye wrought, Chris, exchanging dinner music for our fare and meals, but what'll we do when we reach Melbourne? We've nae money to live on and ye said y'rself, the concert in Melbourne will likely not pay well, for I still be unknown. It frightens me, traveling with nae money."

He smiled gently, warmly. "You still don't trust the gifts God gave you. This tour to Sydney is laying the groundwork." He draped his arm across her shoulders and directed her down the street. "We'll be getting people to hear your name. Familiarity. After Sydney, and your appearance with Giambone, you'll return in victory! You'll be celebrated, Linn."

She snorted. "So be Guy Fawkes. That dinnae make it lovely."

They walked out into Commercial Road and down to Queen's Wharf. *Rustbucket*, Chris called their little steamer, and if you looked at it with a cold, uncaring eye, it probably was. As the son of a well-traveled diplomat, Chris no doubt knew lovely ships from ugly ones. But Linnet had sailed from Cork on a steamer not much bigger than this, and far dirtier. She preferred to see the good of it, its sleek lines and jaunty tilted prow. As they stepped aboard, a steward called, "All ashore who's going ashore." Five minutes later the little steamer cast off and slipped out into the channel.

She leaned hard against the forerail to watch green water boil around the little steamer's cutwater. She banished to the nether corners of her mind the worrisome fact they were traveling without funds. Her adventure had begun.

Samantha unlocked the office door and threw it open to the breezes of dawn, not to mention the flow of commerce. These March winds were a delightful change from the heat of summer. She welcomed them. Commerce didn't flow much yet, but any week now the Murray's waters would begin to rise. She looked forward with anticipation to her first busy season as assistant to the wharfmaster and welcomed that flow as well.

She had barely completed the morning's correspondence when her son came bounding through the open door.

"G'day, luv!" She rubbed his head. "Off to school, eh?"

He grinned wide enough to admit his pencil sideways.

"This fall we commence long division and advanced story problems." He sobered. "Do you know, mum, by winter, I shall know more arithmetic than my father. That doesn't seem right."

"Sure'n 'tis perfectly right! Y'r father wants a better life for ye than he has; all parents dream that. He'll be immensely proud of ye."

He shrugged. "That's what he says. Still . . ."

"Knowing how to cipher and possessing wisdom be two very different things, lad. Ye'll never surpass y'r father for wisdom."

The grin returned. "I'll be in at noon with the postings."

"Good lad! Off ye go now."

He was scarcely out the door before his piercing soprano bade Mr. Drummond good day. The man's bulk filled the doorway.

Jovial in the morning brightness, he crossed to her desk. "G'day, Samantha."

"Top of the morning, sir. Your schedule." She handed him her prepared list of his day's activities.

He scanned it, squinting. The man really ought to consider reading glasses. "Who is this Dr. Stoney I'm to meet at ten?"

"He runs the consumptive house out on the Campaspe. Let's see; 'Echuca Private Sanitorium for Open-air Treatment of Consumption.' According to the note he sent round last week, he's seeking a special excursion rate for passengers residing in his sanitorium. As an inducement, I presume."

"How much is he charging for that palace?"

"Four guineas a week, sir."

"If they can pay that, they can afford a boat ride. Anything else I should know?"

"He claims the consumptive house barely pays its way, being that several others, newly opened, are cutting into his business. The barber in Hare Street tells me that Dr.

Stoney's been boasting of the grand new house he just bought in Melbourne."

Mr. Drummond smiled. "Thank you very much, Samantha. I believe I'll use the time until ten getting my hair trimmed. See what else I can learn prior to our appointment."

"Time well spent, I trow. G'day, sir."

The poor man ought to walk more, too, for he was growing ever heavier. Samantha noted as he passed through the open door that he had no lateral clearance to speak of.

By the time the train whistle hooted in the distance, she had completed the few papers needing Mr. Drummond's signature. She had arranged on his desk the papers and proceedings he ought to read. Her duties for the day lay behind her. She adjusted her broad-brimmed hat on the way out the door to meet the train.

Because Echuca's trade had dwindled so drastically, even in good times, the wharfmaster was also the stationmaster. It would behoove Samantha, when things got busy, to know all the engineers and conductors on the Melbourne-Echuca run personally. Therefore she met most of the arriving trains.

They were running Engine 137. That meant Mr. Dumont was probably at the throttle. There he was, waving; she smiled and waved in return.

Half a dozen passengers were detraining, in no apparent hurry. The stevedores began loading and unloading the few cars behind. Short train today.

As she paused to pass the time of day with Mr. Dumont, they were joined by Mr. Casper, the conductor. There is a close camaraderie among railroad men, and Samantha enjoyed listening to the banter. Rivermen—officers and common laborers alike—shared a similar comradeship. Railroad men, though, possessed a certain formality and finesse the rivermen lacked entirely. Samantha never felt this same ease when she moved among the river runners.

"G'day, Sam."

She wheeled.

His face looked normal again; the cut above his eye had left only the slightest trace of a scar. To the indiscriminate eye, Cole Sloan looked healthy and fit. But in that first brief moment, Samantha saw desperation and despair hiding behind his somber eyes.

Was she imagining things? No. "G'day, Cole. I'm surprised and most pleased to see ye."

"I'm nearly as surprised as you that I'm here. But I'm in a bit of a bind, and I need your help."

"Of course!" She took leave of the railroad men and led the way back to the office. They stepped from bright morning sun into stuffy gloom, both literally and figuratively.

Cole flopped into the straight-backed chair as Samantha sat down at her desk. "Sam . . ." He sighed and his voice dropped. "Sam, I was operating on a shoestring when I left Sugarlea. The string just broke. I have to get something moving. Now. I mean, right now. My get-started fund is gone, and Beckerstaff tied up the last of the Sugarlea payments in court actions. It's been one thing after another. Weird things. I have nothing to make money with, and it's getting worse. I don't even have an office anymore."

She studied his face and saw utter defeat. He was giving up. She could see it.

"Why come to meself, Cole? I be but a humble assistant, an office drone. I have nae power."

"You have all the power here, Sam. Drummond's a figurehead. You do his thinking for him, his planning for him, and you cut his deals and hand them to him. I looked into the wharf a bit during the holiday. Talked to people about things besides business, the rivermen in particular. They know you're bunging on this turn, you're the power in this office."

"Eh, sure 'n ye be overst—"

"There's not a boatman on the river who wouldn't do

anything you asked of him," he interrupted. "And there's not a riverman who will pass the time of day with Drummond. They see him as a spineless political appointee and not worth spit. You can help me, Sam. No one else can."

She sat back and stared at her desk top a few minutes. "Ye made certain contacts with foresters and others while ye were here over the holiday. What might be available to transport right now?"

"Not wool. Not timber until the water rises. A little wine that would come through Mannum."

Just then Ah Loo came whisking in the door. He stopped cold and changed instantly from a vivacious little boy into a sedate young man. He bowed slightly to Samantha.

"Ah Loo." *Ah Loo! Perhaps . . .* "Have ye the latest?"

"Yes, mum!" He plopped a student's tablet on her desk. "I checked the post office and all the agents."

"Good." She ran her eyes down the page of neat handwriting. Ah Loo was, if nothing else, precise. She smiled. "Bring me the river map." She raised her eyes to Cole. "The sales agents, wholesalers, and the post office all post news of upstream water levels on their doors, by means of which local rivermen may judge the water level here in advance. One of me son's chores is to bring me the postings that I might know when traffic will begin to move."

"You see something?" Cole frowned slightly, but it could not be called a spark of interest.

"Aye! Ah Loo, ye seek expertise in arithmetic. Meself has been told it takes a week for rising water to travel thus far," she said, pointing to the map. "If that be so, how long will it take for a rise in the Darling here below Bourke—as the post office posting promises—to reach our river?"

Ah Loo shook his head. "No good, mum. The Darling enters the river west of Mildura. Way downstream of us. Won't do us no good at all."

"Mr. Sloan here wants to bring up cargo from Mannum."

The snapping black eyes held hers for a long moment. His mobile little face shaped itself into bright sunshine. He snatched up the tablet and pointed. "Look! Here's rain with water rising above Albury! By the time the river rises from above us, the Darling water should have reached beyond Mannum. That is, if it keeps raining."

"Calculate it out more precisely, lad. We must know the earliest a boat could have Mr. Sloan's wine on the way, but not a moment before it."

The lad bent low over the map and table. He set hard at work, the tip of his tongue peeking out the corner of his mouth as he penciled figures, most of them hash marks, and carefully measured map points with his thumbnails.

Samantha glanced at Cole. He was watching the boy with nothing short of wonder on his face. He looked at her and the hope was back; his face had softened.

She smiled. "Telegraph y'r vintner, aye? Meself shall telegraph the skipper of the *Mayflower*. Methinks she was in Swan Hill when the water ran out from under her. She can ride the crest down to Mannum, pick up y'r goods and bring them here, if the current be nae too strong for her. She's small but plucky."

Ah Loo snapped erect, triumphant as a knight victorious. "The water will reach Mannum a day before ours reaches us." He held his figures before her. "Six and a half days. Does that look right?"

"If y'r ciphers be correct, meself shall write a letter to y'r teacher describing y'r exploits and demanding ye receive a perfect score in math."

He grinned. The grin fled. "And if I'm wrong?"

"Why sure'n I'll throw ye back in the river. 'Twas where I found ye, aye? Now I've an errand for ye; then ye must hie y'rself back to class. Run down to the Bridge Hotel and ask the desk to send over any skipper they come across. Especially Captains Runyan or Sykes."

Ah Loo bowed slightly to Cole and like a flash was gone.

Samantha stood up. "And now, Mr. Sloan, we shall apply the balm that we seem always to apply: tea at the garden."

He smiled wanly. "I can't even afford that."

"Is that nae what friends be for?" She knew she had at least four shillings in her little change purse. She dug it out and dumped it uncounted into his hand. She stepped back and extended her elbow and waited. *Escort me.*

He stood. He smiled. He kissed her hand and offered her his arm. Ever the gentleman, he saw her to the door. But his shoulders, sagging with all that weight, remained bowed.

Reginald remembered reading about the conversation somewhere but he could not recall which evangelist had been quoted. The incident itself, though, was so emblazoned in his memory he could recite it word for word. A young preacher approached the noted evangelist and said, "Sir, I preach the same message you do verbatim. I even use the same gestures. Yet hundreds come to your call and I get few or none."

The evangelist studied the young man intently. "Well, you certainly don't expect to win souls *every* single time you preach, do you?"

"Oh. Well, uh, I guess not."

"And that, young man, is exactly why you fail."

Reginald possessed that hunger for evangelizing. He *expected* to reach souls with every message. Why had he no success? Ellen, faithful Ellen, remained. She tried to keep the garden and the books and the school. Half a dozen elderly blacks, men and women too infirm to travel, still hung about Barmah. Three half-caste fellows kept showing up for meals; Reginald knew they'd be gone as soon as the waters rose and the boats, their seasonal livelihood, ran again. Everyone else had disappeared. Even Toby and

Polly were gone. "No doubt honeymooning," Ellen had said. No doubt.

Apparently the home office was ignoring him. That wasn't bad. Whenever they sent some word from their position of ignorance half a world away, it created crisis. But then, neither were funds forthcoming.

Funds. This was God's work. Why did He not provide funds? *Or was this God's work?* Reginald had been assuming to this point that he operated in God's will, following prayerful consideration. Was this Barmah Mission project actually as that Sloan fellow painted it—a reach for glory? An attempt to big-note Reginald Otis on a grand scale?

Assailed by both doubt and an acute lack of operating capital, Reginald Otis tipped his head out the open window of his railway car to see the first of the river red gums in the distance. Ahead lay Echuca and the one bright spot in his life. *Dear God, you know what a matchless team Samantha and I would make for your service. She's sensible, efficient and wise. We worked together so well at the first. I perceive we were literally made for each other. God, guide me in approaching her effectively, at just the right moment, regarding marriage.*

Marty Frobel watched the flatness zip past his window. The mallee down here looked a lot like the brigelow on his own place in Queensland—a lot, but not exactly. He'd be in Echuca in another two hours. Victoria and New South Wales could take some lessons from Queensland when it came to laying railways. He had crossed the Murray at Albury. It was ridiculous that he had to ride south practically to Melbourne before heading north again to the river.

Was Sloan there? He couldn't be found in Sydney. By the time Marty made contact with Margaret's sister, either by telegraph or by mail, he could be in Echuca. But then,

Marty had always wanted to see this part of the country. The richness of its grazing land was legendary, especially up in central Queensland, the land of fat-or-famine. Right now his cattle wandered belly deep in Mitchell grass; this country, just coming off the summer dry, didn't look half so good.

"Bulldog," Marty's pop called Sloan. "Don't trust him any further than you can throw a bullock. But he's tough."

All right. Pop knew. Marty wouldn't trust Sloan. But he did need the bloke. Meatworks in his Mitchell District perched on the brink of collapse, even the boomer companies that had been around for twenty years, in Lakes Creek and Gladstone. Markets. They had to have new markets. The old, established brokers wagged their heads sadly at Queensland's plight and politely suggested that those banana benders up there would be wise to move south with their sheep and cattle.

Sloan, though, was new blood. He possessed no ties to the old school, the inner ring of mates and old men in the brokerages. More so than the Sydney silvertails, he knew Queensland; he'd lived there for years. He just might find new markets, new ways to market. Frozen beef transported by freezer ships wasn't economical. Maybe Sloan could find some new angle on that.

He had to. Things could not continue this way for long.

Linnet stepped forward and bowed politely in response to the polite applause. Thirteen persons does not make an enthusiastic audience. The modest hall echoed, essentially empty.

She waited beyond the wings. No one came back to congratulate her. No flowers. No well-wishes. She felt near tears.

She heard the piano lid slam shut in the pit. Was Chris

angry with her? He shouldn't be. She'd done her best despite the poor attendance.

He came back, then, from the silence of the auditorium. The scowl on his fine features made her wince.

He tossed her carpetbag at her feet. "We're canceled."

"Canceled? All of them?"

"The impresario feels you're not ready for the concert circuit. The drongo claims you can't draw a crowd. I know better, but I couldn't convince him. No engagements, no pay."

"We could play our way back to Adelaide on the steamer, dual pianos in the dining room." Linnet brightened. "Mr. Giambone's company will pay our way to Sydney when the time comes. They said so. We've nae lost that."

"But no tour." He sighed heavily and flopped into a prop chair in the corner. "Linn . . ." He licked his lips. "Linn, it's not just the thrill of the chase anymore. At first, I wanted the satisfaction of finding an unknown and turning her into a world-class artist. But that was just at the first." His marvelous, warm, classic eyes held hers. "It's more than that now. I never before cared for a woman the way I care for you."

She watched his face, looking for some sign of mockery. She could hardly be called a woman. What was he *really* saying?

"I never intended to say anything about it. I don't know why I'm talking about it now. I believe in you, Linn, and I love you. The only reason I haven't touched you is that Guli Hack is right: the one thing that will destroy your career is to get mucked up with a man. Babies and footlights don't go together. That's why you got the job in Sydney to start with; their soprano tried to have it both ways. I could never forgive myself if I were responsible for destroying your budding career with my own selfishness."

Her mouth gaped open, and she had no strength to close it. She shook her head. "Chris, ye ken nae what y're saying."

"I ken every word, gentle Linnet. I ken every word."

Chapter Fifteen

Counterpoint on a Heart's Theme

For various reasons, none of them savory, the Esplanade Hotel had been delicensed years before. No grog was to be served on the premises, decreed the government, save certain harmless semi-alcoholic accompaniments to dining-room meals. The bar by the registration window had long since been converted to a simple but elegant reading salon. The government's will be done.

Economists and other prominent blokes said that Australia rode on the sheep's back. No such thing. Australia floated on beer. Booze, with its mysterious attraction, thereby gave a fresh twist to an even older adage. "Man proposes but God disposes" became "The government proposes, but customers dispose."

Cole Sloan, along with half a dozen other patrons disposed toward having a cool drop on a warm afternoon, draped himself at the bar in the Esplanade's hidden cellar. Underground by several definitions, the covert pub provided a tidy income for what in the public eye was a struggling hotel in a depressed area and well past its prime. Sloan should have a slice of something this lucrative.

But for a feeble and jittery little light over the bar, the place dripped gloom. The rough-cut earthen walls were damp and clammy and discolored by seepage from the last rain. Everything about the premises smelled moldy. Eighteen inches above Cole's head a pall of tobacco smoke hung itself upon nothing. A legion of black flies waded about in a spill near his elbow.

Behind the bar to Cole's right a small, tight passageway dissolved in blackness. That passage emerged into light and air not far from the tea garden, provided you didn't splack into a shoring timber. The passage these days stood forsaken and festooned with cobwebs, for the local constable had just about given up raiding the joint.

Beside Cole, Captain August Runyan wagged his shaggy, unkempt head. "A beaut, that one. Far and going away, the biggest, most impressive flood I can recall in the last thirty-five years, and I've a trove of recollections, for I've resided in these environs since infancy. It crested in all its fury just about a year ago this time."

"Floods the usual thing right along the river here?"

"They're the exception. You can expect high water—by which I mean a river level raised enough to flood into the forests here about—once in, say, four or five years."

"You're telling me, then, no flood this year."

"You can wager your life savings on it. It just doesn't happen twice in a row, as if the Almighty uses all His rain up in one glorious deluge and then stores up for the next one."

"Floods make good trade for you rivermen, I'll bet."

The crusty old man drained the last of his glass. "Last year was one of the most profitable in decades. Not only did we move goods during the flood to and from places we can never reach in a normal year, we also had a record wool clip. Barges laden so bounteously they could scarcely fit under the bridges. More wool than would fit on the river.

"That, you see"—he wagged a finger at Sloan—"is why I bunged on such an act when my sweet *Charlene* ran aground. I didn't need the money. I had no business taking her upriver on that low water. Your fair Irish lass, with her eyes as deep as the ocean, bewitched me. You, you bloody dill, could go jump in the river. I would never've done it for you. But when she asked, I was all yesses. 'Yes, I'll take your supplies out to the mission.' 'Yes, I'll give your mates a ride, wherever you wish.' Blast! My weakness still makes me crook."

"I assume your *Echuca Charlene* is still perched on that mud bar."

"You assume correctly. And there she shall remain, stripped of the dignity and glory of her kind, until the water comes. I see, though, that we can expect water any moment; your delicate flower of Erin has taken to posting the latest word right outside the wharfmaster's office. Saves us who toil upon the river from having to wander all about town finding a bit of news here, another bit there."

He kept referring to Sam as Sloan's. If only it were so! Sloan needed the subject changed. "Think I'll have enough water to move a ton or so up from Mannum?"

"Maybe. Don't count on it. This will be a down year." He was staring morosely at his empty glass, so Sloan signalled the barman for a refill. "Hear this, city lad," the riverman continued; "you can never count on the river for anything, except trouble. She'll have you thanking your lucky stars for a good and profitable run; and the next bend round, she'll hang you up on a snag. She'll change her course in the middle of the night and fill in the old channel without the courtesy of telling you. She'll give you a smooth run or she'll yank the water right out from under you; makes no difference to her either way. A mind of her own has the mighty Murray, and a lady she's not."

With bells and mournful hooting, the train lurched to a halt. The car jerked and nearly threw Reginald back into his seat as he pulled his carpetbag off the overhead rack.

He followed a handsome, sun-tanned young fellow down the aisle. They stepped together out into the bright sun. The young man turned back toward the baggage car and Reginald went the other way, toward the wharfmaster's office.

There she was. She stood by the engine as the engineer hung out his window. The conductor handed her a paper of some sort. She signed it and handed it back, smiling. They were all three nodding and laughing. No surprise there; wherever Samantha stood the whole world beamed.

She spied him as he approached. The smile on her lovely face absolutely melted him. How could he be so smitten this late in life?

She extended her hand. "Welcome back, sir."

He seized the opportunity to kiss that lovely hand. "May I whisk you away to lunch, or are you engaged in business?"

"Sure'n I'll nae turn down a lunch!" She took her leave of the railroad men and walked beside him out across the wharf toward what he knew to be her favorite place, the tea garden. "Ah Loo and I've been paying daily visits to y'r roan down at the livery. We take him a carrot or whatever Ah Loo's uncle provides. He's in fine fettle, and ready to be ridden home. However, check before ye leave; Captain Runyan thinks to float his *Charlene* free tonight or tomorrow. Ye might not have to make the journey on horseback."

"I'll stop by your office for the latest on my way out."

"And how went y'r trip to Melbourne?"

"Since you ask, disastrously. No church board in Victoria has funds to spare for Barmah Mission. I tried the cathedral in Bendigo in the bargain."

Silence. He glanced at her. Her brow had puckered in that way of hers. She was thinking about something. "Might a secular source underwrite ye, for the good will of it? The *Herald*, mayhap, or the local commissioners? Barmah Mission be a feather in any community's cap, aye?"

"Do you think?"

"Sure 'n 'tis worth the try. Mr. Drummond is the one to approach the commissioners. We'll write up a proposal after lunch. Have ye tried the government offices?"

"Federal and state both. They have their own projects in place, they say."

"Philanthropists?"

"For that I need contacts. I have none."

"Eh, nae big thing. Take an evening stroll, noting addresses of the finest houses. Then go down to the lands office and look up the owners' names. 'Twill give ye someone to write to as ye sit in lovely isolation. Also, ye might have y'r hair trimmed before ye return to Barmah. We have a barber who knows everything about everybody."

He chuckled. "I'll try them all."

She was frowning again. "I shall make contribution out of me wages. Well I know from working for ye that every bit counts. But I cannae give ye a sum. I recently made a loan to a friend in need, and it's cut me account quite low."

"I certainly don't expect that of you!"

"Were ye expecting it, meself'd think much the less of ye."

They arrived at the tea garden, and conversation ceased as they were seated and served. She was still thinking when the serving girl left with their order. Reginald didn't mind the quiet a bit. Basking in her presence sufficed.

The sandwiches and tea arrived, and still she had not spoken. Reginald offered a blessing and took over as mother of the pot.

She spread her napkin in her lap. "Now that the office be in order, me duties are nae nearly so demanding as I would have imagined when first I took this job. Most afternoons be free. I've been using them to become better acquainted with the persons with whom we shall do business once the slack picks up."

He nodded and bit into a sandwich.

She leaned forward, her forearms on the edge of the table, and laced her fingers together. "And now meself shall be an utter hussy and a froward woman. I recall when first I began work for ye, I read y'r charter, issued from London and approved by New South Wales. Among the other allowances it provides y'r salary, and a stipend for y'r wife, the reasoning being, I presume, that she be a co-worker with equally onerous duties."

"That's true." Was she headed where he thought she was?

She swallowed, and her cheeks flushed pink. "Were we man and wife, ye would collect both y'r salary and the stipend, a needed addition to y'r operating budget. Meself could keep me job here and work for the mission in me spare time, which as I said is ample. 'Twould justify the stipend, ye see. If y'r budget be similar today to what I remember from last year, the stipend would make a welcome addition, as would whatever part of me salary was left after living expenses. Indeed, if ye suffer a month like last October, it could mean the difference between black ink and red. Ye'd have a place here in town whenever ye come in, and would nae shoulder the cost of an accommodation and meals taken out. There be all sorts of financial advantages."

He could not suppress his grin, his happiness. "What a unique proposal!"

The pink flush turned vivid red. "I be nae proposing, ye blackguard. I be suggesting a possibility to think about. Nae more."

He sobered, but only a little. "We've not discussed love."

"Nor need we. Love is a skill to be learned, if what I read in Scripture be true, and well ye know it is. Over and over, we are commanded to love. We are nae to wait until some mysterious emotion comes upon us. We're to *love*. Now. Since God made nae distinction in His Word between one sort of love or another, I have nae doubt it refers to the love of man and wife as well as any other."

Reginald's eyes burned hot. He must not allow an embarrassing display now! He managed to stammer a self-evident "I'm speechless" as he fought it back. This woman, brought into the fold through his influence, was absorbing the wisdom of God more quickly and more completely than he could ever have hoped or dreamed.

He completed the luncheon in something of a daze. He was still half numb when they returned to her office and drafted a proposal for the commissioners. He saddled the roan and paid the livery tab with nearly his last farthing, accepted a picnic supper from Samantha's hand, and set out east toward Barmah. He could take the road, essentially the long way around, or he could strike out overland, following more or less the course of the river. The moon would be entering first quarter tonight. Once the roan got close enough, its homing instinct would surely take over and they could finish the trek in the dark. He chose the short, rough route.

He sang. His heart sang. His soul sang. Samantha!

A bit over eight miles out of town a boat whistle hooted in response to Toplady's "Rock of Ages." He turned the roan aside and rode down to the river shore. There sat the *Echuca Charlene*, four feet from the New South Wales bank, huffing smoke and puffing steam.

Gus Runyan threw a line ashore. "Gimme a bit of a tug, man of God, not to mention a brief prayer. She's just on the verge of freeing herself. One more straw on the camel's back should do it."

Reginald obliged with both the prayer and the tug. *On the verge* was overstating it considerably. It took the roan and the river current and *Charlene*'s straining engine nearly an hour to shake her free. With a raucous hoot of her whistle, she steamed west toward home.

The east had turned pink and the kookaburras were issuing their first call for the sun when Reginald saw the roofs of Barmah Mission shining in the distance. The roan picked up the pace. Even so, it was another half hour before he rode, bone weary, into the dooryard. The roan slogged, just as weary, to its shelter and fumbled to a halt.

What a staggering week this had been—rebuff on all sides, the long hours of travel by train and horse, a night without sleep, and most of all, Samantha's startling plan. Samantha. She lingered on his mind as he unsaddled the roan and turned it into its paddock. He tossed it a fork of hay and pointed his exhausted body toward the house.

He gasped and paused. Ellen stood two rods away in the gray-pink dawn. She wore a dark dress, true, but that was no excuse. Why had he not seen her immediately? She came to him and he altered course to join her. She extended her hands and he grasped them. They were warm and soft, and they gripped his firmly.

"Welcome back, Reginald."

"Ta. Good to be home, Ellen. And what disasters happened in my absence?"

She fell in beside him and they continued toward the house. "Disasters! What is the word? Pessimist. That's it."

"Very well, what blessings were bestowed in my absence?"

"Your safe travels."

An uncomfortable silence descended that even the kookaburras honored. The dust beneath his feet felt firm and settled. It had rained here recently.

He paused by his verandah. "What is it, Ellen?"

"I've a matter I must discuss with you, but it will wait until you've rested."

He sighed and watched the pink sky turn yellow. "Dawn. Wake-up time. No, I'll not go to bed today. I'll retire early tonight to make up for it." He plunked down on the verandah step. "Come. Sit here with me. I've a matter to discuss with you as well. We'll discuss together."

"You're sure you don't want to take a nap?"

"Sit."

She sat. She looked at the dust, the verandah floorboards, the quickening sky, the distant trees.

"You first," he prodded.

She shook her head. "I had it all so carefully rehearsed; I knew exactly what must be said; and it's all fled. I don't—" She bit her lip and started over. Her black eyes held his firmly. "Ever since you left I've been rising very early, like this morning, for prayer. I've a hideous problem, Reginald, with jealousy. I can't control myself. I can't rid myself of it. And prayer isn't working, no matter how much of it I do."

"Jealousy! Of whom could you be jealous? Toby's Polly?"

"Samantha Connolly." The dark eyes fell away.

He felt himself staring, and he could not muster the presence of mind to stop. *If the object be Samantha, that meant—*

The black eyes rose to meet his again. "I've loved you since the first day I came. I told myself it's a fatch—a fatchi—"

"Infatuation."

"Thank you. It's not. It grows each day. I know you well enough that I'm aware of your shortcomings as well as your virtues, and I love you no less. I want to serve you and be a part of your life. I want you to be my life." Her lip trembled. "And I understand that you do not return this love. I don't fault you for that; it's the way things are. But I had to tell you the way things are with me. I'm sorry if it troubles you."

"Troubles me? No, not that. I had no idea, Ellen. I didn't—" His head spun. Perhaps he ought take a nap. He was reeling, unable to think.

"You have a matter to discuss, you said."

He shook his head. "I must first make decisions regarding the matter, and I must make them alone. You can't help me. No one can, save God. I must talk to Him first before I say or do anything. As for your jealousy, the first step is to recognize it and confess it. You've done that. I suggest now that you not bother giving your jealousy to God. He doesn't want it any more than you do. Rather, give into His care the situation precipitating the jealousy. I think if you give that to Him, the jealousy will pretty much take care of itself. He can handle any situation, you know."

"Shall I pray for what I want, do you mean?"

"I cannot advise you on that. You must pray as the Holy Spirit leads, not as Reginald Otis leads. Don't let your heart drown out the Spirit, though. Do you know what I mean?"

"I understand, but I'm not sure I can do it. You don't know how loudly my heart is crying out."

"Yes I do, Ellen. Yes I do."

Samantha.

From clear out in the summer kitchen, the teakettle shrieked loud enough to interrupt their conversation. Samantha left Cole to finish his berry pie and hurried out to fetch the kettle before it called all the cats in Echuca to her door. She filled the teapot, dunked the little porcelain tea infuser and returned to the table.

She sat looking at the teapot intently, pretending she could watch the tea steep. "I be nae sure why I told ye all this. It does seem the best way out for Barmah Mission. He'll ne'er get as much money as he really needs to run the place right. This would help." She glanced up.

He was glaring at her. "The lurk merchant's taking you, Sam. Can't you see that? He's using you!"

"Nae, Cole. 'Twas me own idea, nae his."

"Does the word *persuasive* mean anything to you? He makes a business out of persuading people. Believe this. Do that. And one of the important tricks of persuasion is to make the person you're manipulating think it was all his own idea. His or hers. You're being led down a primrose path, and it scorches my hair just thinking about it."

She should have known better than to think he might be open and understanding about it. How foolish she was to believe he'd be helpful, or offer some additional point. "Meself has been reading Scripture daily since I gave meself over to Christ, and I found the perfect verse for ye." She rose to fetch her Bible from the bedroom, but he didn't stand up. He usually had better manners than that.

Samantha sat again at the table and began thumbing. It took her a while to find it. He poured himself another cup of tea and did not bother to warm up her cup. The grouch. The supreme grouch!

"Here 'tis. Titus one, verse fifteen: 'Unto the pure all things are pure; but unto them that are defiled and unbelieving is nothing pure; but even their mind and conscience is defiled.' When I refused ye up at Sugarlea, 'twas because I could nae trust ye. Ye cannae see the purity in Reginald for y'r own blindness." She closed the book. "At least, now I know 'tis y'r own skewed view and not Reginald. Nae too long ago, I would've let ye plant doubts in me, for I place so much weight upon y'r opinions and y're good will."

He scowled black as death at the Bible. "At least there's nothing in the verse about straying."

Straying? Someone was knocking at the door. She abandoned the discussion—it was fruitless, anyway—and went to answer it. She opened the door and gasped, delighted.

"Why, look here! Martin Frobel, a thousand miles from home. Do come in, and welcome!"

Chapter Sixteen

Betrayal

Marty Frobel. Sloan studied the young pastoralist and tried to add two and two. It wasn't adding. They sat across from each other at Sam's table. Sloan was doing that a lot lately—sitting at her table. This happened to be breakfast. It could as well be lunch or dinner. He had come over here from the hotel at dawn because he couldn't afford to eat there. She was so open and friendly, so eager to assist—to a point. Reach that point, and you slam into a steel wall. She was in essence holding him at arms' length, and the torture was killing him.

And Frobel. Frobel was staying at the Cattlemen's. If Sloan got attacked by toughs again tonight . . . Sloan still couldn't decide whether to hold Frobel responsible for that incident or not. His denial seemed genuine, but that meant nothing. The very best liars can make it sound *ex cathedra*. But then, essentially the same thing happened in Adelaide, and Frobel wasn't anywhere near there. Was he?

"Frobel. Have you ever been to Adelaide?"

"No. Farthest west I've ever been is Cloncurry. Understand Adelaide's a nice place. Not much of a cattle district, though."

Samantha brought the kettle in from out back. "Is that what makes a place worth being in, Marty? Cows?"

"Used to think so. Not so sure these days. Beginning to look as if we've a few more cows than we need. What I was talking about with Sloan here yesterday afternoon and evening: you see, the cattlemen and some private developers built meatworks. There were eighteen of them in Queensland for a while. It's a good idea, but they just can't seem to get profitable."

"Meatworks. Abattoirs?"

"Partly. There's been boiling-down works for fifty years. In drought years, when your cattle are dying anyway, you sell them for a few pennies to the boiling-down works, and they take the hides and tallow. Waste the meat, essentially. So we put in freezing plants. Gladstone and Lakes Creek are two big ones. Freeze the carcasses, put them on freezer ships, and send them all over the world."

Samantha stared at him wide-eyed. "They can do that?"

"We're getting better at it, but there are still a lot of problems with the mechanical end of it. A freezing plant needs a steady cast and a steady—"

"What is a cast?"

"The cattle out of your herd that are ready for market. The crop. The product. That fluctuates up and down, depending on the weather. Dry year, wet year. But the market doesn't fluctuate. You have a given number of people eating just so much beef a year. There are other complications, but mostly, we need markets to make it pay."

"Sure'n ye'd nae ask a better man than this." Sam was looking at Sloan with what could only be described as admiration. "Ye give him the facts; help him learn all about it; and he'll find what ye need."

Sloan desperately wished it were true in this case. He wished that Australia were not already glutted with beef and lamb. He'd love to sell Frobel's beef. But where?

Sam turned to Frobel. "I thank ye again, ever so much, for bringing me trunks and saddle. With all me worldly possessions here at last, sure'n I can feel a bit more at home."

Frobel casually waved a hand. "They arrived at Pop's for some reason, and Mum sent them on to me. Mum has this feeling that if I'm in Sydney, I'm only a few miles from anything in southern Australia. She understands that Queensland has distance, but she doesn't think any other state has any."

Sloan watched Sam's face. He savored the memory of her clear and overflowing delight when her saddle had arrived here on her doorstep. She obviously treasured it, his gift to her. So why didn't she treasure Sloan as much?

She stood up and pulled her hat off the rack by the door. "Gentlemen, feel free to relax as ye wish. I must hie meself off to work. Ye need nae worry about locking the door. Just pull it to when ye leave. G'day." She stepped outside and took the sunshine with her.

The men talked a few minutes more of inconsequential things. Frobel mentioned taking a horse out into the countryside to look the area over. They shook hands and went their separate ways, pulling the door shut behind them.

The overcast sky promised rain. Frobel was going to get wet if he went out there today. Sloan wanted to send telegrams to Henscke, to Basedows' and Hamilton wineries so badly he could taste it. "Are the wines I ordered on the way? Will I be saved from ruin by a timely river rising?"

For want of something better to do on so glum a morning, he wandered over to the wharf. After its summer sleep, the wharf was stirring. Skippers on the larger boats were starting to come in now. He ought get to know them. He wished it would rain and get it over with. The sullen cloud cover weighed down upon him. Everything weighed down upon him. Sam was such a sensible woman. What could she possibly be thinking of?!

She could never be happy with Reginald Otis!

Yes, she could, too. When he talked to Sam, Sloan undermined Otis every chance he got, trying in vain to convince her of something he knew was false. For although he might sling off at Otis on every opportunity, he knew the man was real. Sam needed a stable man, a sensible man, an everyday, down-to-earth man. Otis was all those things. Sloan was none of them. She could trust Otis, and probably with justification. And she was absolutely convinced she could not trust Sloan.

An intense jealousy seized his heart and turned the gray day black. Sam had found the kind of man she wanted and needed. And it wasn't Sloan.

He heard his name called. At the far end of the wharf, a portly gentleman he did not know beckoned. This was not Drummond. Sam had introduced him to Drummond.

The fellow shifted a batch of papers from his right hand to his left and gravely offered a handshake. "My name is Wiersby. I'm one of the port commissioners. I wonder if we might talk to you a few minutes in chambers?"

"Certainly." Now what?

Sloan followed him past Sam's vacant office into the street and across the esplanade to a bluestone building. Their footsteps ticked on the varnished red gum floor down the building's long, echoing hall. They entered a narrow meeting room. The door clicked shut behind them.

At a miles' long polished table sat Drummond, two other puffed-up gents, and Samantha. Her face was drawn tight as a drumhead. Sloan felt his anger rise, and he had no idea what to be angry about. But they were giving Sam a bad time; he could tell that much just from her expression. How dare they cause a splendid woman like this a hard moment? You could see by looking at them that they were a fair prize themselves. Pompous, overweening, self-important shysters, the whole lot of them.

Commissioner Wiersby introduced the other two strangers as commissioners also, but their names didn't register. Sloan was too busy trying to figure out the situation.

Finally, Commissioner Wiersby waved toward a chair. "Do be seated. We convened this morning to investigate certain activities involving Miss Connolly. I saw you by chance as I was gathering some papers from her office, an opportune happenstance. You figure prominently in the accusations against her."

"Accusations?"

"The port commission is the most crucial governing body in this area, Mr. Sloan, because trade and transport are our lifeblood. Only the finest citizens, unblemished by scandal, are chosen as commissioners, reflecting the immense importance of the post."

"I'm sure."

"The wharfmaster is the extension of the commission, the link between authority and the trade itself. The wharfmaster and those he would hire must be absolutely above reproach."

"Absolutely."

"Despite damning evidence against her, Miss Connolly insists so strongly upon her innocence that we felt a hearing was necessary—to clear the air, as it were."

"Evidence of what? Innocence from what?"

"A number of things. Foremost, the wharfmaster is never to use the influence of his position to further his friends' fortunes or his own. And his assistant no less so."

"You mean, set up good deals for his mates."

"Precisely. Miss Connolly has been working behind the scenes, contrary to regulations, to arrange special favors for the Barmah Mission and, frankly, for you yourself."

"She's not done a thing illegal. She introduced me to some boatmen, showed me a few things—"

"She is a clerk, Mr. Sloan. That's all. A clerk. She has neither power nor authority to influence trade on the wharf. If her activities were not suspect, she would have worked properly, through Mr. Drummond. And then, again involving you, Mr. Sloan, there is the question of her moral conduct. We—"

"Why, you lazy galahs! How can you sit there and—" *Hold your tongue, Sloan boy! Think before you attack these rats! THINK!*

If she lost her job here, she would be far less inclined toward that marriage of convenience with Otis. In fact, if the stigma of a dishonorable release plagued her badly enough, she'd have to leave the area and seek work elsewhere. Surely Sloan would be doing her a favor were he to destroy her plan to wed Otis, for he'd be saving her from a horrible mistake.

Sloan dropped his voice. From the looks on these drongos' faces, they weren't accustomed to being called galahs. "My apologies, gentlemen. I was overcome with the enormity of the moment. What specifically do you need from me?"

"Are you engaged in an unwholesome relationship with this young woman?"

"I prefer to keep private matters private, gentlemen. I'll not discuss it."

"We would appreciate a yes or no. A no on your part would clear it."

"You've no authority to expect any answer from me that I'm not ready to give. What is your next question?"

Wiersby laid a sheet of tissue out on the table, a list of some sort that Sloan couldn't read at this angle. "Miss Connolly sent telegrams to the skipper of the *Mayflower* at Swan Hill and to the wharf at Mannum. No Echuca Wharf business would require those messages. Were they to promote your personal business?"

"She lined up a shipment for me, yes."

"Without going through proper channels."

"I neither know nor care what the proper channels are." Had he done enough damage? Probably the damage was complete before he'd even gotten here. He was the frosting on the cake, his testimony their final justification for sacking her. "I don't like the accusatory nature of your remarks toward me, and I choose not to participate further. Good day, gentlemen." He started to rise.

Wiersby raised a fat, ugly paw. "The inquiry is not directed toward you in any way, Mr. Sloan. Please, just a few more points."

Sam stood up suddenly. "Do as ye will. I'm past caring." She sounded shocked, her voice taut and razor thin. Sloan couldn't look at her face. He felt her brush past his chair; the door clicked; she was gone.

Sloan stood up. "You don't need me."

Wiersby, that nark, was still thanking him for his cooperation as he walked out.

Why was he following her? She'd never speak to him again. He didn't want her to; at least not for a while. Would she go running to Otis's arms anyway? It was a possibility. Not a probability.

Out at the east end of the wharf the train hooted. So it was that time of day already. Sloan followed her, keeping a respectable distance between them. Sam stopped at her office—her ex-office—only long enough to retrieve a broad-brimmed hat on a rack. As she stepped outside, a sweet, familiar voice called her name.

It couldn't be! Sloan took a dozen jogging steps to get in closer, to see better. It *was*. Linnet had just detrained and that Chris What's-his-name was with her. Linnet and Sam ran to each other and embraced. If Chris was responsible for that attack in Adelaide, and Frobel for the one in Sydney, Sloan was in a barrel of trouble; both were in town now.

Sloan could not make out words; he could only hear the voices. The women were still locked in embrace. Sam sank to her knees, then sat heavily on the worn and rough-hewn platform, her legs folded under her. Linnet knelt, cradling her, hugging her, rocking her back and forth. Sloan had never heard a woman weep as Sam was mourning now.

It did rain later that day, but whether Frobel got wet Sloan neither knew nor cared. Wearied for no discernible reason, he took a nap in his hotel room. He ate a cheap dinner at a little dive of a place. About dark it began to rain in earnest. He slipped down the backstairs to the cellar of the Esplanade, where the rain didn't matter, and there he stopped cold, two feet short of the bar.

Chris "Whoever" was perched on a stool right by the door. He wore a great, black, musty-smelling opera cape. What was it with this lair, anyway?

Sloan grimaced, an adequate substitute for a smile, and parked himself two stools away. He glanced at Chris. The lad was looking at him. He might as well speak. "So, how's she doing?"

"She's getting on. She and Linn are at her place. Girl-talk. I got a room at the Bridge."

"I'm at the Esplanade."

Silence. "You're despicable, Sloan. You know that, don't you? In fact, I'm spending a pleasant evening here making a mental list of all the unflattering names you are."

"What'd she tell you?"

"Nothing. She told Linn plenty, and I listened. She was all primed to fight Drummond until you killed her chance of winning."

"Fight Drummond? I thought it was the commissioners."

"Drummond dropped his bundle. Told them she came to him for a job when it was actually the other way around; told them he knew nothing about her activities when she kept him informed all the way. The spineless lizard told them anything they wanted to hear. And then you turned on her." Chris shook his head. "I've met moles and white ants you wouldn't believe; the diplomatic corps is riddled with them. But they can't top you."

"And now she hates me."

"Maybe later. Right now, she's numb. Glassy-eyed, like someone punched her up."

"Speaking of which . . ." What good would it do? "Never mind."

"Speaking of what?"

"A couple of jacks in Adelaide jumped me, right after you left. You wouldn't know anything about that, would you?"

Chris looked at him mildly, his face loose and relaxed. "No. Sounds like a good idea, though. Who won?"

"I got done like a dinner."

"Good on them."

The barman set a beer in front of Sloan, but he didn't want it. He didn't want anything. Yes, he did, too. But he couldn't tell what it was. "You ever been in love, Chris?"

"I am now."

"Enough to lie and cheat for her?"

"I don't know. Maybe. I suppose."

Through the foggy, sweating glass, Sloan watched the little bubbles rise in his beer. "Me, too."

They sat there, suspended in unmeasured time. Finally Chris lurched erect and wished the barman good night. Not a bad idea. Sloan pushed away and followed the silly black opera cape upstairs and out into the rainy night.

Chris had expressed his opinion. Sloan took it from that the ocker didn't want company on his way back to the hotel. He dropped back thirty feet. They walked together apart.

A shadow in the darkness between two buildings, the merest hint of movement, caught Sloan's attention. Had he been drinking tonight, he no doubt would not have seen it. He wheeled to face the movement as an arm snaked out and grabbed his sleeve. He only got half a yell out as he was yanked into the blackness, but at least he had seen it coming.

He folded his legs, ducking low; he felt an arm swing past his head, flailing the air. He leaped up with both arms out stiff before him. He connected fairly, heard the fellow go *oof!* He ducked again and pivoted. He could see nothing; his adversaries' eyes were probably better attuned to the dark than his own. How many were there? He couldn't tell.

He crab-walked two feet sideways toward the street, his knees bent nearly double. No good! He was now exposed in better light than they. A fist from nowhere knocked him onto his bottom.

A black cape came flying past, exuding musty odor. Sloan heard the kid connect solidly. Voices cried out. Sloan was back on his feet now. He waded into the melee, boots and all. The exhilaration was there again, the scintillating urge to show these drongos the folly of attacking a simple, peace-loving man like Sloan. His blood had come to life.

He could see somewhat now, too, as his eyes adjusted better and better. A face not Chris's loomed before him; he socked it. A set of frantic footsteps beat a retreat down the alley. Someone in the darkness thunked against a wall. The face at Sloan's feet was starting to rise. He kicked it. He circled around lest he be silhouetted.

Ten feet away someone grunted. Another set of feet beat their way to safety down the alley. Suddenly a black presence loomed beside him, too near and too advanced in its swing for him to stop it. He was going to get pasted fair with this one. An arm and hand whistled inches past his nose and slammed solidly into the black nemesis, then pulled back in pain. The gent let out a surprised "huh!" on his way down.

Chris stood beside him and studied the fallen oaf. "Any notion who they are?"

"I was about to ask you."

"You really do think I set some sort of war dogs on you."

"You were cheering for the good guys an hour ago. Now here you are defending me."

"If these louts would attack you, what of the gentle ladies? Just making the streets safe. Besides, I need something to punch. It's been frustrating the last few weeks."

"That's a tune I can whistle, mate!" Sloan hauled the blackguard on the ground to his feet. "Let's get some answers."

With the groggy ratbag propped between them, Sloan led Chris out to the wharf. Here the streetlights were most distant. And yet, it was as light here as anywhere, with nothing but open sky overhead. He recognized the clown the moment the light was strong enough; the pencil mustache from Sydney! They walked through the rain to the very edge of the wharf.

Sloan laid a hand on the man's throat. "Make a sound any louder than my voice now and we drop you. Understand?" He whipped a leg out and caught the back of the fellow's knees. The lout went down like a hod of bricks.

Chris caught on instantly. Together they shoved the fellow backward out over the edge until he hung head down with only his feet and calves touching solid wharf. He struggled a moment and reduced his attempts to a continuous litany of begging and pleading.

Sloan sat on one shin, and Chris on the other. "Now, fair cow, you can dive head first onto someone's boat deck, or possibly the river, or you can cooperate. Your name?"

"Vernon B-B-Bower."

"Your occupation?"

"Thief. Naught but a thief."

Sloan lifted his weight slightly. The leg slipped a hair. "I remember you on that bay horse. You and your knife. Your occupation? And why no knife tonight?"

"We just wanted to f-f-f-frighten ye, Mr. Sloan. I wasn't going to k-k-k-kill ye with me knife, just mark ye up a bit. I swear it, Mr. Sloan; w-w-we'd never kill ye!"

Chris twisted around to look Sloan in the face. "Sounds like he's more your cobber than mine. He doesn't know my name." Chris bounced his weight a bit. "Or do you?"

"We-we-we-we got nothin' 'gainst ye, sir. Just Mr. Sloan."

"And why Mr. Sloan?"

" 'Tis what we're paid for, sir."

"Paid by whom?"

Silence.

Sloan spent a few minutes just watching all around. Apparently this Vernon Bower's mates were a cowardly lot not about to save their accomplice. Sloan shifted his weight. "Hope you get paid enough to die for it. Your boss lives in comfort while you plunge off the end of the Echuca Wharf. Doesn't seem fair to me."

"W-w-w-will ye promise ye'll not tell me boss I cracked? And will ye p-p-promise ye'll not let me fall?"

"I don't have to cut a deal, cove. I'm on top."

"You don't want to cut a deal with him anyway," Chris chimed in. "You can't trust him worth a brass razoo. He's been known to dob in his best friend, and recently, too. But my word's good. I'll warrant you I won't let him toss you over the side. *If* you give us the dinkum oil—the truth, now."

"Beckerstaff. Horace Beckerstaff hired us at thirty-five a month plus railway fares."

Sloan snorted. "I don't believe you. He's got me knocked down in the courts. He doesn't have to spend money like that to send a couple of pie-faced drongos out into the bush after me. That's foolish. You really think I'd believe that?"

"It's the ch-ch-ch-ch-truth, I swear! His orders were to make your life miserable. He kept saying it over. He seemed to take a delight in it, ye know? Little annoyances and big ones. The more miserable, the better. And we were to write reports."

"So did you write reports?"

"That's when we got our bonuses. But we were truthful. Didn't dare lie to Mr. Beckerstaff."

"How good are you at arson?"

"Bit of k-k-kerosene in y'r filing cabinet. We did it by d-d-d-day so's the bombers would get on it quick. Even left a window open so's someone would see the s-s-smoke right off."

"Clever of you. Follow me around all over?"

"Follow ye around and cause ye p-p-problems. The bag ye lost in Melbourne? We threw it in the river. And the time in Adelaide, at y'r lady friend's b-b-b-boardinghouse? Cleaning out your hotel room got us a fat bonus. And at the track in S-S-S-Sydney. That was us. Y're a hard man to follow. Lost ye—lost ye a couple times. And we was a day behind ye most of the time. Would've done a lot more if we coulda caught up. But that's over now, sir, over and done, I swear. We'll not b-b-b-bother ye again."

"You caused me all this trouble. Now tell me why I shouldn't just stand up right now."

"Ye wanted the dinkum oil, sir, and I bared me soul, sir. Have m-m-m-mercy, sir!"

Chris was staring at Sloan, bemused. "Sounds as if you have a world class enemy in this Beckerstaff. You never do things by halves, do you, Sloan?"

"If it's worth doing, it's worth doing well. Since the constable hasn't found us, let's go find the constable. Let our fizzgig here sing for the law and sign a statement."

Chris nodded. "And, it will probably pay to muster up the other two before they go running to their boss. It'll save him the effort of destroying some of his files."

"Wouldn't want to put him to any extra effort on my behalf."

Getting Bower out of his predicament was a lot more taxing than putting him into it.

Beckerstaff. Sloan's mind gazed with admiration upon the purity of Beckerstaff's hatred, and of his power to indulge that hatred. Sloan had heard it said that hatred is a more powerful driving force than love. He believed it. If love were such a strong controlling factor, he would not have done what he did to the one true love of his life.

In the rain on that dark wharf, at just about that moment, the dull numbness Sloan had felt all day began to lift. In its place came pain.

By the time Vernon Bower was ensconced in the local gaol, Sloan's pain had grown until its hot fingers probed into every fiber of his existence. Excruciating emotional pain. Look what he had done! He remembered her voice as she had left that council chamber. An honest and upright woman, a noble woman, and he had sullied her. Her honor was important to her. He knew that. And to serve his own interests he had glibly impugned it. By his very silence he had condemned her. On purpose.

Late, late that night, when the goblins of the mind have their turn at designing one's dreams, Sloan awoke to a hideous nightmare. He found himself drenched in sweat.

And he was weeping.

CHAPTER SEVENTEEN

IN PURSUIT OF FAME AND FORTUNE

A white cockatoo lit in the yard outside Samantha's window. She straightened at her writing desk and paused a moment, admiring it. It flashed its yellow crest and began waddling about in search of breakfast. Samantha finished this latest release. "Here ye go, Linnet. This one will be for the Swan Hill paper. I believe 'tis a weekly."

From the dining table, Chris passed Linnet another envelope. "And here's the envelope addressed to us, so they can send the press clippings."

Linnet paused in her envelope stuffing. "Chris, what if the press clippings be bad? The Melbourne papers said naething a tall, and that's even worse."

"Then we excerpt and quote it separately. 'Miss Connolly is a wondrously lousy singer, adept at wrecking even so great a composer as Handel' becomes 'Miss Connolly is wondrously dot adept dot, period.' It's done all the time."

"How dreadful!" Linnet went back to her work. She looked up again. "We'll not resort to such flummery, will we?"

"We won't have to. You'll be glorious!"

Samantha giggled. That pleased her. It was the first time she had felt like giggling since . . . since . . . "Your boat will be one of the first on the new water. That is to say, one of the first calling at these towns. These people are starving for entertainment, not to mention flour and salt. You could be a roller-skating goat, and they'd love you."

Linnet brightened. "They've had roller skating in Adelaide over a year now; we've gone a couple of times. And they're planning to bring it to Sydney this year." She turned to Chris. "If it be open by the time we get there, perhaps we might go?"

"We'll cross that bridge when we roll over it. Linn, you've mastered the *non sequitur* like no one else I've ever known."

She smiled demurely. "Thank ye, Chris."

Samantha rose and reached for her hat. "I be off to the post office. I'll send these and the telegrams. Sure'n ye'll be a celebrity before ever y'r boat arrives, Linnet."

"We're going over to the arts school to practice. They're renting us a baby grand to use on the tour." Chris scooped up a batch of papers and rather roughly ushered Linnet toward the door.

They went their separate ways. Samantha lingered a bit to watch Chris and Linnet as they walked upstreet and turned the corner. He was gesticulating wildly, she nodding vigorously. What a strange, sweet fellow was Linnet's Chris! But then, so was Linnet, in her own way. Samantha felt very happy for her.

She consulted her list, making certain she had everything she needed. All here. Away she went.

Already she had arranged for the *Mayflower* to charter as Linnet's showboat. It was a tiny vessel, and sprightly, and would serve nicely on this still-low water. Now she must mail out these news bulletins of Linnet's appearance to each of the towns along the way. Each packet contained details of the event, background on Linnet for the local editors and reporters, and a return envelope with the request for clippings. If this worked—if even half the towns responded—Linnet would soon have quite a sheaf of recent clippings with which to influence impresarios in the big cities.

The pain of Cole's betrayal stabbed as deeply as ever, but Samantha could at least see a reason now that God might not mind that she'd been sacked. She could spend her full energies on setting up Linnet's tour, and of orchestrating the news items and publicity it would generate.

She thought only briefly of the staid, regular, unremarkable life she had left behind in Cork, the life her parents still pursued. Whatever would Mum and Papa think of this wild land and of Linnet and Samantha's constant employment adventures?

Cole, Cole, Cole. Why?

Her postal duties completed for the moment, she turned almost by habit toward the wharf. Who had come in this morning? She walked down the steep, endless stairs to the lower level. But the lowest level was under water now. Boats were tying up at the next level.

The *Adelaide* was back in the water now. She worked logging barges between the wharf here and Barmah forest. Apparently they were planning to use her, so perhaps water was up in the forest also. At the far end, Samantha could barely make out the *Gem*. And outboard of her was tied the *Pyap*.

This was exciting! That was it exactly. The rebirth of the river trade excited Samantha. She regretted being robbed of the chance to take part in it. Sadly, bitterly, she turned and climbed back up the stairs.

Her spirits had lifted by the time she reached the top. Late this morning the *Mayflower* would arrive with Cole's wine shipment. That shipment would be transferred to the train, and the skipper of the *Mayflower* would take on the sweet-voiced Adelaide Lark, with her accompanist, Mr.

Yorke, for a triumphant musical tour of the Murray drainage. Already, here came Chris and Linnet, and look at that: they had employed Ah Loo's cousin to move the piano from the church to the wharf.

"Miss Connolly!"

She wheeled. "Mr. Wiersby."

"I've learned you've been in contact with the skipper of the *Mayflower,* Captain Husting. At least one letter, and several telegrams."

"Which friends I send letters to, or telegrams, be a private matter and nae longer a concern of y'rs, Mr. Wiersby. Ye'll nae accuse me of using me position unwisely, for I've nae position left to use, thanks to y'r own fine meddling." She watched his face redden, and it delighted her in a perverse way.

He puffed up visibly. "Your lack of deference toward your superiors confirms our decision, young woman."

"An opinion meself'd expect of ye, sir. However, sir, when ye discover who really kept the wharf's affairs in order, I may or may nae be interested in being rehired. 'Twill depend upon me sister's success and the time required in tending to her needs."

A familiar and welcome whistle hooted out on the river. Samantha dipped her head. "Enjoy this fine weather, Mr. Wiersby, and g'day." She hurried off down the wharf and stood at its far end, watching the *Echuca Charlene* come churning up, her ugly tin smokestack spitting sparks.

Reginald waved from *Charlene*'s foredeck, the roan standing stolidly beside him. Samantha waved back. Captain Runyan waved and tooted the whistle again. Samantha waved back. It was very difficult to remain sad and depressed on this river when comical little boats like this, or stately power horses like the *Rothbury* across the way, churned about with their huffing and hooting. And the men who ran them were no less comical and stately. Samantha loved this whole milieu.

Cole, Cole, Cole. Why?

Captain Runyan beckoned with an arm. Samantha descended the stairs hastily and stepped out across the rickety planks.

"Come aboard!" the captain shouted. "I'm dumping him down by the mill!"

With a mighty leap, Samantha barely made it onto *Charlene's* deck. Reginald's strong arms steadied her.

She smiled and Reginald smiled and they shook hands. She was his fiancee? She crossed to greet the captain. "Top of the morning, sir! Good trip?"

"Didn't beach her once!" the captain laughed. The season was off and running!

Samantha realized now that they could not have offloaded the roan at the wharf without expecting the stodgy horse to negotiate the loose planks like a tightrope walker. *Echuca Charlene* nudged herself against the bank downstream on the New South Wales side, and as Reginald applied encouragement to the roan's rump, Samantha guided the front end ashore. The horse's disposition matched its ungainly head quite well.

With a final wave and a toot, *Charlene* backpaddled toward the wharf, and Samantha joined Reginald for the walk upstream to the bridge.

He told her the almost utter lack of news at Barmah Mission. She told him about Linnet and Chris. She told him about Marty Frobel, a man Reginald would enjoy meeting. And she told him, without detail, about the wharf job. She neglected mentioning Cole's part, and kept on neglecting it. That was foolish. Why protect the beast? And yet, she did.

He expressed shock at the commission action, properly aghast, and Samantha could see it was genuine. All those critical claims Cole had made against this gentle and caring man said far more about Cole than about Reginald.

They paused on the New South Wales bank beside the

bridge. Of occasionally painted iron, the bridge, another wonder of the modern age, arched high over the river, perched on great paired, braced columns. The railway to Deniliquin took up a part of it. The rest served road traffic.

Samantha hung on Reginald's arm and smiled. "Sure'n the bureaucrats I ran afoul of are only keeping up history. Captain Runyan was a boy when this bridge was completed, in '79. He says the locals were all ready for the big bridge-opening ceremony. But the bureaucrats wouldn't open it, for they were squabbling among themselves over who would inspect it and what traffic would be allowed and all."

"Some things don't change."

"Aye! The locals finally broke through the barricades one night and spent hours parading back and forth across it. The Bridge Riot, 'twas called. From then on, they just sort of used it. The good captain says the bridge never was officially opened."

"Life goes on in spite of the bureaucrats."

"As shall me own." She watched the distant shore. It seemed serene, for buildings and trees hid its bustle, and the wharf was not visible from here. From this side, her troubles and responsibilities all seemed to dwell at arms' length. In moments she would cross the bridge and plunge herself back into them.

He entwined her arm in his and began exploring her hand with his fingertips. "Samantha. You've heard, I trust, the adage that a man thinks from his head and a woman from her heart."

"Aye—the notion of it, at least."

"Yes. Well, I can nowhere in Scripture find the notion of it. When God told Isaiah, 'Come, let us reason together,' He called all mankind. Still, I rather cling to it. Cultural, I suppose." He licked his lips nervously. "I, uh, just recently learned that I have not one but two prospects for marriage."

"Aye, Ellen."

"Ellen, yes. I should have known you women would be miles ahead of me in this area. I struggled, in a quandary. I even called God to question for putting this decision upon me. Finally, I sifted it out. My heart loves you; my head loves Ellen. Your head loves me, Ellen's heart loves me. Uh, er . . ."

Samantha knew what was coming. In a way, she knew the moment he linked his arm in hers. Curious, the way she could almost read his thoughts, when she so inaccurately read Cole Sloan that she was frequently flabbergasted—or appalled. Did that not indicate she was literally made for this man?

She finished the thought for him. "Ye'd feel much more comfortable with a—how shall we say it? He-head, she-heart relationship than with one the other way around. Aye?"

He sighed. "The matter's not cut in stone. When I came down just now it was more to explore the situation with you than to declare a decision. But yes; that's pretty much it." For the first time he turned to face her squarely, eye to eye. "I love you too much to hurt you . . ."

Would that Cole could say the same.

"But I perceive that whatever choice I make will inflict pain on someone. I regret that. I so wish it weren't unavoidable."

"Meself greatly admires ye. To follow y'r head down the straight road when y'r heart goes skipping off across the meadow calls for a powerful discipline."

"Legend gives the Irish a gift for beautiful pictures. That's it exactly! The road and the meadow." He kissed her hand tenderly. "Thank you."

Samantha felt herself very near tears, and that would never do. To break down now would make this man feel terrible, and he of all men did not deserve that. She forged a smile deep inside and let it surface. "I received me severance pay late yesterday. If y'rself be like the rest of the swarmy mob I've been running with, y're utterly impecunious. Might I treat ye to lunch?"

" 'Impecunious.' You've been listening to the verbal excesses of our August Runyan. You called the game indeed; impecunious is my middle name. Completely penniless." He turned and began the stroll to the bridge. "Eighteen-seventy-nine, eh? Not yet thirty years old, and already she looks worn as an old shoe." He squeezed her hand. "Regardless of my final decision, I shall love you always, Samantha Connolly."

Sloan leaned back against the wall of the Esplanade's cellar and didn't mind that its dampness was probably ruining his coat. He stared at the drink on the table in front of him and didn't really see it. It was something else, an abstract. Everything was an abstract these last few days.

How could he have done that?

You poison everything you touch, Cole boy. Sugarlea was one of Queensland's great plantations when you took it over; you left it bankrupt and in ashes. You destroyed John Butts' dreams and then you destroyed Butts. He was an honest man, good-hearted. You're not in Sydney six months before you ruin Clyde Armbruster without half trying. One of your oldest, most caring friends. Boyhood mentor. And Sam. How the blazes could you ever let yourself do that to Sam? You tell yourself you love her. But you're not capable of anything but hate and treachery.

He took a sip simply because the glass sat before him.

In fact, you're not even capable of hate. What did you do about Beckerstaff? Turned Bower over to the Victoria police and let it go. That's all. If you were the man you used to think you were, you'd have Beckerstaff in the crosshairs of a pistol.

He took another sip.

Pistols don't have crosshairs, idiot.

He tossed the last of it down.

You're tonked. You're not worth a brass razoo, Cole, old man. You can't do anything right, and everything you look at goes crook. What are you doing, taking up space? You're not worth the air you're breathing, you flaming ratbag.

Cole thought of all the people who would have had happier lives if he'd never been born—especially Samantha. He tried to think of people who were better off for his being here. Nary a one. Nobody. And that, mate, about summed it up.

He pushed the table away and stood. His sleeve was damp clear through; it must be raining outside. There beyond the bar to the right stood the narrow black entry to that passageway, beckoning. He ducked under its lintel beam and stepped inside.

Dark. Moist. The dirt floor gritched beneath his boots. He extended his arms; his fingers touched rough-cut wall on each side. He took a step forward. Blackness like a cocoon enveloped him. He did not look back. Another step. His fingers hit shoring timbers. He passed his hands around them and continued.

Spider webs slashed sticky, painless lines across his face. He paused to brush them away and walked on. The passageway curved, curved back again. As he perceived first light ahead, his boot toe struck a riser. He began ascending stairs cut into the living rock.

With each step the light grew brighter. When at last he emerged into the gray-green alley behind the tea garden, the light forced him to squint.

The tea garden. He entered its shady bower from the rear, from the alleyway. They were closed now. He sat down in the wet iron chair at Samantha's favorite table. So familiar. Samantha.

He sat there a long time, with the rainwater dripping through the leaves of these arching vines, and he found this place far more conducive to rational thought than the Esplanade's cellar. Whether or not he decided simply to hang it up, there were amends to be made first. And the first was to the victim of his most heinous act of treachery.

He walked out into the rain, across the Esplanade to the wharf, seeking Samantha.

Chapter Eighteen

Hymn for Him

The sun skated in and out among fluffy cloud-blobs against a marvelously blue sky. To the one side of the little boat stretched brown rolling land. A patina of new grass tinged it green. To the other side, cliffs with ragged faces rose straight close to the boat, arcing high into the blue. What a lovely, serene, majestic view!

Linnet could see why Samantha had fallen in love with the riverboats. This little *Mayflower*, as clunky and noisy as it was, echoed the mystery and charm of the Murray itself. Linnet loved just standing on deck watching the beauty slide by.

The whistle hooted. It hooted again. Chris came out with a comb and arranged Linnet's hair just so. Linnet adjusted her elaborate, ruffled, lace-detailed dress and the little ribbon at her neck. They were getting pretty good at these arrivals.

Swan Hill was larger than most of their ports of call. For the tiny settlements, they simply set up chairs on the deck of the *Mayflower* and used the covered space between the paddle wheels as the proscenium. Captain Husting frequently stacked his fresh supply of firewood neatly around and under the piano. Swan Hill being larger than the deck could accommodate, Linnet would sing tonight in a local union hall, the only place in town besides the church with a piano. Linnet always felt funny about singing "Brennan on the Moor" in churches.

Samantha's advance notices were doing their job. More people awaited Linnet than she could ever have imagined! They lined the wharf; they stood on the street beyond. *Mayflower* hooted one long whistle and reversed her paddles. So many people!

With all the usual churning, roaring, shuddering mayhem, *Mayflower* drifted in and nudged against the wharf right at a—what was this? A red carpet!

Now Linnet must act. And indeed it was acting. She was playing the part of a famous singer greeting her admirers, for these people couldn't possibly be interested in a simple servant girl. She smiled. She blew some shy little kisses. She waved.

They were clapping. They had not yet heard her sing, and they were clapping. A small boy even more shy than she came running up with a bouquet of wildflowers. She accepted it, plucked one from the bouquet, and handed it to Chris beside her.

And now she was to walk up to the union hall. She stepped out onto the wharf still waving and onto the red carpet, albeit a very short one. Honestly! She smiled and happily greeted those nearest who caught her eye. This was beyond dreaming! This was beyond imagining, and certainly beyond reason.

"Miss Connolly! This way, please!" The mayor himself beckoned from an open carriage. It had to be the mayor; he was wearing a handsome top hat. Linnet was to be conducted to the hall! How unimaginably grand.

Close to her right, a little girl's voice cried out, "Oh, Mum, she's *so* beautiful!" Linnet froze. This was Linnet Connolly the lass was talking about! Chris nudged her on.

The rest of the evening proceeded just as dreamlike as this unexpected welcome. Linnet sang her best. It wasn't difficult; she felt *good*. A warm and happy amazement spurred her on. Chris was never better as his fingers glissaded up and down the keys.

The audience applauded. The couple encored. They encored again. Lacking a backstage, Linnet stepped out the back door into near darkness. Moments later the enthusiastic admirers found her.

The mayor, magnificent in his top hat, swept her hand to his lips and kissed it. "My dear, you were marvelous!"

She closed her eyes. To the dip of her head she added the slightest of bows, a tiny movement of the shoulders. As she raised her head, slowly opening her eyes, she beheld the silliest awed-little-boy gaze on the bedazzled mayor's face.

This is it, this is it, Linnet thought. This is the reality for which I've prepared. Chris was right; I do have gifts. Her heart shouted, drowning out her thoughts, *This cannot possibly be happening to a simple Irish working-class girl. How dreadful I will feel when they discover the truth about this "celebrity."* She answered questions from the news editor—she remembered his name from one of those envelopes they had sent out—while her heart cried *Sham!* No matter how her head reasoned, her heart shouted louder.

Very late that night, Linnet returned to the *Mayflower.* The curtains in the dark, silent cabin windows had not been drawn; the captain was still ashore. So was Chris—probably handling the last of business details and counting the money. Money. They were making money.

She looked at the sheltered space between the wheelhouse, where she conducted the very personal, intimate concerts for small groups of people in the villages. She enjoyed pleasing a big crowd, but in a different way she enjoyed just as much the eye-to-eye, smile-to-smile concerts here on deck.

Captain Husting had stacked firewood all around the piano again. She climbed over and through the wood and lifted the lid. She seated herself and began to play.

Sister Bertrand. *Dear, sweet Sister Bertrand. If you could see me now! How patient you were, teaching theory and technique to a cabinetmaker's daughter for no other reason than that the girl enjoyed music. What a wonderful gift you gave me!*

She ran through her warm-ups and began at the beginning of her present Czerny book, from memory. Of the thousands of homilies she heard in her life, Linnet could recall only two or three, and they didn't seem memorable at the time. In one of them, the parish priest preached respect for the nuns, for they were gifts to the common folk from God. *Thank you, God, for your gift of Sister Bertrand.*

And Chris. Yes, Chris. Of all the hundreds of people at the university, he was the one to notice her first. She could play tonight, at one with the music, because of Chris as much as Sister Bertrand. Chris had taught her to see not the notes and notations but the work itself. Sister Bertrand had taught her to read the music. Chris had taught her to feel it. Both of them pushed her to excellence.

Chris. Did she love him? She let her heart think about that awhile. It didn't take long. Yes. What about him would she not love?

Her fingers continued. The music flowed freely now into the darkness and the starlight. *In fact, thank you, God, for all of this!* This adventure had to be God's work; it certainly could be none of her own doing. She thought of Sam and how she had talked for hours about her new awareness of Jesus Christ. It was a different tune in the same symphony Meg played. Was Linnet missing something important?

Joy. Plain old happiness. The pure, sweet pleasure of living. She wasn't really thinking about what her fingers were doing. They responded to something deeper, more profound than her thoughts. Joy sang in her heart and expressed itself in a parade of all the piano pieces she had ever learned, simple and advanced. No longer was she Linnet *at* the piano. She was Linnet *and* the piano.

The darkness beside her moved. She recognized him, and the musty odor of his cape confirmed her identification. He climbed over the firewood and settled onto the bench at her left. She shifted up an octave to accommodate him.

They had to make some adjustments; one piano and four hands cannot be played with the same range as two pianos. And yet, adjust they did, with no thought at all on Linnet's part. It happened. They played beginning to end that first program they presented on South Terrace in lieu of the Bach master. The music sounded so much sweeter and happier now, flowing spontaneously from her joy.

"You were wonderful tonight," he said.

"Eh, no less'n y'rself."

He played in arpeggios as she completed a melody line.

"Will you marry me?"

Her fingers stopped.

She twisted around to stare at him, gaping.

He moved smoothly into a lovely air she had not heard before. "Those first moments, when you sang 'Brennan on the Moor,' I fell in love with your voice. Melodic, sweet. As we worked together I fell in love with you. All of you, to your very depths, is just as sweet as your voice."

"Miss Hack warned me . . . warned us . . ."

"And she's right. Of course, the battleaxe never married, so she holds a rather jaundiced view. Most female artists marry, even the most successful ones. They do just fine."

The melody ceased, faded into the liquid night. He turned to her. "I want to be part of your life forever, and I want you to be mine. Please, Linnet?" In the compassing darkness his black eyes disappeared into infinity.

"Yes," she whispered, and that moment her joy multiplied itself beyond imagination. "Yes."

Marty Frobel arrived at the Bridge as wet as a Murray cod. This country did dump the rain! He didn't mind the warm rains of summer up in central Queensland. The cold rain of autumn down here penetrated to his very bones. He pulled his hat off and slapped it against his leg as he stepped into the lobby.

"Mail for ye, sir." The desk clerk smiled. The desk clerk constantly smiled. *Leads you to wonder about the bloke,* Marty mused.

He leafed rapidly through the four or five letters and ripped open Pearl's on the spot. She loved him and missed him. No news there; he longed for her, too. She had found a darling church not far from her accommodation; its vicar preached the gospel; its congregation received her warmly.

She was still in Sydney. She had spoken with all the people whose names Sloan had suggested. Two prospects seemed bright and a third proved to be a real bottler. Through this third, she had already arranged a shipping schedule for a regular supply of frozen sides of beef to Hong Kong. She hoped Marty would be able to talk to Sloan some more; the man seemed to have a special knack for coming up with obscure and promising contacts. The weather was pleasant.

Marty jogged up the stairs to his room. Sloan was still in town somewhere, he thought. He'd look the chap up later. Right now he was going to peel out of these wet clothes and try to find someplace—anyplace—that was warm. The weather was almost surely pleasant up home. Pearl said it was pleasant in Sydney. What was he doing in Echuca?

Samantha wasn't home. Ah Loo had no idea where she was. The post office was holding her mail, for there was no forwarding address. The conductors didn't see her leave the area by railway. That left the riverboats as the most likely choice, for Sam did love the cranky boats. Sloan stood on the wharf in a pressing wind, endured the pounding rain, and contemplated side wheelers.

Along Rotten Row, an unsightly stretch of river shore, a score of derelict side wheelers and barges lay beached, weathering in the harsh summers, and the winter rains. In their heyday the riverboats enjoyed a trade monopoly stretching through the heart of Australia's most productive and picturesque country. Then the railways, finger by finger, poked their sleek and greedy hands into the Riverina to steal away the cream of the trade. Now, no longer profitable, these sorry hulks sprawled, ignominiously abandoned, on the shoulders of the river they once served.

The weather was being exceptionally cruel to them these days. After broiling all summer under the dry sun, more and more of Rotten Row was now disappearing below the flood. Many hulks sat with their rear decks submerged and their bows sticking out.

Sad it was that the railways could shove a whole way of life to the brink of extinction. The few steamers left afloat, those plucky vessels still earning their keep off the river, allowed Sloan to cut a deal. The railways would not.

Echuca was the logical place to find Sam. She was not here. The next logical place was Barmah Mission. Quite probably Sloan's ill-considered move, a move she could quite accurately interpret as deliberate betrayal, had driven her into Otis's arms. Almost certainly, Sloan had precipitated the one thing he had sought so desperately to avoid.

He would go to her. He would beg her forgiveness. Was it too late to keep her out of Otis's hands? Probably, but no matter. He must at least seek her forgiveness face-to-face. If nothing else, he must do that.

He started down the stairs toward the shore and was

startled to find the water lapping so high. It must be a good third of the way up the wharf pilings—maybe more. But then, what else would you expect from all this rain?

By chance might *Echuca Charlene* be in port? He walked the length of the wharf on its temporary plank catwalks. Several boats of different sizes bobbed in the water. Not Gus's. He booked a ride on a little snagging steamer called the *Industry* that just happened to be working its way upstream.

The *Industry* stopped at the second of several makeshift barge slips serving the Barmah Forest. Sloan stood in the rain two hours because the loggers he was talking to stood passively about in the rain. The bravado paid off. They introduced him to the mill boss. When Sloan casually dropped the name of his prior contact, the top gun, this chap sold him five thousand feet of box and two of red gum.

Now if he just had some money to pay for it . . .

For a few minutes more, until the *Industry*'s captain completed his tea, Sloan watched curious pontoon rafts—platforms floated by two rowboat hulls, it appeared—bring out the massive logs. Red gum, his new logger chums explained, was too dense to float. They cut the timber during the dry season and marked it with withes. Now they were hauling it out upside down, as it were, suspended beneath the pontoon rafts. One at a time, log by log, the bounty of the forest was loaded upon barges to be carried to the mills.

Where was Gus? Sloan couldn't wait to call him on his casual promise that the river never floods like this two years running. More important, infinitely more important, where was Sam?

The *Industry* pushed out into channel, seeking snags and other navigational hazards. Woodlands lined the bank on both sides. But even in this shelter, the wind buffeted the husky boat about.

Five thousand feet of box, two of red gum. The mental math involved was child's play. All the wine in South Australia would not pay for that much lumber. The red gum he could sell in Sydney; he knew to whom; but five thousand board feet of box was four too many. What could he have been thinking of?

As his shining-bright deal of an hour ago dulled to lead, Sloan's spirit dropped, and dropped. Already he owed the world. Now he owed twice the world, and no clear way to recoup. So jaded was he that he could be taken for a drongo by a man with half his brain. That mill boss had just shellacked him.

Did he fancy himself a prudent businessman? Where did he dig up that foolish notion? Every business decision he ever made came to no good. This was just the latest and most blatant example of all.

He almost failed to recognize the temporary Barmah Mission slip. The flood was forcing it farther and farther back into the trees. No wonder Otis built so far from the river; had he built near shore, he'd be under water now.

The *Industry* never did come to a complete stop. Sloan leaped from the moving deck onto the shaky little floating pier and almost dumped himself in the drink. He waved perfunctorily at the departing boat and started walking through the wind and rain. She had to be here. She wasn't anywhere else.

He blurted out a choice expletive as his hat left his head. Before he could grab it, it sailed in a graceful, tumbling arc right into the water. That hat was an old friend. Why didn't he care more that it was lost?

Slippery, gummy mud clung in big globs to his boots and made footing treacherous on this crude track up from the river. The treetops swayed high above him. Somewhere in the woodland to his right, a limb went crashing down. Cold, steely rain pelted his face. What a miserable evening! But it was worth it if he could find Sam.

As the trees thinned, the wind's fury picked up. And now Sloan trudged through a bared, open stump field, with no bushes higher than his waist. Almost certainly the next big gust would rip the hair right off his head. Possibly it would take his head the way it had taken his hat.

The rain-slicked tin roofs up ahead reflected what little light the sky offered. They were the only bright new thing in the whole district. This place was a dump. Dismal. There were a thousand ways Otis could find glory easier than to put all that hard work into this rubbish pile of a place. Look at the makeshift buildings, the coarse-plowed ground. Their pea plants weren't up more than a couple of inches.

The wind shifted and renewed its determination to make Sloan's life as miserable as possible. It drove the rain right through to his skin.

He paused in the middle of the dooryard. The government house up ahead looked deserted. Nothing stirred around the outbuildings. Except for half a dozen sheep in a brake behind the summer kitchen, not a living thing moved. But wait! Four or five saddled horses stood dozing in the lee of that squarish stone building. With the wind buffeting his face, Sloan walked over.

Try as it would, the wind could not sweep away the music growing louder as Sloan approached. This amateurish stone building, this mason's nightmare, must be a church or chapel. The stonemasonry might not be the grandest, but their choir was second to none.

Chapel, hymns—this must be a worship service. Sam had been talking lately about some sort of new experience of faith. If she were anywhere near, she'd surely be here. Cole stepped inside.

It was a chapel, all right—a stark, colorless parody of a respectable church. No vestry linens, no ornamentation, no fine woodwork graced this interior. Peeled poles supported the rafters, for obviously no one was trusting the weight of the roof to these shaky walls. The tin sheeting had been nailed directly to the bare rafters. Nail holes leaked here and there. The choir, most of them abos, wore plain old clothes. No choir robes, not even a choir loft. They stood on risers behind the lectern.

A dozen people formed the choir; they sounded like a hundred, clear and pure. That they competed successfully with the rain drumming on the tin roof was a miracle in itself.

In the main room, three dozen abos with at least as many children sat on benches and stools in ragged rows. Sloan spotted seven white faces, and none of them was Sam.

In spite of himself, Sloan practically memorized the words of the chorus; this was the third time the choir had repeated it; *Praise the Lord! Praise the Lord! Let the earth hear His voice! Praise the Lord! Praise the Lord! Let the people rejoice! O come to the Father through Jesus the Son, and give Him the glory, great things He has done.*

Amid a cloud of enthusiastic "Amens" from the congregation, the choir wandered off rather willy-nilly and sat down. Otis stood up, beaming happiness the way the sun pours out light.

He stepped to the lectern. "To God be the glory. Yes. The woman who wrote the words to that magnificent hymn of praise has been blind since infancy. Her name is Fanny Crosby. She's written many songs, wonderful songs, and she does it all within her memory, for she cannot see to read or write. What she does see, friends, is God's majesty. Beyond eyesight, and through His Son, that vision is available to any person. Let us pray."

All heads save Sloan's bowed. Did Otis spot him? If he did, the missionary gave no sign. This was as good a time as any to leave. Sloan backed toward the door.

The door opened behind him; a gust of wind cut through his wet clothes and reminded him he was getting chilled standing around. A black family—mum, father, and three small children—stepped inside and pushed the door shut. Then they just stood there like doorstops, blocking the way.

Otis's voice could probably charm a snake right out of its hole. In normal conversation the fellow's enunciation was smooth enough. But when he raised the volume in order to fill the room, his voice took on a ringing clarity.

"Our reading is from Jeremiah nine, verse one and following. This first verse is one of several that earned Jeremiah the nickname 'Weeping Prophet.' "

Sloan should just elbow his way through that family and leave. Suddenly Toby—bridegroom Toby—appeared from nowhere at his side. His teeth gleaming in a wide smile, he gripped Sloan by the arm. Still grinning, he piloted Sloan to a bench and sat him down. Polly smiled beside him just as happily. The bench was warm; Toby had just given up his own seat.

The last thing in the world Sloan wanted was a seat. He wanted out. A whistling gust shook the tin roof; it thundered and rattled above the roar of the rain. On second thought, it was fairly snug and warm in here.

It occurred to Sloan he had been wrong. Otis could not possibly be in this for the glory. There was nothing glorious about this place. And yet, it wasn't quite the dump Sloan first took it to be.

Otis was still reading. "Take ye heed every one of his neighbor, and trust ye not in any brother; for every brother will utterly supplant, and every neighbor will walk with slanders. And they will deceive every one his neighbor, and will not speak the truth: they have taught their tongue to speak lies, and weary themselves to commit iniquity."

Get tired committing sin? Actually, the prophet wasn't too far off there. Sloan had never thought of it that way before, but it was true. He knew, for he had committed sin more than once. It was not restful.

"They refuse to know me, saith the Lord. Therefore thus saith the Lord of hosts, Behold, I will melt them, and try them; for how shall I do for the daughter of my people. . . ?"

Not just *don't know me*. He said *refuse to know me*. A considered decision.

Otis held up a smudgy, unremarkable rock. "This is iron ore." He held aloft a gleaming steel knife, the kind of all-purpose knife abos love. "To make this sharp, useful steel, you have to melt this rock. That is, you make it into a liquid that pours, like water. For that you need a special furnace that makes more heat than a campfire. The iron you want separates from the rock, the way cream separates out in milk. You pour off the molten iron and let it cool down into metal, and you throw away the useless rock. That useless rock is called dross."

Sloan smiled to himself. Of course Otis must explain it. Not only did these people know nothing of smelting, probably not a one of them had ever seen anything melt, except maybe some morning frost.

Otis flipped to the back of his Bible and started quoting from first Cor—something, about building on the foundation of Jesus Christ and trying all the foundations with fire. Something like that. Like Otis said before, it all fit together. Jeremiah: *I shall melt them and try them*—the beleaguered prophet, weeping for his people who refused to know God. There was a beauty and poignancy to the Bible Sloan had not suspected before.

Now Otis was re-reading the part about how no one can trust anyone else. When Sam had refused Sloan's offer of marriage (it seemed like painful ages ago) she said, "I cannae trust ye." She was right. Sloan proved her right. He could not be trusted. Neither did he dare trust Frobel, who might well be bent for retribution. Every person he knew, including himself, with the notable exception of Sam, was out to advance his or her own interests. He certainly could not trust shallow, selfish Hilary. Jeremiah had Cole Sloan pegged exactly.

And Jeremiah condemned all untrustworthiness to destruction.

"Those of you who are believers—those of you who embrace Jesus Christ as your Lord and master: Paul and Jeremiah are talking to *you!* They're telling you that everything you do that isn't grouse, that isn't done for Jesus, is going to get burned up. And don't you doubt a minute you aren't going to get blisters from the heat. You'll be tried, like this iron, until you're pure. What? You lied? You can't be trusted in everything? You change your ways! God doesn't want that!"

Otis was staring straight at Sloan. Out of this roomful of people, he singled out Sloan. "Now, for those of you who have not committed your lives to Jesus Christ—" He leaned on the lectern. "Somebody must have told those sheep out behind the kitchen what we had in mind for them because one of them bolted yesterday. Jumped the brake and headed for Queensland. There are two kinds of strays, you know—the kind that sort of wanders off accidentally, like a child wanders away from camp, and the kind that goes galloping off in a determined way."

Sloan had mentioned the stray sheep idea once, and he never said anything about it other than those two words. How did Otis manage to read his mind?

"You're both equally lost. Ah, but Jesus Christ is the Lamb of God, and the Lamb is going to take a bride. His church. Hear the invitation: 'You are invited to the marriage feast of the Lamb, to be held in the King's hall in His heavenly kingdom. Pure wedding garments will be provided.' "

Sloan's body, his mind, his spirit—all begged him, *Get out of here! Now!* Agitated. That's how he felt. Agitated. Anxious. Upset. He didn't want to hear this.

Otis's voice rang above the wind and the rattling roof. "That's one invitation you want to RSVP right away! But believe it or not, there are some here today who will answer,

'I decline your invitation to the wedding feast. I prefer being cast into outer darkness where I can wail and gnash my teeth. I don't want your spotless wedding garment. Count me out!' Would you ever respond to the King that way? Not if you know what's good for you."

They refuse to know me.

Sam had met Jesus Christ. She said so.

Vinson and Otis knew Him. Marty and Pearl Frobel knew Him, though Sloan could not remember how Frobel phrased it in the stall at the track that day. Sam's sister knew Him.

The tin roof rattled and clanked. Rain came blopping down faster than a simple drip. No one seemed to care.

Sloan had been so engrossed that he had not noticed the choir gathering behind Otis, back up on its risers. With the choir as his accompaniment, Otis lifted a solid, golden tenor voice in the loveliest song Sloan had ever heard. "Softly and tenderly, Jesus is calling" it began.

The vibrant voice beckoned "Come home, come home, ye who are weary, come home" as the choir sang a sweet, echoing counterpoint. "Earnestly, tenderly, Jesus is calling, calling, O sinner, come home!"

Weary. Of all the things Sloan was, including straying, he was weary. Intensely weary.

"Though we have sinned He has mercy and pardon, pardon for you and for me. . . ." The man's voice seized Sloan, compelled him. The whole idea of rest, of pardon gripped him. What if it was true? Sloan needed pardon!

As the choir repeated the last verse and chorus, Otis raised his hands in prayer. The music lifted the prayer and the prayer lifted the music, higher than either could go alone. Was it possible Sloan could pray, and that his prayer would get past the ceiling? He had never in his life prayed. Who'd listen?

With a long, moaning shriek, the right half of the roof gave way. A whole sheet peeled back. It ripped loose the one beside it and clanged against the intact side of the roof, disappearing noisily on the straining wind. The sheet next to it banged, one side whanging loose against the rafters. Rain came cascading in by the bucket.

No one seemed to notice. The building was being torn asunder and no one cared, least of all Otis. The prayer continued, for the saved and for the lost, for these people and for those. The wind howled, the rain came pelting in gleefully to drench the worshipers.

As prayer and choir ended together, the whole congregation launched unbidden into another tune Sloan had never heard. "Blessed be the tie that binds," they sang, "our hearts in Christian love."

The song ended. Instantly laughing and milling, the chapelful of celebrants mingled beneath the driving rain. Sloan sat. He could do nothing more. He wasn't numb now; he was beaten, as if with a club. Too many sorrows weighed on him. Too many unexpected and unusual sensations had just assaulted him. Too many ideas clamored to be heard, ideas he had been resisting arduously for a lifetime. It all, all, all was pounding upon him at once.

A brown presence hovered at his side. He extended his hand mechanically—not a handshake, but a reaching. "Otis. Help me."

Chapter Nineteen

Tangled Threads

Rain and wind battered the roof of the government house, but somehow Sloan felt safer here. Maybe this roof had been nailed on by different carpenters. He listened to the steady drumming and considered how cold it sounded compared with the warm crackle of the fire before him. A gust of wind back-drafted the chimney, puffing smoke into the room.

"You'll have to add some more height to your chimney." This box-frame-and-rawhide chair felt remarkably comfortable. Sloan stretched his legs out toward the gentle fire.

"That and about seventy-eleven other projects." Reginald sobered. "I went through a deep, deep valley of doubt there for a while, when so many people took off on walkabout. I can't express the joy I feel now that they've returned—a sense of wresting victory from defeat."

Sloan looked at the mild-bearded face, the warm eyes. "I can't imagine you plagued by doubts. You're supposed to be a man of God. Isn't doubt beneath your dignity, so to speak?"

Reginald's laugh rang warm and genuine. "Uncertainty is human. You'll never vanquish it completely. Expect it."

"I'm human, all right. When your roan went lame with that slice on its pastern, I—"

"I never thanked you properly for that, to my shame.

I've come to like that old roan, as humorless and sluggish as he is, not to mention that we need the horse desperately and could ill afford to lose him. We're grateful."

"I didn't do it for the roan, or even for Sam. I did it to get one up on you. It gave me great pleasure to show you up. Intense satisfaction. That's hardly an attitude worth thanking me for."

"The fact that you confess it now is a beautiful testimony to your change of heart."

Change of heart. Sloan's mind and emotions churned in such turmoil he didn't know what his heart was changing to, or from. He was too smart, too modern, to fall for this religious nonsense. It must have been a moment of weakness. And yet, he knew that what he had just experienced was powerful and real. And that in itself confused him. What a mess he was inside!

It would help if he could have some clear sign of some sort that this experience was genuine. All his life he had doubted God's existence—or ignored it—and now God had put the hard word on him. He was either going to have to accept the Almighty or admit he had just been deceived. And yet, he was not one to believe in signs, not when random circumstance so clearly directed the fortunes of men. Or did it? More confusion.

"Reginald, you're probably not the one to be asking, but what do I do for Sam, to make amends? How do I make up for that?"

"Make up for what?"

Sloan stared. "She didn't tell you?"

Reginald frowned. "A lot of things have happened to her, all hard. The jobs especially. You weren't a part of any of the troubles she told me about. Curious, in a twisted way. Her trials began in earnest after she came to the Lord, and yours multiplied before you yielded to Him." He shrugged. "Just an observation."

Here sat the man Sam was considering marrying. Why

didn't she tell this Reginald everything on her heart; why wasn't she open with him? Hope stirred anew, hope absolutely unmerited.

"You talked about confession and restitution, Reginald. You're saying it's necessary for me to correct the effects of my sins as much as possible."

"Correct the effects of sin. Good concept. Yes."

"Those commissioners have got tickets on themselves, but they aren't stupid. If they don't know Drummond's a dill, they'll soon figure the fool out. I'll go to them directly. Tell them I lied for personal reasons. Give them the drum. Whether or not it gets her job back for her, at least I can wash some of the mud off her reputation."

Reginald was staring at him oddly.

"Now what do I do about Beckerstaff?"

"Who?"

"A man who has done me great wrong and threatens to ruin me."

"Nothing illegal or extra-legal. Let God and the law handle him. Also, restitution for your transgressions against others should take precedence over your actions against him, if it comes down to priorities."

"I see what you're saying. I filed a statement and complaint with the constable. He said he'd send it on, but I doubt anything will come of it. He's Victorian police and Beckerstaff's in New South Wales." Sloan snapped forward and propped both elbows on his knees. He stared a while at the fire as it danced its lazy saraband, and he stared at the light patterns it cast upon his clasped hands. What could he be thinking of, exalting himself? He learned to treat the commoner horse problems, like that infected pastern, from Clyde Armbruster. If as a boy he hadn't spent all that time behind the track . . .

Clyde Armbruster. Somehow, he must buy Clyde another horse, a good horse; ideally, the colt he covets. And John Butts . . .

"Some sins can't be corrected. Dead is dead."

"You mentioned once that Samantha thinks you killed a man on purpose. I asked, 'Did you?' and you didn't answer. So, did you?"

"Yes." An anchor of weight lifted from him. Another anchor of weight remained. His hands began vibrating subtly as the enormity of that moment crashed down upon him. *Yes. God forgive me, yes.* When two hours ago Sloan asked forgiveness for all his sins, and professed his faith in Jesus Christ, did that include the death of John Butts? Reason said yes, but his heart could not squirm out from under the guilt. He would need much advice and guidance for that one.

He sat up straight. "I'd like to catch a downstream boat as early as possible tomorrow. I have things to do. And for once, they're not things to further Cole Sloan's dreams of empire."

———

"This is kinda fun." Marty Frobel leaned back against a crate of melons and stretched his legs out along *Echuca Charlene*'s deck. "And here I always thought that if you couldn't get there on a horse, it wasn't worth going."

Samantha plopped down cross-legged beside him. "Sure'n I've fallen in love with these crotchety things. With rail freight so cheap, and the railways being built all over the Riverina, I fear the old boat days are numbered. A sad day indeed when the last of them be beached on some mud bank."

The trees lining the riverbank stood several feet in water. Clumps of dry yellow weeds in their branches told Marty that this flood was nothing compared to some past deluge that swept flotsam along that high up.

Practically overhead, the steam whistle blared.

Marty jumped. "What does that mean?"

Samantha hadn't moved a muscle. "Either we be ten

minutes away from Albury or Captain Runyan is greeting someone he knows along the shore."

"What are you going to do next, Sam? Know yet?"

"Nae. I thought of waiting about a bit, to see if they might offer me old position, but chances be slim to nil. I be nae deferential enough to men, so I've been told."

"Neither is Pearl. It's one of the nicest things about her." *Pearl. Soon.* At Albury he would take the train into Sydney and join Pearl. In a way he wished the Murray flowed to Sydney. These noisy, dirty, vibrating boats were a lot more enjoyable than the noisy, dirty, vibrating trains.

Sam tucked her long black skirt around her ankles as she drew her knees up. Marty was not an ankle-ogler, as were some, but he did notice there was not a thing wrong with hers. She crossed her arms across her knees and rested her chin on them. "If ye be torn betwixt the head and the heart, Marty, which wins?"

He considered the question a moment, not to frame an answer but to nut out why she should ask it. "My heart's clever enough to make my head think it does."

She smiled and lapsed into thought.

Marty had it figured out, he was pretty sure. "I got a telegram from Pearl as I was checking out of the hotel. She arranged another deal with one of the contacts Sloan gave us. That's three now. He'll have some bonzer brokerage commissions waiting for him when he gets back to town. Big sales. That doesn't make him an endearing marriage prospect, I know, but it shows he has his good points." He glanced at her. "That it?"

"I would nae have guessed I be so transparent." She shook her lovely head. "Why did ye come to Echuca?"

"To see Sloan and get his help with our problems. I guess it's because he grew up in Sydney's high society that he knows so many people. And he has new ideas. Also, to check out the competition; the Riverina is Australia's biggest wool-and-mutton producer, and we'd like to sell a little wool and mutton ourselves. And then, just to look at the place. I've never seen a river this big before, let alone floated on it."

Somewhere back there the firedoor clanked. Thunks and crackles suggested more wood was being tossed into the boiler. Train locomotives were just as noisy when being fired, but passengers were considerably more removed from the action. Here you almost sat right on top of the boiler. It provided a sense of immediacy lacking on trains.

Sam stared pensively at the passing scene. Did she see its beauty at all? "*Through the Looking Glass*. The queen makes Alice run ever so hard just to stay in one place. I feel like that."

"Yair. Still, it's better'n being bored." He pondered the original question. "Head or heart. Why does it have to be either/or? Why can't it be both? Most either/or choices turn out to be some third thing anyway." He shrugged. "Go with both."

She twisted around to study him. "Aye, of course! I believe 'tis somewhere in the gospel of St. John, Jesus promises abundance. I've aught but to accept it!"

The whistle hooted again, and the paddles changed their rhythm. Pearl. Pearl and home—that was abundance!

Marty smiled. "Does that mean Sloan has a chance with you?"

"Nae." Her face darkened. "He cannae be trusted."

"Who can?"

"Ye know what I mean."

"But you're missing what *I* mean. Nobody's perfect. You work with imperfection. You don't wait for the perfect hand, you play the hand you're dealt."

"Ye dinnae ken the sin he's done!"

"We all have, one way or another. That's what the gospel's all about. What if he were forgiven?"

"Eh, if only he were!"

Another hair lost. Horace Beckerstaff scowled at the loose hair on his lapel and plucked it away. He paused at his reflection in a shop window and smoothed the few hairs left on his balding pate. Hair loss had to be related to genius—how many bald derelicts did one run across? But he rued his fate anyway. In a bad mood he continued his walk to work.

A small man with a bushy mustache was polishing the brass handrail as Beckerstaff approached the steps to his building foyer. The man looked Italian. The very thought of "Italian" set his anger to boiling all over again. Ship the Kanakas out of north Queensland, ship the Italians in, all at Beckerstaff's expense.

Sugarlea. What had looked like such an eagle of a deal turned out to be an albatross around his neck.

The moment he stepped inside he could feel it—a tension in the air, almost a danger. What was this? He paused beside his secretary's desk.

"Your mail, sir." Richard Thomas had served as a clerk for three years and as his personal secretary for seven. The man stood up, as he always did when Beckerstaff approached, and passed across a sheaf of letters. His voice today was tight, guarded.

Beckerstaff took the sheaf without looking at it. "Anything from Vernon Bower?"

"No, sir."

"I haven't heard a pip from that lout in nearly a month. I'd better not receive word he lost him."

"Sir . . ." The man closed his mouth again. "Nothing, sir." He sat down.

Beckerstaff strode on down the marbled hall to his office. He swung the doors open and stopped. "Who the blazes are you?"

The neatly dressed gentleman displayed a badge. "Detective Inspector Marsh, New South Wales Police. Horace Beckerstaff?"

Behind him another man entered, in the tunic and helmet of the rank-and-file policeman. The man laid a hand on Beckerstaff's shoulder.

The inspector's voice purred the litany; he'd done this a thousand times. "We've reason to believe, Mr. Beckerstaff, you are involved in a conspiracy to inflict harassment and bodily harm. We're authorized to examine your files. Specifically, we are seeking correspondence to and from a Vernon Bower and associates regarding a Cole Sloan. Symonds, begin with the *B*'s."

Beckerstaff glanced involuntarily at his near cabinet. He didn't mean to do that. "Bower? Don't believe anything that crook told you! It's nonsense!"

Marsh's voice didn't change a bit. "Be advised we shall be writing down everything you say, Mr. Beckerstaff. Be advised also, this is a joint investigation with the Victorian Police and the security officials at the racetrack here in town." The man held up a packet of papers. "Interesting connections with an unprovoked attack occurring at the track. Unsolved. We don't like unsolved cases, sir, and the Victorian officers don't appreciate Sydney's problems being exported to their jurisdiction. You'd best make contact with your solicitor."

Samantha braced herself in the doorway of the wheelhouse. *Echuca Charlene* seemed so stable when one sat on her deck, but she tended to sway a bit up here in the second story, so to speak. She watched the river ahead, felt its surging power. She enjoyed the river nearly as much on a dull, moody, overcast day as in sparkling sun.

Captain Runyan worked his wheel this morning as his steersman fired the boiler below them. "Insurance carriers run the rivers now, lass, and that's the truth of it. A prime example: A skipper is enjoined from leaving the established channel. Now peer about you. Just how does one recognize the established channel in a section of the countryside such as this?"

"I see y'r point, sir. Nae trees to mark the banks, and the water spread out across the plain. How *do* ye find the channel?"

"Magic," the whiskered captain whispered hoarsely. "Another example: You recall we had to tie up come true darkness, and could not enter again into our journey westward until first light this morning."

"Ye be a one-watch boat. Meself assumed that to be the reason."

"No. Insurance carriers. We are forbidden to navigate downstream at night. The sad fate of any downstream-bound vessel is to tie up and sit idle, watching the play of sulphur light upon the trees and banks as her luckier counterparts forge their way upstream. We may navigate upstream by headlamp, as we ourselves did on the run to Albury, but not downstream."

"Ye'll nae gull me into thinking there be nae reason for such a rule."

He chuckled. "It's far harder, keeping to the channel and staying ahead of the current, while moving downstream. You see, we must without fail and at all times move faster than the current, or we lose steerage. There are few fates dreaded more than riding a current helplessly."

"Y're towing a loaded wool barge. Might that make it all the more difficult?"

"Quick lass! Clever lass. Dragging the beast down from Albury has been easy so far; once we pass the narrows, the game will move into a new level of play."

"New water moves downstream about thirty miles a day. That be nae much more than a mile each hour."

He nodded. "That's the usual speed, with allowance for variation on different stretches at different times, and depending upon the volume flow already in the channel. Yes. To maintain control of this noble craft, I must surpass in speed the normal current, plus the press of any new water coming down. And as you can so easily surmise, the river is rising still."

"So the insurance carriers be nae so willy, after all."

He snorted. "I prefer to look upon them as the scum of the earth, since I've been paying the piper for years, although I have never possessed the want or need to make a claim. *Charlene*, bless her bollards, has had nary a sick day in her life."

They cruised in silence—if *Charlene*'s huffing and puffing and clanging and creaking could be called silence. The bare, open land closed in, and the familiar trees appeared. Soon the shores below the water were marked with wattle, red gum and box. Along most stretches the shore itself still protruded above the flood.

Samantha looked out the back window at their wool barge. It loomed as big as a building off their stern. Five tiers of huge bales, massive bales, made her taller than wide. Her steersman perched on top of the load, three-fourths of the way toward the back. Her wheel, as Samantha understood it, was mounted on loose boards. As a tier was added the wheel was set on top of the load and the steering cables lengthened appropriately. Samantha was not the least certain she'd like to be plopped out on top of a monster like that, exposed like a shag on a rock.

The captain reached for the cord and blasted his whistle.

Samantha happened to glance back. "Hold, sir! Ye've lost y'r barge! 'Tis adrift!"

The hirsute skipper snickered. "My steersman just turned her loose, like a retired old cab horse sent to pasture. She'll drift along down the way and we'll catch up to her after we've called at the mission slip. It would never do to try to drag her through the trees here out of channel.

Certainly we wouldn't want to displease the high and mighty moguls in the insurance industry, aye?"

"If ye cannae steer *Echuca Charlene* when adrift, how can y'r barge steersman?"

"Magic."

The hulking barge drifted silently, surely, down the channel and around a bend.

Charlene scuffed past low-hanging box trees. Leafy branches slashed at Samantha. Although the boat reversed her paddles early, Samantha was absolutely convinced they would overshoot the Barmah Mission wharf. At the last possible moment, Captain Runyan wrenched his wheel around, then wrenched it back again. The little boat slipped sideways out of the current and eased, churning mightily, into the trees to the right. Samantha had learned that rivermen did not use nautical terms like *port* or *starboard, bow* and *stern*. If it was off to the right, they said so.

"Ah, the pain and shame of it! I am about to be castigated for an error of judgment voiced not two weeks ago when I told your Sydneyside businessman friend that this would be a low-water year. My spotless reputation for prognostication will be sullied the moment he opens his cavernous mouth." Captain Runyan pointed toward the bank beyond the floating slip.

Samantha's businessman friend stood on the shore beside the slip with his cavernous mouth gaping open. Apparently he did not expect her here. But then, he was the last person she would expect on the mission wharf. Beside him stood Reginald and Ellen, very close together. Ellen looked happy, even triumphant, and Reginald absolutely glowed. Samantha was not certain she wanted to see them. She was positive she did not want to see Cole.

He shook hands warmly with Reginald, nodding and smiling. He and Ellen hugged, albeit with propriety. She handed him the mailbag.

The backwash from *Charlene*'s paddles set the floating wharf to lunging. Cole jogged the length of it like a drunken man. *Charlene*'s paddle wheel housing skimmed past the wharf, her tail dipped toward the slip, and he came aboard with a wild, theatrical leap. *Charlene* headed back out into channel.

Cole came up the tight little ladder to the wheelhouse immediately. Samantha stepped inside, and he braced himself in the door.

"G'day, Sam," he smiled broadly. As he reached across her to shake Captain Runyan's hand, he was still smiling. And that smile was different. Cole was different. Samantha did not know how, but he was *different*, not the same man who did—did that to her.

He must have heard about the fat commissions awaiting him in Sydney. But that wasn't likely. How could he? Marty had been unable to reach him, and news of the latest deal came just as Marty was leaving.

His breath lingered right by her ear. "Sam, I've been looking for you. I'd like to speak to you privately."

Why put off the inevitable? "As ye wish."

He backed down the little ladder and held her hand as she descended. She folded her legs and settled down on the deck next to the paddle wheel housing. He took the cue and hunkered down beside her.

"I looked everywhere for you," he began. "Finally, I figured you must've gone out to Barmah. When you weren't there I didn't know where to look. Reginald said, 'Pray to find her.' I did, and there you were in the wheelhouse."

"Pray to. . . ?" She gaped at him. Pray? *Cole?*

He was looking out across the water. "Gus in a hurry?"

"He be catching up to a wool barge he took on at Albury."

"It doesn't feel right—or is that just my imagination?"

"Then 'tis me own imagination as well. But Captain Runyan turned the wheel over to his steersman and the captain be fiddling about in back, so it cannae be too much out of kilter."

She knew more about it than he. He let it go. "Where were you, Sam, if I may ask?"

"Marty Frobel wanted to ride the river—there be nae like this in his country—so meself arranged privately for him with Captain Runyan, who was taking melons to Albury. The good captain suggested I come along for the company, and delighted I am that I did. 'Twas a delightful trip. Relaxing. Being unemployed, I could do that, ye see." She watched his face a moment. "That be an ironic reference, in case ye dinnae notice."

"I noticed." He pursed his lips. "Reginald suggested looking for threads—ways God arranges something completely unexpected. If you hadn't disappeared up the river to Albury, I wouldn't have gone to Barmah. . . ." His voice trailed off.

"Cole, why be ye here?"

"On my way back to Echuca, to make amends. I may not be able to restore your job, but I'll do my best."

"Why the change of heart?"

"Change of heart. That's it. Remember how you explained to me about your own change of heart? The difference between being a Christian and being a Christian? I've experienced that myself. And I can't explain what happened or why. But I did."

Those incomparable opalescent eyes studied him. Why wasn't she elated? Why wasn't she gushing *Oh, that's so wonderful!*? The eyes fell away. Disappointment ripped into Sloan. He expected a happier reaction than this.

"You seemed to want me to at the time, Sam. Changed your mind?"

"Nae, by nae means. But, ah . . ."

He scooted in closer. "But what?"

"Meself told ye in the long past, I cannae trust ye. I know y'r ways, Cole Sloan, and the devious way ye think. Y'r heart may be brand new, as Reginald explains it, or ye may for some reason be saying the one thing ye ken would sway me."

"You think I'm lying."

"Nae, 'tis more difficult than that. I've nae way of knowing whether ye be lying or nae. Sometimes ye do, sometimes ye dinnae. And sometimes . . ." Her voice caught. "Sometimes ye say naething atal, which can be the most telling lie. I've learned to me sorrow I cannae trust the words ye speak."

The gall of this woman! Here he was trying his best to pour his heart out to her and she was snubbing his efforts! She turned, then, presenting her profile as she studied the brown water and the rushing river. What a lovely face, serene and sad.

Sad. Think how many times he had made her sad. Why should she believe him? He didn't believe him either, at least not completely. In his desire to sway this woman worth loving, he could be fooling himself in some colossal way. What if this faith, so-called, were a sham of his own mind, generated not by the Holy Spirit but by his yearning for a woman who believed in such things?

Cole Sloan was not one to despair, but he did now. He had damaged his trustworthiness irreparably. He might as well give it away; he was never going to win the trust of this solid, practical lady—and for good reason. She had no reason to trust him now. And the sense of loss nearly drove him to tears.

He shuddered. "You're the only woman I've ever met who actually deserves a perfect man. Nearer perfect than me, at any rate. And you're right. I can't be trusted. I want to change. I want to be a man known for my word. I never have been, but from now on . . . Maybe someday . . ." Someday. Tomorrow.

She was studying him. Not staring. Studying. "I be nae perfect either."

"Who is? You know what I mean—oh." He dug into his pocket. "The postmaster decided I'd probably see you before he did, so he asked me to give you this copy of a telegram you received." He handed her the thin yellow envelope.

She ripped it open, paused, grinned. " 'Tis from Chris. Fine news! 'Roller-skating goat a complete success.' "

Chapter Twenty

Flood and Crescendo

Dateline Sydney:

Miss Linnet Connolly, popularly known as the Adelaide Lark, arrived in town today to commence rehearsals for Ricardo Giambone's lavish Easter production of Handel's beloved *Messiah*. Miss Connolly, a musical prodigy discovered and nurtured at the University of Adelaide, has just completed a victorious concert tour through the Riverina. When an interviewer suggested that playing to small audiences in bush hamlets was not exactly an accolade, she replied through her spokesman, "Should these people, who are the backbone of Australia's primary industry, expect and receive anything less than the best simply because there are fewer of them?"

Who would guess that hundreds and hundreds of people would turn out for an afternoon performance? Extraordinary!

Even more extraordinary, look at them rise and applaud! These people were Sydneyites, the most sophisticated, cultured, discerning arts patrons in all Australia. See how enthusiastically they responded to the Giambone *Messiah*! And here stood Linnet in the heart of it, basking in the footlights, receiving accolade. Extraordinary? Far more than that. Fantastic!

Linnet felt her cheeks flush as she raised an arm in

gratitude. Her smile threatened to break her face in half, so wide and irrepressible was it. She looked to the wings. There stood Chris with a grin as broad as her own. He was clapping wildly, and with his eager clamor was saying, *I believe in you! I love you!*

Chris. Dear Chris!

The singers exited stage right as the crowd quieted.

Mr. Giambone hugged her, burying her in his massive bulk. "Tomorrow, fair lass, you shall be the toast of Sydney, soon as the newspapers and the *Bulletin* write you up! And no woman deserves it more! How magnificent you were! This will be the finest Giambone production ever!" He bubbled a few more exclamations, but Linnet didn't hear them. She could only see Chris's face, that marvelous, glowing face. He loved her. He approved her performance. That was all that mattered.

Chris pushed in beside her to pump Mr. Giambone's hand. "We appreciate immensely your trust in us, sir, in Linnet here. Her career is well on the road thanks to you."

"Now that you mention . . ." Mr. Giambone received a towel from some faceless minion and began wiping at his makeup and perspiration. "We are taking *Handel* back to Europe, to Britain. The Adelaide Lark here must accompany us. You will, will you not? You and your swain here, of course."

Linnet's world hesitated in its spinning. To Britain . . . Extraordinary was hardly describing it.

Chris beamed like the sun. "We would be honored! An international tour."

Linnet's heart was pounding. "Ye mean London?"

"Dublin, then London. We're setting it up now."

She glanced at Chris. For months he had counseled her to act boldly, to assume her place as a world-class soprano. Now she garnered her courage for the boldest request she had ever made. "Please, sir, be there a chance we might do a performance in Cork as well?"

Chris, bless him, picked it up instantly. "Of course! Her

family lives in Cork, and her grandmother is very frail. The trip to Dublin would tax the old lady sorely. Is it possible?"

Mr. Giambone was laughing. "That, lass, is what makes you so charming. No pretense. No false airs, nor false modesty. And the first thing you think of is your family. Of course. We can schedule there as well. Your parents and grandmama, eh?"

"Aye, sir. And most particularly, if she be still alive, a nun at me old school."

We're coming, Sister Bertrand, that you might learn how much your patient love has wrought. For with your generosity and caring you gave me more than you will ever know.

Sloan was not a boat enthusiast. He loved driving a snappy little sulky, or a shiny, pin-striped enameled trap, and he enjoyed the blatant elegance of an open brougham. He didn't mind trains. Boats were something else—dull, pedestrian, sluggish.

Listen to *Echuca Charlene*'s steam engine strain and struggle. She had taken her wool barge back under tow hours ago. Now she was roaring along all out, canting a bit on the curves, and still she wasn't going much faster than the pace of a man running.

Sloan was not a rain enthusiast, either. He had abhorred the rains during those years at Sugarlea. And it was raining now, inside and out. Outside, the rain was drumming on *Charlene*'s deck and dripping off the roof three feet in front of his nose. Inside, Sam was in a pensive mood. She sat near Cole's feet under the shelter of the roof, saying hardly a word. She professed the same sort of new faith in Jesus Christ that he had just discovered. He had hoped her reaction to his story would be jubilant. No such luck. If anything, his news deepened her introspection.

Sloan sprawled in a nest of firewood that just happened to be shaped more or less like a chair seat. He shifted a bit to avoid a sharp edge that had been poking him for the last ten minutes. "Know what hurt most of all? Having to accept your charity. Not having a brass razoo—anything— of my own. Every penny I spent was yours. Being forced to accept a woman's largess really twisted a knife in me. It's not natural, a man living off a woman's money."

She shrugged. "Meself prefers to think of it as a friend rendering temporary assistance to a friend. There was nae man-and-woman aspect to it, at least nae for me."

She stood up suddenly. For a moment she watched the trees moving by, and then she walked over to where, by craning her neck, she could glimpse the wool barge behind them. She was frowning.

"What's going on?"

"We be moving too fast to be so near Echuca, unless the rules have changed since last I traveled this stretch."

"*This* is too fast?" Sloan lurched to his feet, as much to give his body a rest from the woodpile as to see what was going on.

Somewhere in the nether reaches behind the firewood, the firebox door clanged shut. Steam hissed.

From up in the wheelhouse the steersman yelled something Sloan could not discern.

"A pox on all insurance brokers!" rang the cry from beyond the boiler. "May they follow each other in a long, unbroken queue to Abaddon! Head for the trees, Harry! Head for the trees!"

"Vic or Wales?"

"Vic!"

Charlene leaned left. As little as Sloan knew about riverboats, he knew that normally they didn't tilt.

From upriver came a distant plaintive cry—the barge steersman was calling to them.

Charlene convulsed in a single giant, jolting shudder. It threw Sloan against the paddle-wheel housing and flung Sam to her knees. Instantly glass shattered. Lions from hell roared as something from the rear of the vessel crashed into the woodpile. Sticks of firewood came scudding forward, filling the chair-shaped depression where Sloan had been sitting moments ago.

"Gus! Captain! Gus!" Sam screamed. She was as close to hysteria as Sloan had ever seen her. She charged past him and scrambled across a low spot in the wall of the firewood, heading toward the rear. Didn't she realize that was absolutely the most dangerous place she could be? Sloan reached out to grab her, but he wasn't quick enough. What could he do? He clambered over the wood, too.

The flimsy tongue-and-groove walls housing the boiler system were gone, blown away. Sloan thought that one of the walls, jammed against the woodpile, might be burning. Acrid black smoke billowed out so thickly he couldn't see anything for certain, nor could he say for sure what was afire and what was not. His eyes filled with tears.

Curled up in a corner by the firewood, Gus started to move. He shrieked and started flailing wildly as Sloan reached him. Sloan grabbed the first flying wrist he could get a hold of and began pulling. He had to get Gus out of here, out of the smoke, if nothing else. Already all three of them were coughing.

The firebox lid banged and fell away. No wonder the old man shrieked; ripped from the firebox, the nearly red-hot lid had slammed against the woodpile, thrusting loose firewood into Sloan's vacated chair, and then fallen to pin Gus's leg to the deck. Sloan grabbed a piece of wood and pried Gus loose. Sam had seized Gus's other arm. Together she and Cole hauled the old man up over the firewood and out to the rain-slick foredeck.

Blood and soot had made a mess of Gus's face. The bushy, silken beard was burned crisp, reduced to a black and stinking remnant of frizz. "My leg . . ." He reached out, groping toward his leg.

The firebox lid had gone through his dungarees almost

instantly, obliterating a big square patch. Half of Gus's shin and calf were quite literally cooked. He'd lose his leg below the knee; Sloan knew it, as no doubt Gus did.

The singed head shook. "Blew a tube. Musta blown a tube. Only thing would do that . . . blow the firebox like that . . ." Suddenly, as if a new man were inserted into the beaten old body, Gus came to life. His voice, though still shrill, took on a ring of authority. "We can save the old girl yet. There's a chain coiled under the wood in the back, Sloan. Drag it out, loop it over the back bollard and let it drag behind. It'll keep us nosed downstream."

As Sloan clawed his way back over the firewood to the rear of the boat, he heard Gus telling Sam, "That was the magic, lass. Dragging a chain behind us kept us in the channel back there. Helped us feel the bottom, hold to the deepest part. Same with the barge."

The chain. Here it was, a monstrous thing with links three inches long. Sloan flung aside the few sticks of wood stacked upon it. Bollard. What's a bollard? The stern post there, likely. He found the end of the chain and started pulling.

Charlene was definitely afire. Sloan could hear crackling beyond the expected noises of the firebox. Was this steady rain heavy enough to put it out? Probably not. The conky chain kept kinking and tangling.

With a whishing, sibilant crash, *Charlene* flipped her tail ninety degrees, yanking Sloan's feet right out from under him. He sprawled across that unforgiving, iron-hard pile of chain. Pieces of big, heavy, slimy wet wood fell across him. Wheelhousing! *Charlene* must have hit the trees, for she had just taken out her port wheelhousing and possibly the paddle wheel itself.

Cole tried to fight his way out of the debris. He finally freed his head, caught a swift look off the stern, and buried his head in his arms. The wool barge was coming on at full speed!

Rushing, smashing noise drowned out Sloan's thoughts. *Charlene* leaped beneath the blow. This boat was being torn apart, ripped into shreds out from under him. If he couldn't free himself, he'd drown in the next few minutes, dragged under in the wreckage. And Sam! *Oh, God, Sam!*

A few eternities of struggling got his head and shoulder free. The wool barge hung off their stern, listing badly. She had dumped her top tier of bales, her steering wheel and her steersman. The second tier was just now avalanching down off the massive wreck.

The towline must have snapped. *Charlene* spiralled away from her ruined barge. Sloan could feel them hit a solid, unyielding tree trunk, bounce off, reel away. It wasn't a tree; the iron bridge, like the shadow of death, drifted past above them. *Charlene* listed savagely; Cole lay head uphill, but he couldn't tell if he was crosswise or lengthwise on the deck.

This close to the wharf they might well be saved; half the town had surely been drawn by their roaring black cloud of smoke and were coming to help.

The steersman screamed above, and in the distance Sam cried out. With a splintering crash the upper-story wheelhouse tangled with a tree and lost. The whole superstructure was coming down on Sloan. With nowhere to go, he pulled in his head and shoulders and pressed himself farther under the slimy timbers that pinned him.

The world—nothing less than the whole world, it seemed—came smashing down upon him. There was no way he could come out on top this time. Any rescuers who came would come too late. He had that same feeling he felt when Bower and his nong mates beat the stuffing out of him in Adelaide. He faced certain defeat, and the certainty of it enraged him. This, though, was ultimate defeat. This time he was going to die.

Sam. Sloan deserved whatever befell him, but Sam . . . *Dear God, save Sam!*

Fire sirens howled somewhere afar.

Sloan squirmed back deeper beneath the tumbled, slimy beams as the debris above him shifted ominously. He felt no resistance. Nothing barred his way. He scooted back farther. One boot went under water. He scooted forward quickly.

God help me! God save Sam! The plea rang in his mind, poured out of his heart, and he couldn't tell if he was speaking the words aloud or not.

Wait! The water . . . *Charlene* was sinking; Sloan would find himself under water soon in any case, and he seemed to have a clear way behind. He scooted backward again.

Both his boots went under. About a yard of the deck had submerged, it seemed. His toes could feel the low little gunwale. Beyond that he could find nothing solid. He kept scooting. His legs were under. He kicked wildly and felt no debris, nothing to trap him. He took a deep, deep breath and shoved himself backward. His head went under, his belly scraped over the gunwale. He kicked and flailed, trying to clear the wreck. It would help if he could open his eyes, but they remained tightly shut and would not cooperate.

His head broke the surface. "Sam!" His lungs filled up; he gagged and coughed. "Sam!"

Charlene was still spiralling. Her bow came swinging around toward him. Still coughing, Cole thrust one arm out to fend it off. It caught him and swept him along.

Sam! Her lovely face, twisted and dirt-streaked, appeared right above him. Her eyes looked straight at him unseeing. Sam? *Charlene* hit something stationary; the boat jerked and shuddered and tilted to a steeper list. Sam came sliding. Sloan couldn't catch her in time, couldn't help her. She slid down on top of him and drove him under.

He couldn't let go of her. He kicked; he surfaced. She was alive; she moved, feebly. She was still wrapped in his arm. He must not let go.

A soprano voice from heaven pierced his awareness. A rope splashed into the water beside him. He didn't pause to wonder where it came from. He just grabbed it.

The rope dragged him through the water; his head only went under a time or two. Half a dozen men's voices were telling him what to do, but he couldn't understand any of them. A life ring came dropping down beside him. He pulled it over Sam's head and shoved her arms through it. He was getting cold, and his hands didn't grip well anymore.

They were at the wharf, its grayed timbers looming above him. He bobbed less than fifteen feet below its top deck. Willing hands were hauling Sam up, up. When a looped rope fell into the water beside him, he simply grabbed it and hung on.

He rose out of the water slowly, steadily, gratefully. As he rotated on the end of the rope, he watched first the maze of beams in the wharf's underbelly, then the bending river shore, then the open river. Out in the open river a steam fireboat was spraying water upon the stunned, crippled, smoking *Echuca Charlene*. Her green and slimy underside showed to starboard. The port wheel was gone, the upper-story wheelhouse was gone. Although it wasn't patently obvious, Sloan knew the boat's boiler was gone, too.

A few more rotations, and eager hands hauled Sloan up over the side. He was safe.

Beside him Sam had already struggled to a sitting position. "Gus!" she sobbed. She looked at Cole. "He fell over the side. I couldn't hold him."

"Was he alive?"

She nodded numbly and crawled the two feet over to him. He gathered her in against him and held her tight, and her warmth strengthened him.

Reginald had talked about the power of God. When chance did not permit Sloan to live, he lived. When chance decreed Sam's sure death, she hugged against him now.

Sloan could easily have been maimed or killed in those first seconds of the blast when the firewood was driven forward by the exploded firebox door. He could have been, but he wasn't there.

All right. You win. Foolishly, God, I thought I wanted a sign from you. You've given it to me. I accept. I accept you, Jesus Christ—all of it. You're real. You're you. I ask you to forgive me for doubting your existence all these years. Thanks for not dealing with me any harsher than you did. Now I'm going to ask a favor from you. Bring Gus back. Don't do this to Sam. Spare him. Bring Gus back, God.

Ah Loo hovered anxiously beside Sam. He looked at Sloan. "She all right?"

Sloan nodded. A Chinese man knelt beside Ah Loo and wrapped an arm around the boy's shoulders.

Ah Loo smiled through incipient tears. "She pulled me out of the water, and I belong to her. Now I helped save her, so I'm her papa? This is getting very confused."

It wasn't raining anymore, Sloan noticed. He watched the *Charlene* a few moments longer. Sagging hawse lines tied her securely to the fireboat and to another vessel off her starboard flank. She lay motionless, no longer at the mercy of the current. Most of the cloud billowing up off her now was white. Steam and water, not smoke.

Sam shuddered and burrowed deeper into his arms. "I saw his face, Cole, when he went over the side. 'Twas a sight I cannae—" She shuddered again.

Just then Sloan happened to look out beyond the *Charlene*. Two men were rowing toward the dock in a punt. A third fellow sat erect in the stern seat of the little boat, and Sloan's heart leaped.

He gave Sam an extra squeeze. "His face looks a lot better when it's washed."

The sobbing became a startled breath caught in her throat. She lifted her head away to look at him. "Wha—?"

He dipped his head toward the punt.

Like the king himself out for a cruise upon the water, Augustus Runyan rode in regal splendor down the rushing brown current. Nearly all the town of Echuca stood crowded here on the wharf and along the muddy banks, watching the fireworks, watching the captain come ashore. As his rescuers brought the punt into the wharf, a few scattered "hurrahs" became a crescendo of applause.

In that moment Sloan's mind worked out two lessons: one, prayer works; two, don't ever ask for a sign. You might get it.

Chapter Twenty-One

Coda

Palm Sunday, 1907

Me dearest Linnet,

After the long, newsy letter I sent you some days ago, this will be short and uneventful. I am so grateful that it is uneventful! I've had quite enough events to last awhile, as you know.

Cole wishes that we marry in Sydney, and that is fine with me. So if you and Chris are able, remain in Sydney beyond Easter, at least long enough to attend the wedding.

I understand that Chris has been invited to be the new organist at the university. You described to me the wondrous two-story organ they have their conservatory. I be so pleased for him! A news release here in the *Riverine Herald* says you've been invited on a tour to England with Mr. Giambone's group. How exciting! Will you go?

When Cole first described his visit to Barmah Mission, and his conversion, I was very skeptical. I thought perhaps he had said that to win my hand, or to somehow persuade me to grant some boon, for he was always so adamantly against Reginald's religion. But it is very real, Linnet. He could not, I believe, maintain a false mien for this long—not when the whole idea was previously repugnant to him. He still does not use pious words and phrases. He has never learned them, and I love him all the more for that. Jesus is real in him. It amazes me.

Samantha paused and put down her pen. She linked her fingers together and stared vacantly across the room. So much had changed, so much . . .

Cole reached over her shoulder and took her hand in his own. Her eyes met his, full of warmth and promise.

"What are you thinking, luv?" he asked quietly.

Samantha smiled. "I be thinkin' about trust," she said simply. "Trust and love. Both can be learned, ye know . . ."

She picked up her pen and began to write again.

> Linnet, and you, too, Chris: I pray daily that the two of you will know the completeness we have found. Incidentally, Chris, since I did not study Greek in school, I only just learned that your name, Christenikos, means Christ's victory. I'm sure you knew all along.
>
> Ah Loo sends greetings. We have decided that one rescue cancels another; I have lost a son and gained a friend.
>
> Cole sends his greetings.
>
> We stopped by the hospital this morning and learned that Gus's steersman will survive. He will probably regain full use of his hand. Gus is healing well and has already begun whittling his wooden leg. He is considering wearing a patch over one eye so as to look even more like a pirate.
>
> Mr. Wiersby and the commissioners made their verbal job offer a formal written one, but I refused it. Cole and I have decided we will live in Sydney. We will box my belongings and travel to Sydney by train. Praise God it will not be by stagecoach.